THE A

THE ACADEMY

Arabella Knight

This book is a work of fiction.
In real life, make sure you practise safe sex.

First published in 1995 by
Nexus
332 Ladbroke Grove
London W10 5AH

Typeset by TW Typesetting, Plymouth, Devon
Printed and bound in Great Britain by
Cox & Wyman Ltd, Reading, Berks

ISBN 0 352 32968 8

Chapter One

The deep blue Daimler purred effortlessly through the early morning London traffic. Miranda sat back, her soft, full bottom snuggling into the sumptuously dimpled leather seat. She was tired. Although the luxurious car was pleasantly warm, she shivered. The events of the previous hours flashed through her mind like a silent film. Caught red-handed on a dare-devil shoplifting spree. Bringing her boredom to Bond Street, as Rollo had smirked ironically. Being arrested – Rollo had vanished and abandoned her to her fate – then the helpless moments in the back of the grim police van. Interminable hours overnight in the sordid police station. The belated arrival of the family solicitor to haggle for her release. Worse still, being caught by those freelance press photographers (How did they get there? How did they know?) snapping their gleeful fill of her utter disgrace. Hours of shame and humiliation, severe enough to ruffle the confidence of Lady Miranda Davinia Gordon-George. Only eighteen summers old, she was already a svelte beauty, oozing the poise, the arrogance and the haughty pride bred by successive generations of sound money and social rank. Remembering her shame, Miranda shivered deeply.

1

Behind her, the winking lights of the Telecom Tower were glowing faintly in the pale dawn. Ahead, she saw the blaze of orange sodium lights that marked the M4 as it rose up out of Paddington and strode on concrete legs westwards. The opulent Daimler nosed down Praed Street, whispered along beneath shimmering plane trees and came to a stop at the Notting Hill lights seven minutes later. London was stirring. The traffic was thickening.

'Where are we going?' Miranda asked. Her tone was sure and certain, for she spoke with a voice accustomed to command. Courtesy and politeness were unnecessary when one was either very rich or very privileged. Preferably both – which she was.

'Your Aunt Emma has cancelled her Rome trip. She's coming down to Wiltshire,' the unctuous voice of Mr Porteous replied. 'We're picking her up at her Kensington flat before going on directly to Sandstones.'

Miranda winced. What a common little man. Picking up Aunt Emma, indeed! One simply did not say such things. One called for, or perhaps collected, Aunt Emma. He really was a terrible little bore.

Miranda shuddered suddenly. If Aunt Emma was coming down to Sandstones it looked as though a family conference was on the horizon. With her parents abroad so much – Hong Kong, and now the Gulf – Aunt Emma and her husband, Sir Peter Cranbourne (tipped for the Cabinet soon) had acted as Miranda's guardians for several years.

'Was she cross? About having to miss Rome?'

'Quite furious, I'm afraid,' Mr Porteous, the family solicitor, replied with every evidence of relish.

Miranda groaned inwardly. There was going to be a terrific row. Aunt Emma had cancelled her trip to

Rome. Sleazy snaps would soon be in the papers. Things were looking grim. Just because Rollo, a young blood despised by Miranda's guardians, had dared to go shoplifting, an escapade that had ended in ignominy for her. Aunt Emma would scold her. Aunt Emma.

The Daimler purred piously down Church Street, Kensington. Miranda dozed lightly, lulled into a fitful reverie in the warm, silent womb of the car. *Aunt Emma*. The engine murmured the refrain softly. Miranda stirred uneasily. In her sleep, she frowned.

When she was almost sixteen, Miranda had blithely taken two twenty-pound notes from a desk drawer in the estate office in order to buy a new martingale for Toast, one of her two ponies stabled down at Sandstones, the family seat. Before she had time to replace the missing money from her own very generous and liberal allowance, the loss had been noticed. Aunt Emma had been in residence, running a rough shoot for Sir Peter's political chums. There had been a little bit of unpleasantness with a Minister's valet over the loss – Aunt Emma had been firmly insistent on conducting an inquest in the servants' hall. Having grilled the household staff thoroughly, and drawn a complete blank, she summonsed Miranda for what proved to be an awkward interview. Unaware of the cloud of embarrassment created by her aunt's heavy-handedness, and dismissing the sum as a mere trifle, Miranda had made the mistake of lying. But the piercing blue eyes of her indomitable aunt had been unsettling, and impossible to evade. More insouciant than penitent, and with vague explanations and no apologies, Miranda admitted to taking the money.

3

The consequences were both painful and humiliating. Ordered up to her bedroom, Miranda had sat with growing unease for an anxious hour and a half. At long last, Miranda had heard her aunt striding along the corridor. Then the bedroom door had opened sharply and Aunt Emma had marched in. She had been wearing a snow-white silk dressing gown over a crisp basque. A satin sash was drawn tightly around her waist. A grim, inscrutable smile played on her pursed, full red lips. Miranda was taken firmly by the mop of her thick, blonde hair and spread across her aunt's soft thighs. With her tummy nestling into the silk-sheathed lap, Miranda gasped in disbelief as her denim jeans and white knickers were peeled off slowly.

The late afternoon sun of a warm, Wiltshire summer had been shining in through the leaded glass of her bedroom window, bathing Miranda's pale, naked bottom in a warm swathe of shimmering gold. Then the severe spanking had commenced. Six firm slaps in rapid succession for having even dared to think of taking the wretched forty pounds. A brief but equally stinging sermon had followed, with Aunt Emma's hot hand resting gently on Miranda's burning cheeks. Six more harsh slaps, three on each upturned buttock, had then exploded in the afternoon summer silence, each fierce slap seeking and finding the tender, reddening curves of her exposed, joggling bottom. Those, her aunt had curtly explained, were a punishment for actually stealing the money. Miranda had squirmed and wriggled, but there was to be no escaping the burning shame and blazing humiliation of the chastisement. Aunt Emma spoke in low, curt tones, and all the time her flat palm had been stroking and rubbing Miranda's hot bottom.

As the brief, scolding lecture came to its conclusion, Miranda had felt her aunt's thumb sweep across the surface of her satin-soft buttocks, pause and then come to rest in the gently sloping valley between her fiery cheeks. Time seemed to stand still. Even the doves in the stableyard held their sweet notes in their soft throats. Only the solid gold carriage clock on the dressing table had refused to be daunted and had ticked softly but determinedly onwards to the hour.

Miranda, with all the fierce pride of a fifteen-year-old, bit her lip, suppressing the instinct to squeak with surprise at the outrage to her buttocks or squeal with discomfort at the painful punishment meted down upon them. She had not shed a single teardrop. Silence reigned. Thankful that the punishment was over, Miranda had slipped off her aunt's soft lap.

'Now bring me your hairbrush,' Aunt Emma had commanded, her tone quite neutral and completely free from menace or rancour.

Obediently, Miranda had pulled up her knickers and denim jeans and, scooping up the broad-backed, long-handled hairbrush which was fashioned out of hard, polished cherrywood, almost skipped back to her aunt. Kneeling down at her punisher's feet, she bowed her crop of blonde hair into the lap she had moments before been stretched across, and waited for her hair to be lovingly, soothingly brushed. Instead of the anticipated reconciliation, more harsh words of admonishment bruised the sunbeam-heavy air.

'Across the bed, young lady,' came the stern command. 'Jeans and knickers down. At once, please,' her aunt had firmly instructed. Confused, and a little fearful, Miranda unzipped her jeans and wriggled out of them. Once more, her tight, white cotton panties were peeled off to flutter helplessly down to her ankles.

'Over the bed. Right over. Hands out in front. Bottom up, young lady,' came the crisp order.

Stretched out fully across the bed, her golden hair splayed out along the deep, silk eiderdown into which her anxious face was buried, Miranda presented her already ruby bottom for what threatened to be an even more scorching punishment. Involuntarily, her small hands gripped the edge of the soft, silk eiderdown.

'Lying is something we simply do not do. Stealing, that is of course wicked but understandable. Often necessary. Indeed, this family would not have got to where it is today if some of our illustrious ancestors had not been more than a little imaginative in their acquisitions of tithes, rents, land deeds and revenues from surrounding estates. But lying . . .' *Crack.* The hairbrush spoke with a cruel note of cherrywood on naked flesh. 'Lying . . .' *Crack.* Again, the hairbrush had hissed through the air and savagely kissed the soft, clenched cheeks resoundingly. 'Lying is simply bad form.'

Aunt Emma had paused, the polished back of the cherrywood hairbrush hovering in mid-air over the squirming bottom.

'Stay still, or I will double the punishment,' Aunt Emma had warned in a voice of icy control. 'Raise your bottom up a little. A little more. Dip your tummy.'

Miranda had obeyed instantly.

'That's better,' Aunt Emma had remarked with grim satisfaction.

6

Four more times the wicked hairbrush, once an instrument of comfort and now a fierce tormentor, sliced the air to splat down across the juddering, rubescent buttocks. Girlish buttocks, soft and rounded as they suffered the stinging punishment, raised and offered in timid obedience to the cruel wood . . .

Vrrrmmm. A dispatch rider, eager to turn right into Kensington High Street, revved his BMW bike harshly. Miranda opened her eyes, realised that she had been dreaming, and sighed with relief. The Daimler, dignified and unperturbed by the harsh motorbike, sat ticking gently opposite Barkers store. Miranda blinked away her fretful sleep and glimpsed the reassuring ears of Freddie, the family chauffeur, over his creased neck and blue serge collar.

'Left here, we'll cut across the Cromwell Road,' Mr Porteous said with unnecessary urgency. Miranda noticed that the voice trembled slightly, betraying the fact that its owner enjoyed a brief taste of command. In Miranda's circle, family solicitors kept silent and sipped pale sherry. Commandeering the Daimler had been quite an adventure for the little weasel, she reflected. Freddie nosed the big, silent car left, past the frenzied windows of Hyper-Hyper. Miranda gazed into the displays of silver, black and gold. A year ago she had spent a little over four thousand in one summer splash at the exclusive boutique, but now minor Royals frequented it the place was becoming far too middle-class for her. Similarly, at Henley and Wimbledon she did not bother attending the Leander Tent or Centre Court any more, but simply went to the champagne and champions' supper parties secluded from the common gaze.

As the stately Daimler whispered to a silent halt in a leafy square deep in South Kensington, Miranda pretended to be asleep. It would be simply hell, she thought, if her stern Aunt Emma and the odious Mr Porteous started to go to work on her en route to Sandstones. She really needed to shower and dine before all of that tiresome business. A splendidly liveried doorman, one of the very few retained in London, ushered Aunt Emma into the confessional silence and gloom of the Daimler. The door clunked expensively and reassuringly behind her. She fussed with her mink stole impatiently.

'Wretched girl. Wretched business,' she fumed, vigorously closing the partition glass to deny Freddie the chauffeur the opportunity to take any further pleasure in the family crisis. From under her fluttering eyelids, Miranda saw Freddie glimpse back at her in his mirror. He winked. Despite herself, she grinned.

The family conference proved to be sticky going.

After arriving at Sandstones, Miranda had luxuriated in a fifteen-minute shower. The icy sluicing left her invigorated. Then, towelled and softly talcumed, she had slipped into tight, pale, thigh-hugging, bottom-moulding, powder blue Shantung silk slacks and had eased herself into the embrace of a cherry pink cashmere jumper. Splashing orange water liberally onto her wrists, between her breasts, across her pale white belly, she took the familiar sweeping oak staircase of the Wiltshire residence three steps at a time down to the spacious dining room. She had deliberately not worn a brassière, planning to sit

8

directly opposite the toad, Porteous, and relish his turning pink as her soft bosoms bounced within their loose cashmere bondage.

She really was a bitch, she thought, laughing to herself. But the atmosphere in the dining room was markedly strained. Tense, even. Aunt Emma sat next to Mr Porteous, chivvying grilled oysters onto a solid silver fork. She sighed impatiently between each liquid mouthful. Her diffident husband, Sir Peter Cranbourne, sat slightly apart, a green ministerial box stamped with three crowns open at his elbow. He slowly consumed Treasury statistics together with the celery and Stilton soup before him. Lunch was underway, and taken in the main in a loud silence that became oppressive as the warm lobster salad was cleared and mango water-ices were served. Miranda played safe with black grapes and coffee. As ever, Mr Porteous ate loudly and greedily. When Sir Peter had swilled his balloon glass expertly to judge the cognac, his increasingly impatient wife broke the lowering silence.

'Scandalous,' she commenced with a harsh bark.

'We certainly have been hearing some worrying things, to be sure. Most worrying,' Sir Peter bleated mildly.

'Nonsense,' Aunt Emma snapped. 'The girl's completely out of hand.'

'If I may say so,' chimed in the weasel Porteous, unctuously dabbing his thin lips with a white napkin, 'the charges were certainly of a very embarrassing if not actually grave nature, I venture to suggest.'

Miranda detected the accusing whine in his tone. As ever, he was anxious to keep well within the Aunt Emma camp. She drew a deep breath. It was

9

going to be a tedious afternoon. Boring. Boring. Boring.

Playing absently with her coffee spoon, Miranda glanced up briefly and caught a glimpse of the majestically angry frown that glowered on her aunt's stern face. She shivered slightly. Thank goodness she was now too old for another apppointment with that cherrywood hairbrush. Miranda giggled slightly, stopping abruptly when she caught her aunt's fierce eye resting on her.

'Well,' Sir Peter drawled, opening his hands expansively. 'I've been on the phone to Dubai and I've managed to square things with your parents. They were most perturbed. Most perturbed. Your mother was quite relieved to learn that the charges have been dropped.'

'Put aside,' Mr Porteous interjected. 'Merely put aside, Sir Peter.'

'Quite so, quite so.' Her uncle nodded vaguely.

A sudden sense of relief swept over Miranda.

'I have taken care of all the details,' the toad solicitor simpered.

The details. Shoplifting with Rollo of whom they disapproved. And the press there on the spot, as if by some black miracle, for the disgrace. Miranda studied the squat, oily solicitor carefully, and with a sudden rush of apprehension realised how she would hate to be indebted to this weak yet insidious little bully. How merciless and how cruel he would prove to be to anyone in his clutches. The fearful moment passed.

'That Rollo. Bad blood there. Needs a spell in the army,' Aunt Emma thundered, tracing back Miranda's disgrace to the first causes. 'Anything in the Ninth and Twelfth Lancers, Peter?' she trumpeted.

'I'll speak with a chap I know, my dear,' Sir Peter promised vaguely.

Gosh. Poor Rollo, Miranda thought. In a year's time he'll be heading up a line of armoured Saracens as they bounce across Salisbury Plain.

'As for those press photographs, I have concluded my negotiations. The prints and the negatives have been destroyed. For a not inconsiderable sum,' Mr Porteous said, timing his contribution for maximum effect.

'How much?' roared Aunt Emma, purpling.

'Three thousand. A syndicate had put in a bid for sole rights. I had to work quickly. I'm afraid I had to use Sir Peter's name with the editor.'

Damn you, Miranda cursed. The weasel was really putting the knife in now. Why? What possible reason could he have for making things so unpleasantly hot for her?

'Outrageous,' spluttered Aunt Emma. 'Too damn close a call. I've had to cancel Rome. Your parents are distraught.'

'Forgive me, my lady,' Porteous oiled, 'I hope you are not upset by the amount I had to pay, but with Sir Peter so close to the Cabinet . . .' He let the dreadful accusation weigh heavily in the ensuing silence.

Perfect. Bloody well perfect, Miranda thought, bridling. He's done me now.

'Do you realise . . . ?' thundered Aunt Emma, returning to her onslaught on Miranda. 'I said, do you realise just how much mayhem and havoc your selfish and beastly misbehaviour is causing? Well, girl, do you?'

Despite her discomfort under the torrent of scolding words, Miranda managed to detect a gleam of

11

triumph mixed with almost sensual pleasure glinting in the solicitor's beady little eyes. She squirmed.

'You really are impossible, Miranda,' her aunt boomed.

Miranda thought it wiser to keep silent. She lowered her head in a gesture of atonement and fiddled awkwardly with her napkin.

'Last month there was that wretched Brompton Road party. I believe the police were involved.'

'Quite so, my lady,' Mr Porteous said obsequiously.

'And only last year you were thrown out of quite the most exlusive school in France. I think it is time to take serious stock. Mr Porteous?'

'The position is a little tricky, to be sure, my lady. The charges will remain, I believe, on file. Perhaps if Lady Miranda were to move out of circulation for a little while . . .' His unctuous tones seemed to fill the vast dining room.

Boring. Boring. Boring. Would it be Gstaad or Antibes? Or even Bermuda. Not Bermuda. All that boring sun, sea and sand.

His voice continued, and she returned her attention to it. 'I have in mind a possible solution to the difficulty, with your permission, my lady. An establishment that promises the most, how shall I put it? The most, er, satisfactory results. By the way, Lady Miranda,' he turned in almost sadistic triumph, 'I have telephoned your friends and acquaintances informing them that you have contracted a chest infection, possibly pleurisy, and so you will be out of circulation, *hors de combat*, for some little time.'

Bugger. Miranda frowned. They were closing in on her. Weasel Porteous seemed almost to be in control. Now that they had whisked her away from

12

London, and put the word out – pleurisy – she would in all likelihood be gated down in Wiltshire, here at Sandstones, for some while to come.

'This establishment you spoke of, Mr Porteous,' Aunt Emma said.

The family solicitor inclined his oily head conspiratorially and beamed a smile of smug satisfaction that made Miranda squirm.

'Most certainly, my lady. If I might have a quiet word?'

'Of course.' She nodded. 'Leave us at once, girl,' she snapped testily at Miranda.

Miranda wandered out to the stables. Toast, her favourite pony, was now too old to be ridden. She patted his broad face gently and fed him the soft, brown sugar she knew he adored. Over the next green, half-open door, her other pony Marmalade waited impatiently to greet her. She tugged the small, expectantly pricked ears affectionately. Picking up a curry comb, she entered the loose box and was soon lost in the soothing, rhythmical actions of grooming the warm flanks. Suddenly a tall shadow loomed large in the doorway, and Miranda looked up.

Her aunt spoke curtly. 'Saddle up, girl. You need a good canter to settle your nerves after last night's little episode. Ride on, Melchior.'

Aunt Emma looked magnificent on her big, chestnut stallion. Her close-fitting green velvet jacket flared out over the swell of her supple hips, and the tight cream jodhpurs flattered her full, rounded bottom. Not bad for 42. Great, in fact, thought Miranda, catching up with her aunt moments later on Marmalade. They took the open track down

13

towards Home Farm, turned into the spinney and emerged onto a secluded bridle path which curved through the coppiced woodland beyond.

'This will do, I think. Dismount.' Her aunt had a curiously brisk note in her voice.

Miranda looked up, startled. Her eyes phrased the unspoken question.

'We're getting down here,' her aunt said briskly. 'Want a little chat, my girl.'

A vague sense of unease uncurled itself deep down inside Miranda's fluttering tummy. Her mind flashed back instantly to the business of the stolen money which had been settled so painfully upstairs with the hairbrush. *I want to have a little chat.* Those were the very words her aunt had used to open up the interview which had concluded with the hairbrush speaking loudly down across her naked buttocks. Still, Miranda reflected ruefully, nobody was going to spank her today. She was a big girl now. Her bottom was surely safe from any painful attentions.

'This one will do.' Her aunt seemed to be examining a beech tree. Miranda dismounted and approached the vast beech.

'Squirrels? Are they doing much damage?' she asked, puzzled.

'Never mind the damn squirrels. You're the one doing all the damage to this estate and the family. Now come here this instant young lady.'

So absolute was the command that Miranda found herself stumbling forward obediently.

'Against that tree. Come along. No, face inwards. That's right. Now, arms around it. Good.'

Unthinkingly, Miranda had embraced the aged beech. Her arms encircled the gnarled girth with a

14

good few inches to spare. The rough, scratchy bark chaffed her tender nipples which enjoyed scant protection under the soft pink cashmere jumper.

'That should hold you steady,' her aunt grunted, having swiftly tied a short length of leather harness around Miranda's wrists on the far side of the beech. Miranda instinctively tugged, but the knotted leather thong had been expertly tied, leaving her completely bound and immobile. Like a flicker of forked lightning in a distant, dark bank of gathering clouds, a stab of fear lit up inside Miranda's mind. Something ominous threatened her. The threat was imminent.

'You've been a bit of a girl over the past few months, haven't you? Hmm? Should have done this twelve months ago. Never mind, better late than never. A good, sound hiding is what you need, young lady, and a jolly good hiding is exactly what I'm going to give you. Never let it be said that I shirk my duty. And in this case, my girl, my duty is both a pleasure and a privilege.'

Miranda's throat went dry. She started to protest, swearing out loud. Her aunt, plucking at the yellow leather gloves as she removed them finger by long, white finger, merely smiled as one would smile at a fractious child. Pocketing the gloves, she strode over to where her stallion, Melchior, nibbled at a tuft of sweet sedge. She took the supple riding crop from where she had slipped it under the warm, leather saddle and turned back towards the beech tree where Miranda, despite the dappled sunlight of the autumn afternoon, shivered in her bondage. The cruel crop sparkled and gleamed, slicing the air with eerie, ominous notes. A thin, harsh sound.

Within the tight leather binding that pinioned her

wrists so firmly, Miranda's helpless fingers splayed
out in a reflex of fear. Miranda writhed as she heard
the approaching crunch of Aunt Emma's polished
boots on the dry bracken underneath. The writhing
caused her nipples to tingle as they scraped against
the rough bark. Miranda's breath started to come
more rapidly and unevenly. The icy talons of an unknown, nameless fear caressed her belly and spine
lingeringly. Suddenly, more human hands were at
her waist, then the cool air of the autumn afternoon
kissed her buttocks and thighs as her aunt briskly
peeled down the silk slacks as far as her trembling
knees. The panties followed with a swift jerk. She
was utterly exposed to whatever was to befall her,
and Miranda knew all too well that it was going to
be very, very painful.

Her feeling of exposure and vulnerability was dis-
turbingly complete. Had the silk slacks fallen to her
ankles, she would have felt merely naked, but having them dragged down to just above her knees
served to remind Miranda that she had been thus
bared and prepared to meet the needs of her chastiser. Indeed, the taut silk fabric served to hamper
and hobble her all the more. The sensation of being
both naked and mercilessly exposed was absolute,
and in her fevered mind she realised that she was in
total thrall to another. Another who now wielded a
supple riding crop and who was to leisurely stripe
her.

'Warm work, punishment. Deuced if it isn't,'
Aunt Emma remarked, shrugging off her taut green
velvet jacket. Her full breasts strained against her
starched, crisp white blouse. 'Pretty hot for you, I'll
wager,' she continued with a mirthless laugh.

'Now look, Aunt Emma,' Miranda whispered

16

urgently, bargaining for all her worth. 'I'll do whatever you say. Scotland. Or Bermuda. I'll go wherever you send me. But don't beat me.'

Aunt Emma was resolute. And said so. Miranda knew she was doomed.

'You have no right to –' she said, impenitently.

'Silence, my girl. You are to be whipped. Soundly. Six strokes for troubling your dear, dear parents. A further five for my missing Rome. Three more for the distress caused to poor Mr Porteous. And a further three strokes for our having to pay out to destroy those pictures of your disgrace. Seventeen. If my mathematics serves me well, a prime number. We'll round it up. Three for almost ditching Uncle Peter's Cabinet chances. He's altogether too soft, that man. Forbade me to beat you. Probably get the Home Office. Too soft on discipline. Law and order needs a sure touch. The firm hand. As for you, my girl, strict discipline is what you both need and deserve to check your profligate misbehaviour.'

Unusually for one so cool and poised, Miranda succumbed to a fleeting sense of panic.

'No, please, Aunt Emma. Don't. I'm sorry . . .'

Once again, in her anxiety, she strained at the leather strap that bound her by the wrists so completely. The rough beech bark scraped her belly, breasts and inner thighs. She squirmed and wriggled, the dread mounting up inside her with an unstoppable surge.

'Silence,' her aunt thundered. 'Of course, you may whimper and squeal. Loud as you like. A remote spot, this. No one around to hear you. In fact, it will please me considerably if you do. It'll simply mean I've not wasted my time and energy with this whip.'

Again, she sliced the air. The menacing swish

17

curdled in Miranda's dark imaginings. She clenched her buttocks in a protective reflex. Drawn by a morbid curiosity, almost impelled yet simultaneously repelled by the desire to look, Miranda strained her head and rested her chin on her soft shoulder. She saw her aunt flex the eighteen-inch cane riding crop. It was so supple and springy it almost seemed alive between her long, pale, tapering fingers. A little wicked loop of ox-blood leather, four inches long, curled from the tip of the clouded yellow bamboo. Miranda was both fascinated and horrified. She felt the surface of the beech tree scrape her cheek as she sank her soft face against it in weary, yet expectant, resignation.

'Don't clench your cheeks, girl. Come along. Up on your toes. Thank you. That's much better.'

As Aunt Emma dispensed these final, pre-punishment instructions, she smartly tapped Miranda's outer curved thigh with the tip of the riding crop.

'What did we say? Hmm? Twenty? Jolly good. Twenty it is.' *Swish. Crack.* 'There's the first. Spot on.'

Miranda yelped, and instinctively hugged the harsh beech bark with her silken inner thighs. The length of cane had come down onto the upper curve of her left buttock, striping it faintly, while the little leather loop stingingly flicked the taut satin swell of her right cheek. She blinked. *Swish. Whomp.*

The next stroke came down exactly an eighth of an inch below the first. *Swish. Whumm.*

The third stroke kissed her softness a fraction below the pink stripe which betrayed the severity of the second. On tiptoe, as instructed, her beautifully rounded buttocks thrust up and out with almost pert coquettishness to meet their appointment with

18

the stinging crop, Miranda suffered the swish and
slice of each successive deliberate and deadly stroke
ten times. She yelped softly after the fourth and
squealed twice, but was determined to deny her
dreadful aunt the satisfaction of any deeper signs of
distress.

Aunt Emma, now breathing somewhat heavily
after the administration of the first half of the measured chastisement, paused. The supple switch
drooped lifelessly along the curve of her jodhpured
thigh. Miranda felt the broad, flat palm of her punisher's cool hand alight gently on her scalding rump
and slowly massage the ravaged buttocks. A mildly
inquisitive thumb seemed to hover lingeringly over
the deep valley that divided her choice cheeks, then,
as if slipping into a powerful temptation, probed
and caressed the deep cleft.

'You've been bad. Very bad, my girl. Disgraceful
behaviour. I'm doing this for your own good. Plenty
of strict discipline, that's what you need.'

Plenty? The word echoed ominously in Miranda's
brain. Plenty? What did this mean? Was she to be
kept under lock and key down here at Sandstones to
be caned like a naughty, pony-tailed schoolgirl at
the whim and will of her dominant aunt? She felt a
sudden, uncontrollable surge of panic tighten at her
throat.

'Of course, you'll have to go away. Tonight, in
fact. Mr Porteous seems to know of some school
that may be prepared to take you on. If we pay them
enough. The family name's good. Just.'

Uttering the final word with a wry grimace, Aunt
Emma slapped the reddened cheeks of her charge as
if for emphasis. Twitching the inert riding crop back
into life, she strode behind Miranda and took up her

stance on the opposite side. Changing the supple length of potent bamboo into her left hand, she tapped her victim's right buttock sharply. It joggled responsively.

'Up on your toes, my girl. Come along. I want that naughty bottom of yours nice and big and round. No. More. Better. Legs together. Better.' *Swish.* 'Jolly good. Nine to come. Take your medicine, girl. You are a . . .' *Swish.* Miranda yelped. 'Gordon-George remember. We were at . . .' *Swish.* 'Agincourt and . . .' *Swish.* 'Balaclava. Put up a damn fine show at Rork's . . .' *Swish.* 'Drift, and were in at the death in the . . .' *Swish.* 'Somme.'

Restrained by her silk slacks that bound her legs together at the shivering knees and by the taut leather thong that welded her pale wrists together, Miranda absorbed each punishing swipe utterly and completely, without even the hope of evasion or protection. She winced at each searching lash of the clouded yellow cane.

Bugger the history lesson, she thought, biting her lower lip. She knew her illustrious family's history all too well. After the fifth slice of crop upon rump, her breath came in short hisses between clenched teeth. The short length of cane rose and fell with an almost hypnotic rhythm, cutting through the air with a low whistle each time to stroke the entire, blushing, rubescent mound of her right buttock. Her left cheek, faintly striped after receiving the force of the first ten strokes, was repeatedly stung by the little curled loop of ox-blood leather at the tip of the crop. It was an accurate, efficient and deadly effective administration of corporal punishment. Miranda's bottom, thoroughly and almost expertly dealt with, throbbed and glowed.

'Two more. Almost there. Buck up, old girl.'

Aunt Emma spoke with almost clinical precision, as though she were overseeing the removal of stitches. Miranda wriggled and squirmed, but the harsh bark of the beech tree against which her soft body was tightly pressed ignited her nipples into delicious agony. With her pelvic delta thrust up into the solid beech by successive swipes of the cane on her naked buttocks, the labia were parted slightly. With a mixture of both curiosity and burning shame, Miranda felt the ooze and gentle trickle of the beginnings of a liquid response. Losing her concentration, she slumped down.

'Up, girl. On your toes, please.'

The confused girl, smarting and shivering, regained the tiptoe posture, jerking her scalding bottom up in an unintentionally, yet undoubtedly provocative, thrust.

Swish. Crack.

'And one more,' Aunt Emma remarked in her tone of ruthless calm. The eager wood swished. *Whomp.* A cutting slice that bit.

The final two strokes were merciless, leaving Miranda's already scalding buttocks ablaze in a seething fire of exquisite torment. And to her utter bewilderment and surprise, she felt a half-formed, half-understood desire welling up from her inner consciousness. That desire, merely a fragile notion, was for . . . more.

Aunt Emma seemed to share the same desire. Tossing her whippy cane crop aside onto the dry bracken beneath her polished boots, she paused for what seemed to Miranda a timeless moment to consider and examine her handiwork. Gazing down, the stern aunt dwelt lingeringly on the beautiful, full buttocks, gorgeously rounded and firm, which had been subjected to her cruel attentions.

Not bad, Aunt Emma reflected. Not bad at all. Haven't lost my touch. She smiled darkly as she tidied her silk blouse back into the elastic waist of her taut jodhpurs.

'Put the blindfold on now, please, my lady,' the oily voice said. Miranda hesitated, reluctant to obey the irksome solicitor's request.

'It is a necessary condition of your acceptance into the Academy. All new entrants must arrive in absolute ignorance of its location.' Miranda submitted to the swathe of black velvet. The last things she saw were the strong beams of the Daimler illuminating a country lane ahead. Bath? Cirencester? The Daimler had left Sandstones in the dark and had prowled the leafy roads for almost an hour. Miranda was at a complete loss as to her precise location and had no idea where she was. She adjusted her tight blindfold.

'That's the way,' Mr Porteous positively simpered, his voice almost betraying a flicker of excitement. Miranda felt a twinge of unease. She hated the trace of smugness in his tone. She was, however, grateful that he had managed to negotiate a place for her at the Academy. It had been difficult but his skills and persuasive arts had, her aunt informed her, won the day. It certainly sounded a rather exclusive place. That fact appealed enormously to Miranda's snobbish pride. So exclusive, it seemed, that she had been advised not to pack or bring anything with her. Absolutely everything would be provided for her on arrival, Mr Porteous explained, causing her to shiver pleasantly with anticipation.

'They have their own methods at the Academy,' Porteous said. 'Just for a term, or two. Possibly a little longer, Lady Miranda. The facilities are excellent and are tailored to meet your exact needs.'

'And who else goes? I must say I haven't heard of it before,' Aunt Emma had asked, adding, 'she won't be mixing with the wrong set, I trust.'

'Good gracious no. All the young ladies at the Academy are very much like Lady Miranda. Very much like her indeed,' the solicitor replied.

'And supervision? One hopes that certain standards are maintained. One is expecting a little discipline in the regime to govern their learning.'

'Be assured of the fact that Lady Miranda will both experience and benefit from constant vigilance and strict supervision,' he had purred.

With these exchanges still fresh in her memory, Miranda sat back in the sumptuous leather seat of the cruising Daimler. Beside her, Mr Porteous, charged with the task of escorting and delivering her to the Academy, remained silent. At last, the luxurious car glided to a whispered halt.

Moments later, Miranda heard large, heavy iron gates being drawn back. The car nosed across a cattle grid and crunched on loose gravel chippings. Gate lodge and drive, Miranda thought. Seems promising so far. And at least we are deep in the countryside. Instead of driving on, as expected, Mr Porteous ordered Freddie to wait. Then, politely but firmly, instructed Miranda to step out of the Daimler. The cold night air made her shiver.

'Keep your blindfold on until given permission to remove it, my lady,' the weasel insisted. 'Merely a security precaution in these turbulent times of terrorism and kidnapping,' he added.

Gosh, Miranda thought. Who on earth actually came to the Academy? Arab princesses? How exciting. Would she have to share a maid? she wondered. And then, suddenly in the cold night air, all her vain and petty fears surfaced. What would become of her glorious blonde hair if it wasn't cossetted by her little Knightsbridge treasure, Julio? And would the clothes and shoes issued by the staff at the Academy be designer items from Milan? The French season was rather disappointing this year, she reflected. Paris was expensive but dull. And would they allow her to have her favourite wild bilberries flown in from Norway? Such a simple pleasure, when laced with vodka and double cream. She sighed.

'Goodbye, Lady Miranda. I am sure that I am leaving you in very capable hands. I trust that you will benefit from your experience here at the Academy. It has, I believe, an excellent reputation for getting results.'

With that, Miranda heard the heavy car door shut and then the Daimler's engine rise in mild protest as Freddie reversed it back out through the gate.

'This way,' a firm female voice said curtly.

Miranda bridled slightly at the churlish tone.

'I would like –' she began, haughtily.

'Silence. No talking.' The sharp tone cut her off in mid-sentence.

Miranda shrugged her shoulders, tossed her head and followed the sound of the retreating feet as they trod gravel.

'Quickly, come along. In here.'

Miranda found herself, as she obeyed the command to remove the blindfold, inside the yellowed, peeling walls of the gate lodge. It had a heavy smell of sour damp and a strong whiff of mice. Miranda's

24

refined nose wrinkled in disgust. The formidable woman, dressed in a loose tracksuit, her hair brushed back into a severe bun, pointed to Miranda's golden watch. A Cartier, from an exclusive limited edition of only 105.

'Watch, and any rings or jewellery. Come along. Quickly,' she snapped impatiently.

Miranda surrendered her Cartier with some misgivings.

'Shoes.'

'My shoes?' Miranda said, puzzled.

'At once.'

Miranda slipped them off and handed them over.

'All these items will be returned to you on your eventual departure from here. A receipt will be issued.'

Elaborate security precautions, Miranda thought. But why? Her shoes, simple gold rope necklace and rare Cartier? Perplexed by this question, and engrossed in its search for an answer, her usually sharp mind failed to pick up on the word 'eventual' which the offensive women had used. If it had, Miranda would have become instantly perturbed. As it was, she remained merely distressed at having been stripped of all her most personal possessions. The dominant woman beckoned. Miranda, awkward in her bare feet, followed her out of the musty gate lodge in silence.

The silence grew more oppressive and became almost unbearable as she sat in the back of a small Fiat which punched the darkness ahead with twin silver beams as the car roared up a twisting gravel drive, flanked by brooding elms, towards a large, eighteenth-century Queen Anne mansion.

'Out,' came the curt command after the Fiat had

25

braked sharply at the imposing, columned front entrance. 'Up the steps. Ring three times and wait.'

Miranda forgot the gruff instructions to maintain absolute silence.

'What shall I –' she began.

'Shut up and get out,' snapped the Fiat driver with a snarl.

Startled more than alarmed by this display of utter rudeness which was alien to her normally genteel circle, Miranda frowned, opened the car door, stepped out into the cool night air and slammed the door behind her testily. The driver sprang out of her seat and strode around the front of the Fiat. Large dark shadows danced against the façade of the mansion as she crossed in front of the headlights.

'Come here,' thundered the woman angrily.

Miranda, taken aback by the flurry of activity, hesitated.

'I said come here, you spoiled little bitch. You need a sharp lesson in manners and obedience, girl, and I'm just the one to give it to you.'

Before Miranda fully realised what was happening, the surprisingly agile and athletic woman grabbed her arm, held her in a powerful grip and deftly spread-eagled her over the warm metal bonnet of the car. Unpocketing a small, leather strap, she pinioned Miranda face down onto the ticking engine hood, one large, capable hand clamped vicelike around the struggling girl's white neck.

Crack. The strap spoke, breaking the brooding silence of the dark night. A flash of red pain seared through Miranda's brain. *Crack. Crack.* The double blows left her soft, fleshy thighs a-tingle. *Crack.* Her bottom, still tender after the attentions paid to it by her aunt, received the scorching fourth lash. *Crack*. The fifth, an evil swipe, stung her scalding cheeks.

A voice, rich and confident in its authoritative tone, spoke out in the night.

'Good evening. Welcome to the Academy, Lady Miranda. I see you are settling in well. Jolly good. Press on, Matron. Chastise the girl.'

The mellow tones rolled down the wide sweep of steps and echoed down the gravel paths and manicured lawns beyond.

'Just teaching the wretched girl a little politeness, ma'am,' the Matron replied, the leather strap dangling limply in between the treacherous strokes.

'Pray continue. Standards must be kept to a rigorously high degree, dear Matron. Let the lesson be a memorable one,' the voice from the entrance porch boomed.

Crack. Crack. Crack.

Writhing under the unerring lash of the deadly strap, Miranda's soft, rounded cheeks blazed as they absorbed three more harsh strokes. The warm bonnet of the Fiat received her squashed breasts and swelling belly as Matron kept a fierce, pinioning grip. Miranda's thick mane of blonde hair tossed wildly as her lithe body jerked responsively to the hot kiss of the cruel leather. The punishment over, the firm grip was relaxed. The punished girl remained spread face down over the Fiat.

'Thank you,' the grim voice of her chastiser said.

Miranda turned her flushed face sideways and looked up, uncomprehending.

'It is our custom to say "thank you" in this establishment, girl,' the stern voice from the top of the stone steps thundered.

Miranda, with gathering understanding, turned to

27

the woman who had just ignited her buttocks with the supple strap.

'Thank you,' Miranda mumbled, not a little sullenly.

'Speak up, you wretched girl,' the unseen speaker boomed.

'Thank you,' Miranda said, distinctly.

Matron furled up the little leather strap and pocketed it, slid behind the wheel of the Fiat and drove off back down towards the gate lodge beyond the towering elms.

'Matron sleeps in the gate lodge. You will meet her again tomorrow during your induction to the Academy. I trust for your bottom's sake that your manners will have significantly improved. Come, girl. I will take care of you tonight.'

Mrs Boydd-Black was a superb specimen of her type. Admitting to 45, but looking eight years younger, she was tall, angular and not without a certain graceful strength. The source of her strength lay generally in her tanned, openly handsome face – and specifically in her piercing eyes made sharper by the glittering pince-nez they sparkled behind.

Miranda studied the headmistress of the Academy guardedly as she stood by the large fumed-oak desk in a vast study warmed by a leaping fire. From the sweet, scented fragrance in the air, Miranda knew that the short logs that yielded so eagerly to the orange and yellow flames were apple. The headmistress wore a heather twill thorn-proof skirt, fine lisle stockings of clouded oyster-grey, a lemon blouse and matching cardigan and strong, sensible brogues. A healthy, outdoor type. Fit enough to tire her gun dogs, probably. Sports bra, suspenders and no knickers, Miranda mused. A powerful woman, certainly not one to be underestimated or crossed. Unaware of her new charge's surreptitious appraisal, Mrs Boydd-Black paced before the fire as she prepared to speak. Planting her sturdy brogues fourteen inches apart on the rich oriental rug, she commenced.

'I have been advised of the details of your illustrious career during the past few months, Miranda. You must, I feel most strongly, change your ways and change them quickly. But before such a change can be seen in your behaviour, there must be a change in your attitude. Rest assured that we shall be taking certain measures to achieve the desired results.'

Miranda gulped and swallowed hard. She knew at once what those certain measures would be. Her rump had just sampled them.

'You have been placed under my charge and supervision here at the Academy and I have given assurances to certain parties . . .'

Aunt Emma and the weasel Porteous no doubt, Miranda thought, mentally grimacing.

'. . . To certain parties. The regime here is simple. Listen and obey. Always obey. The rules are sovereign. Deviation or defiance will warrant instant punishment. We dispense several degrees of punishment, and though they may vary in kind they are blessed with a unique similarity. Severity.'

Miranda trembled imperceptibly, her left hand unconsciously going behind her in a protective gesture to guard the swell of her rump.

'You are headstrong, spoiled, undisciplined and ungovernable. A perfect specimen of privilege gone to the bad. I and my colleagues, together with the

29

regime and range of punishments here at the Academy, will change all of that. Have I made myself perfectly plain? Do you understand me, girl?'

'Yes, Mrs Boydd-Black,' Miranda replied, a little shakily.

'Jolly good. Then we understand one another perfectly. And the length of time you remain here will be determined almost completely by you yourself.'

Miranda looked up in surprise.

'Those placed in our charge must earn their remission and ultimate release. We operate a points system. Merits. All new receptions commence with zero.'

Norway, nul point. The cliché swam into Miranda's brain to taunt her. She had never actually watched the Eurovision song contest, but had a portfolio of preferred shares in a satellite consortium.

'Good behaviour,' continued Mrs Boydd-Black implacably, 'prompt and immediate obedience, all earn merits. Achieve one hundred merits and you will be eligible for discharge from our control and care.'

Miranda rapidly calculated how long her incarceration might actually be. She stared back directly into the magnetic dark eyes that gazed unblinkingly through the glinting pince-nez.

'Each transgression, display of disobedience or symptom of regression will earn both chastisement and a demerit.'

Damn, thought Miranda. Typical bloody catch-22. She suddenly felt a forlorn sense of doom shroud her usually mercurial mind. The last sentence hung heavily in the apple-wood scented air between them. For Miranda, the word chastisement made the peachy soft flesh of her twin buttocks tingle.

'Discipline is the main purpose of the Academy,' the headmistress continued, a warmer, richer note stealing into her voice. 'We dispense with the usual curriculum. A spartan regime is what we aim for. Simple food, vigorous exercise. No fripperies or frills. And rigid discipline.'

Again, for a full two, silent minutes, the protracted pause weighed heavily between the strong, powerful headmistress and the somewhat chastened new girl. Miranda felt a little giddy and stretched out to steady herself against a large chair which stood, incongruously, marooned alone in a sea of richly patterned carpet.

'Do not touch that,' the headmistress snapped. Miranda recoiled and looked up, startled.

'That is a very special piece, my girl. We refer to it only as the Chair.' Mrs Boydd-Black seemed to recover her composure as quickly as she had lost it. Miranda detected a strange, excited note as the headmistress continued.

'That Chair is reserved for the administration of very special punishments. They do not concern you for the moment, girl. Perhaps they never shall. You are not, I am given to understand, a stupid girl. Just spoiled, disobedient and in dire need of discipline. Only those who fail to respond to the strict regime here at the Academy are summoned to the Chair for certain exercises. The Quarter Exercise, a severe reminder. The Half Exercise, a very painful lesson. The Full Exercise, reserved for the very, very wicked . . .'

Suddenly snapping out of her reverie, during which her voice had almost sunk into a trance-like whisper, the headmistress concluded the interview abruptly.

31

'But more of that later. Come, girl, to supper and bed. No questions. Just listen, learn and obey. That is all that we demand of you. Have I made myself perfectly clear? Hmm?'

Chapter Two

Supper was a plain but wholesome repast. No tubs of ice cream or elaborate Thai banquet, Miranda's normal midnight grazing. Just two thick slices of homemade bread spread generously with golden butter and clear, almond-hued honey.

'From our very own bees,' boasted the headmistress, barely concealing her evident pride. 'Such adorable little creatures, but my goodness, how they sting.'

Sting. Miranda's thoughts turned immediately to the little leather strap which had scalded her bottom so thoroughly not an hour since. She was sticky. The honey was thick. She furtively licked her sweet, dripping fingertips and secretly tongued apart her cloyingly webbed fingers.

'Vitamins. And drink your milk,' Mrs Boydd-Black urged in her headmistressy tone. She briskly tapped the table with an extended forefinger. The vitamins danced in their little plastic cup. 'Drink.'

Miranda, head bowed, obeyed.

The basement kitchen was cavernous, though warm and well-lit. Miranda gazed at this alien environment. At the huge Aga, polished and gleaming in the brightness. At the rows of winking saucepans in serried ranks along the scrubbed, white-tiled walls.

Almost a foreign country to Miranda. In her exclusive London penthouse she had a large American Frigidaire with six shades of lipstick and a bottle or two of wine on standby. In town Miranda always dined out, taking breakfast in a brasserie. When at Sandstones all her needs were supplied simply by touching a bell-push, from her early morning mocha – served in a solid silver Georgian coffee pot – to an impromptu supper party for a bevvy of unexpected friends.

'All the work is undertaken by my girls. We do not have any domestics,' the headmistress said. 'Hard work is very character forming. Cook is a tartar. Rules this kitchen with a long, wooden spoon. If you behave yourself, in time you may be lucky enough to get a work detail down here. It can be so cold out in the gardens at this time of the year.'

Miranda shivered slightly, though uncertain as to whether it was at the thought of the tartar cook with the long wooden spoon – just imagine what that could do to one's bare bottom – or weeding gravel pathways with blue fingers on a frosty morning.

'Finished? Good. It is simple but nourishing fare. And no drinking or smoking during your time with us at the Academy. I take a very serious view of any such infringements. A very serious view indeed. Wash and dry those dishes. Quickly.'

Miranda rinsed her plate, knife, spoon and glass and tidied them away.

'We'll see about something for you to wear.'

Miranda followed Mrs Boydd-Black up several flights of stairs and then along a warm, airy landing.

'This is the kit room. You may be assigned to household duties here. I am reliably informed that

Miss Pigeon, our capable seamstress, is a wizard with the clothes brush. Quite expert.'

Miranda gulped. Was Miss Pigeon as expert with her clothes brush as Aunt Emma had been with the cherrywood hair brush? She sincerely hoped not.

'As I said,' the headmistress continued. 'I see to it that everyone works here. And works hard. We are quite a thriving, busy little community. Slackers soon repent. Strip off those rags. Quickly.'

Miranda blinked. After the brisk punishment with the strap, she knew that the Academy might be exclusive, but it was no ordinary private school. Even so, the nonchalance with which Mrs Boydd-Black rummaged through the shelves in a large airing cupboard after instructing Miranda to peel off her clothes, startled her. Hesitantly, the 'rags', some seven hundred pounds worth of silk slacks and cashmere jumper, fluttered down onto the lino beneath her feet.

'No bra? We don't issue them at the Academy, so that's all right. Some of the sillier girls whinge, but a warm bottom or two gives them something else to think about, ha ha.'

Miranda was beginning to find the vibrant woman's heartiness just a little bit too much.

'Panties off.' Again, a command skimpily dressed in the guise of an invitation. But beneath the pleasantness, Miranda knew there lurked both a will of iron and a ruthless resolve.

'Come along, girl. Don't make me have to hurry you. If you do, I warrant you'll regret it bitterly.'

Miranda responded quickly, fearing further punishment. Her naked breasts bulged as she stooped to wriggle out of her flimsy white panties. The briefs caught on her ankle and she had to steady herself against the wall as she hopped indecorously, breasts bouncing, to free herself of the wisp of silk. Mrs Boydd-Black turned, sighed impatiently, and closed the airing cupboard door. Striding towards the struggling girl, she placed one firm hand on a pale, naked shoulder and reached out with her free hand to smack the bare, joggling bottom three times.

'Don't ... *Smack* ... be ... *Smack* ... a silly ... *Smack* ... child.'

Miranda stood, feet and hands together, head slightly bowed, in a passive, contrite posture.

'And don't squeal when you are being so deservedly punished. Stand still. Hands behind your back. Let me look at you.'

Miranda rubbed her reddened cheeks ruefully and stood, legs firmly together, facing the headmistress.

'Matron will be conducting a full medical tomorrow. I need to satisfy myself that there are no immediate problems.'

Miranda squirmed slightly as the glinting pince-nez flashed, raking her soft nakedness avidly. She hotly resented this intimate appraisal and her fierce pride burned intensely as the headmistress seemed to linger over the fulsome swell of her generous breasts before moving across the delightful sweep of her ivory belly and the shadowed delta between her tightly clamped thighs.

'Turn around. No. Sideways, girl.' The order was crisp.

Obediently, but resentfully, Miranda turned the required quarter-circle in her bare feet. Her toes curled up in suppressed fury. Mrs Boydd-Black inspected her profile languidly before placing the controlling tip of her outstretched finger under her chin.

'Head up. No slouching here at the Academy.

Slouchers and slackers are soon licked into shape. Shoulders straight.'

Miranda complied. As she did so, her breasts thrust forward in extended glory. So soft, so supple, so heavy with their trembling, potent promise.

'Turn.' The command was curt.

Miranda, shivering, turned a further quarter-circle, presenting her freshly spanked bottom for her headmistress's perusal.

'Bend over.'

Swallowing hard, she hesitated for a fraction of a moment.

'Quickly girl. Quickly,' rasped Mrs Boydd-Black impatiently in a tone thick with lust, 'and clasp the backs of your knees.'

Stooping down, Miranda adopted the prescribed position.

'That is the First Position. Understand?'

Miranda's ensuing silence was rewarded with a sharp slap.

'I said that is the First Position. Do you understand?'

'Yes,' murmured Miranda.

Smack. The broad palm swept across the soft flesh of the rounded buttocks. A slight pause. The creamy flesh grew softly pink. *Smack.* Skin kissed skin. *Smack.* Again, the firm hand exploded against the juddering cheeks of the exposed, punished buttocks, now dancing fleshily with pain.

'Yes, ma'am,' thundered Mrs Boydd-Black. 'I do hope that you are going to try to settle down quickly at the Academy, girl. We have simple rules. Listen, learn and obey. Simple rules. Kneel.'

Miranda dropped down onto her knees with alacrity.

'Get your bottom up higher. Higher. Good. That is the Second Position. We insist upon it when administering harsher punishments for the more serious transgressions. Much more fitting for the cane or strap, I feel.'

Miranda, both embarrassed and humiliated by the posture which rendered her utterly and completely exposed, clenched her teeth and screwed her eyes up tight.

'The Second Position. Do you understand?'

'Yes, Mrs Boydd-Black.'

Smack. Smack. Smack. The searing spanks echoed along the length of the narrow corridor. Red palm prints appeared on the pale, ivory flesh like rapidly developing negatives.

'Yes what?' came the querulous demand.

'Yes, ma'am,' Miranda corrected herself, fearful of a further flurry of cruel smacks.

The broad, cool hand rested gently on her warm bottom, paused upon alighting and then quickly delivered a final blow. Miranda yelped softly as the smack seared her scalded, satin cheeks.

'Up. And remember. It pays to learn quickly. Listen, learn and obey. You will soon discover that the dull and the defiant suffer much.'

How long? Months? More? A sluggish caterpillar of unease crawled down Miranda's spine. How long would this nightmare last? How quickly could she accumulate the merit points?

The business in hand broke into her thoughts.

'Here. Take your uniform. You must change twice a day. I insist upon the highest standards of personal hygiene here. And you must shower at least twice a day. More, if you are required for any special or specific punishment. I personally prefer to

38

spank a freshly washed bottom. Clean and contrite. That is how I like my girls when I put them over my knee. Pristine and penitent if I am to cane them. Ha ha ha.'

Again, the hearty laugh that irked so much. Miranda took her uniform and started to slip into the brief, white, cool cotton shorts.

'Not now, girl. You sleep in the raw. Much healthier. Vest.'

A simple white, long-sleeved vest with a scalloped neckline was handed over.

'Socks.'

Miranda took the short, white ankle socks.

'And armband. To be worn at all times during the day and evening. As a reception pupil, you will wear beginner's green. Now gather up your things and we'll store them away in here.'

Miranda stooped, gathered up and folded her own clothes and packed them in tissue paper. Mrs Boydd-Black boxed them, wrote her name, Lady G-G, on the box and stored it away in a tall cupboard.

'Time for bed. No questions tonight. You will be fully briefed in the morning. Be sure to be up, showered and dressed by second bell. This means up and doing as soon as first bell sounds. Understand?'

'Yes, ma'am.'

'Good. Remain by your bed until a blueband comes along to take you to your breakfast.'

Miranda, holding her simple uniform against her soft bosom, followed the imposing headmistress down the cool stretch of corridor. Her golden-crowned head was slightly bowed, her usually alert and perky mien now subdued if not actually tamed. Her large, rounded, beautiful bottom bore the blush of faint pink where both leather strap and naked hand had recently visited it. Like the prints of a robin on a snowy window ledge, the instruments of punishment had alighted to leave their discernible traces. Feeling vulnerable in her enforced nakedness, she shivered wretchedly as her bare feet padded silently along the uncarpeted stretch of corridor into which they had turned. It was, Miranda realised, the dormitory wing, at the very end of which Mrs Boydd-Black paused and opened a white door.

'In you go, girl. Straight to bed.'

'Good night, ma'am,' Miranda murmured, quickly remembering to use the correct mode of address.

'Good night.'

Inside, a single cot bed waited forlornly for her. Three others lay folded up inertly on the cold floor. Without another word, the headmistress closed the door firmly. Miranda half expected to hear a key being turned in the lock. To her surprise, and relief, that did not happen.

Gazing around the unprepossessing dormitory, her eyes took in the small, wooden locker, smelling of disinfectant, which stood by her cot bed. The cheap, yellowing door yawned wide open to reveal three bleak and empty shelves. There was no radio, clock or bedside reading lamp. Very spartan, Miranda thought grimly. She pushed aside the memory of her own bedrooms in London and Sandstones with their bright zebra rugs, stereo systems, television and videos, Fabergé carriage clocks, en suite baths. Above all, she shut out the image of her Kadinsky originals on the lemon walls.

Remembering the velvet drapes at Sandstones and the chintz of her flat in town, Miranda shrugged as she pulled up the simple, bottle-green roller blind. Behind it, to her sudden annoyance, she found that the original Queen Anne sash window could only be opened two inches. Wooden blocks firmly precluded any further movement, along with any hope of egress through it.

Miranda suddenly felt trapped and confined. For a girl who enjoyed the utter freedom of diplomatic *laissez-passer* when abroad, and her own chauffeur-driven Audi when at home, this cramped, chilly dormitory was as much as a prison to her as the cell in which she had languished only the night before.

Outside, an owl hooted its melancholy notes in the tall, dark elms. Shuddering, Miranda pulled down the roller blind and carefully arranged her uniform on a chair next to her cot bed. She picked up a fire drill notice, started to read it absently and sighed when, without any warning, the single light bulb was extinguished. Sighing, with an air of resignation unusual in one normally so self-assured and poised, Miranda peeled back the plain bed covers and eased her slightly shivering nakedness in between the cold linen sheets.

Exhausted by all she had recently endured, she slept deeply, a sleep invaded by curious dreams of shameful inspections, in which naked bodies were ruthlessly and intimately examined. Of punishments. Prompt and severe punishments. Punishments in which rounded bottoms suffered.

A shrill bell stole into her already turbulent dreamscape. Her brain stirred. Miranda opened a bleary eye, blinked in dismay, groaned inwardly and rolled over. Within a few seconds, having cursed the stupid bell, she was dozing heavily once more. Never one to be up before eleven, the scarlet and gold streaks of dawn against the cold grey of an early morning

41

sky meant nothing to her. It must all be a vivid nightmare, she mused. Soon her Portuguese maid, pert in her crisp black and snow white uniform, would enter with a large breakfast cup full of her favourite Gunpowder tea. Comforted by the fond illusion, Miranda lapsed into a deep, dreamless sleep.

The dormitory door burst open. Miranda sprang up in her narrow cot bed, rubbing the sleep from her startled eyes. The clamour of the shrill bell broke out for the second time.

'Get up. We're late. Come on!' A tall, pale-skinned brunette bounded over to the cot and shook Miranda vigorously. 'Get up. Get dressed. Quickly,' the lissome girl half pleaded, half commanded.

Miranda examined her, resenting the sudden intrusion. Her human alarm call wore the white, long sleeved vest and tight cotton shorts which were the basic uniform the Academy insisted upon. A king-fisher blue armband encircled her left arm just above the elbow. The close fitting vest accentuated her small, firm breasts and slender waist. The dark nipples peeped through the swathe of taut white fabric almost impudently in their bold shyness. The brief, tight shorts hugged the swell of her hips and thighs, snuggling deeply into the delta between. Miranda thought the little white ankle socks at the end of the girl's slender, tapering legs perfectly sweet.

'Up,' commanded the blueband, who had replaced the note of panic in her voice with a stern smack of authority. Miranda sprang out of her bed and stood, splendid in her full nakedness, before the impatient brunette.

'Get dressed. Hurry up. Breakfast will have started by now.'

Dressing in her own vest and shorts in seconds, Miranda sat down on her bed to don the regulation ankle socks.

'Forget about those. Put your armband on and come with me.'

Down in the refectory, moments later, Miranda gazed at the long, low, oak-panelled room filled with dark polished tables with benches on either side. Some eighteen girls sat in silence as they ate boiled eggs, toast and marmalade, and sipped camomile and raspberry tea with little relish and less enthusiasm. From an austere lectern, a severe-looking woman with tightly braided hair was reading solemnly from one of Tennyson's more dreary odes.

Mrs Boydd-Black sat at the centre of the top table with four female members of staff, including the strap-happy Matron from the night before. Miranda noted that they were all tucking into bacon, sausage, eggs, kidneys and fried bread, helping themselves busily from silver dishes heaped with delicious fare perched on little spirit lamps to keep the feast piping hot.

'Clarissa.'

The tall brunette shivered as the headmistress spoke.

'A very poor start to your duties as a newly appointed blueband. I cannot say that I am not a little disappointed.'

The girl deputed to wake Miranda and deliver her before second bell bit her lower lip apprehensively.

'Loss of one merit point,' pronounced the headmistress gravely.

'Oh, please, ma'am . . .' Clarissa murmured.

'Silence, girl. You know the rules. Never question any decision I, or indeed any member of my loyal staff, deems fit to make. Do you understand?'

43

'Yes, ma'am. I'm sorry, ma'am.' The penitent girl bowed her head.

'Jolly good. However, we are fair. Firm, but fair. Did the new greenband girl cause the delay? Was she not up and dressed as instructed, thus causing you to be so late?'

Miranda looked straight ahead. The refectory fell silent. Matron continued to munch her fried bread dipped in runny egg, as if indifferent to the unfolding drama before her.

'Oh, no ma'am, she . . .' Clarissa refuted the accusation gamely.

'If so, you may instruct her to assume the First Position and teach her the strict meaning of the term punctuality. Six, I believe, would suffice.'

'Thank you, ma'am,' the blueband replied. 'It was not her fault, ma'am. I am to blame, entirely. I should have done my duty better. I promise to try harder.'

'A pretty little speech, Clarissa. I am so glad that you are evidently so resolved to improve your ways. And, my girl, I admire your sense of loyalty and your protective instincts to the wretched new girl. It does you some credit. You shall not lose the merit point –'

'Oh, thank you ma'am,' the brunette gushed.

'Silence! No demerit for Clarissa, Matron. Please note my revised decision. But the new girl, the greenband, will not benefit from being protected and shielded from the harsh realities of her life here at the Academy. She must learn, and learn her lesson quickly. Painfully, if necessary.'

Miranda's mouth went dry. She swallowed awkwardly.

'New girl,' the headmistress said.

44

'Yes, ma'am,' Miranda replied softly, as if in a dream.

'Adopt the First Position.'

Miranda looked at Clarissa questioningly.

'Bend over,' hissed the brunette promptly.

Suddenly remembering, Miranda bent down, presenting her bottom up for discipline, her hands clasped behind her knees.

'Clarissa, it is your duty to teach this wayward girl her responsibilities. As her mentor for the first few weeks, you must discharge your duties well. She has signally failed to obey a simple instruction and so she must be chastised. Six, I think, was what we agreed. Carry on.'

'Shorts off, ma'am?' Clarissa spoke, clearly and slowly.

Miranda felt the crimson blush of shame ignite her worried face. To her momentary relief, she heard the headmistress reply, 'No. Shorts on, my dear. But make it good and hard.'

With what seemed to be her final comment on the proceedings, Mrs Boydd-Black popped a finger of golden toast between her perfect white teeth.

Clarissa walked slowly over to a large mantelpiece beneath which a huge, empty fireplace had been filled with dried autumnal flowers and feathery fern leaves. From the deep shelf of the mantelpiece she picked up an eighteen-inch dull yellow bamboo cane. Miranda, head bent down, her anxious face framed by the curtain of thick, blonde tumbling hair, heard the soft footsteps of her chastiser padding back towards where she waited passively and submissively in the First Position. The stern voice of the severe-looking woman who had been reading from the works of Tennyson at the lectern trailed off into silence. A silence loud and almost tangible in its intensity.

Swish. The thin, supple bamboo sliced the air and bit deeply, almost lovingly, into the tight white cotton shorts stretched tautly across Miranda's bunched, rounded cheeks. Miranda blinked, but sensed that it was not the withering swipe it could well have been had Clarissa put a little more venomous enthusiasm into the matter.

Swish. Miranda blinked again. Once more, the springy cane savagely caressed her taut buttocks. *Swish*. *Swish*. Two more strokes in rapid succession as the bamboo stung her plump rump with a double Judas kiss. *Swish*. Miranda's thick blonde hair tossed and tumbled as her body jerked responsively to the implacable stroke.

'Buck up. Last one,' whispered Clarissa soothingly, softly.

Miranda looked up and saw, upside down as if through an old-fashioned camera viewfinder, the lithe brunette who wielded the short cane gazing down with a half smile of reluctant tenderness on her full, generous mouth.

Swish. The last stroke was a mere token, an affectionate tap of love-play rather than a severe measure of correction.

Miranda remained in the First Position. The brunette paused, the tip of the cane resting quietly in the open palm of her left hand. A chair scraped as its occupant rose. Miranda focused her eyes and saw the strong brogues of Mrs Boydd-Black stride into her field of vision.

'That was a somewhat half-hearted effort, Clarissa. Give me that cane one moment. Thank you.'

Miranda swallowed and shivered expectantly, her thighs clamped firmly together. The tip of the bamboo rested lightly on the upper curves of her buttocks. It remained on her proffered bottom like a delicious, potent threat.

Swipe. In a twinkling, the cane flickered through the dust-spangled sunbeams and cut down across the stretch of white cotton. A cruel, intimately searching stroke. Miranda squeaked her surprised pain.

'There. That is how one canes a naughty bottom, Clarissa. No shilly-shallying. Lift the cane to shoulder height. So. Judge both the angle and the distance of the descent. Yes? Very much like golf, one must keep an eye on the green, not the ball. Then down she comes . . .' *Swish.* Miranda yelped. 'Like so. Sharply, mind. And see to it that you strike both cheeks.'

'Bravo,' cried the stern lector, thumbing her Tennyson frantically. Mrs Boydd-Black executed a mock bow, and then shouldered the cane.

'Thank you, Clarissa,' she purred.

'Ma'am,' acknowledged Clarissa.

'Thank you, Miranda. Please take your allotted place at the breakfast table.'

'Thank you, ma'am,' mumbled Miranda meekly, her bottom ablaze.

Breakfast was resumed. Tennyson was taken up where the grim reader with the braided hair had left off when the punishment commenced. Miranda nibbled a slice of lightly buttered toast and sipped from a cup of the camomile and raspberry tea poured out for her by a thoughtful, dark-eyed Asian beauty with exotic, shining black hair. Silence in the refectory reigned supreme, except for the Matron who continued to make a noisy affair of her bacon, kidneys and sausage. Miranda smiled a thank you at the beautiful Asian girl who returned the smile with large, brown eyes that had golden lights dancing in them.

'Finish your breakfasts, girls, then to work. And no slacking. I will not have slackers. Hurry up,' the headmistress said.

'You. The greenband,' Matron barked, wiping her greasy lips with a large, starched napkin. 'I will see you up in the san straight away.'

The Matron strode out of the refectory. Miranda slipped out of her seat and hurried out after the retreating Matron, who, without looking behind her, swept majestically on up the central staircase to stride resolutely down a white-walled landing hung with several sporting prints of the hunt. Miranda, hurrying to catch up, had a confused sense of packs of hounds, horses leaping over hedgerows and red-faced gentlemen in redder jackets as she passed.

'In here,' barked the imposing Matron who had proved so proficient when plying the leather strap across Miranda's upturned bottom the evening before. Miranda stepped into the cool sanitarium which reeked of TCP.

'Up on the scales,' the Matron snapped briskly.

Miranda obeyed. Matron checked her weight, noting it down on a clinical chart drawn up to record the details of the new girl.

'Height. Against the scale, girl.'

Miranda's five feet ten and a half inches was written down beneath her weight of nine stones by the five-foot six-inch robust Matron who weighed in at a little over fourteen stones.

'Tongue out.'

A wooden spatula, like an ice lolly stick, depressed Miranda's moist, pink healthy tongue.

'Say aahh.'

'Aahh,' Miranda echoed obediently.

'Vest up, girl.'

Miranda's hands fluttered nervously at her side. The Matron, a stethoscope plugged into her ears, raised a questioning eyebrow.

'Vest up, girl. I need to listen to your chest.'

But Miranda still did not comply. Her vest remained tightly drawn down over her breasts and belly.

'Are you disobeying my order, girl?' the Matron half snarled, half whispered.

Miranda remained stubbornly silent, gazing at the tiny lines around her tormentor's mouth. The lips were dry, lipstick free. There were fine, grey creases in the creamy flesh of the thick neck.

'Take a shower,' snapped Matron, turning on her heel abruptly and striding out of the san. 'I will return when you have come to your senses.'

The white door closed soundlessly behind Matron. Miranda glanced around, spotted the opaque plastic shower curtain and stepped gingerly towards it.

The cool tiles behind the shower curtain beckoned invitingly. Miranda relaxed, peeled off her green armband, vest, socks and tightly fitting white shorts and stepped under a stream of warm water which cascaded at the merest twist of a silver tap. The sparkling spray soothed her, drumming gently on her face, shoulders and softly swelling breasts. A warm rivulet coursed down the dark furrow between her recently punished buttocks, and around her pale feet the dancing bubbles eddied and disappeared, carrying away with them memories of the cruel stripes. Miranda sighed contentedly, as she gently soaped her belly and rounded thighs.

'This should cool that warm arse of yours,' snapped Matron, tearing back the plastic shower curtain and twisting the tap over towards cold. Miranda shrieked twice. Once with pure fright at the sudden, silent reappearance of Matron. Again, breathlessly, as the ice cold water sluiced the entire length of her shivering nakedness. Under the cold kisses of the icy deluge, her nipples peaked painfully, rising stiff and erect in rapid response. Fragile diamonds of water droplets sparkled in her pubic delta. The pale pink stripes of punishment across her broad, golden buttocks turned faintly blue as the cold water accelerated the mild bruising.

'Out,' Matron snarled, clearly in no mood to be trifled with.

Miranda, teeth chattering, her eyes screwed tightly shut, stepped out of the freezing shower and found her soft limbs being swathed in a full size bath towel. Almost grateful for the warmth of the unexpected embrace, she yielded up to it completely, only dimly aware at first that Matron's strong hands lay within the fabric to seek out and find her intimate parts. The two hands, firm and brisk, dried her neck, shoulders and arms, pausing after roughly towelling the generous breasts to squeeze and fondle their supple ripeness.

Miranda's breasts, fully and searchingly subjected to the thorough tactile exploration, were abandoned for her belly and inner thighs. The broad palms spread across her dripping wet, firm flesh, frequently straying to her rump to pat her joggling buttocks dry, before pausing to use her fingertips to investigate the cleft that divided the two soft cheeks. Miranda stood rigid, unable to resist the intimate, dominant power to which she was being subjected.

'Turn around,' Matron commanded.

Miranda obeyed.

'Legs apart.'

Miranda cringed as she felt Matron's warm breath on the nape of her neck. Slowly, a quarter of an inch at a time, she parted her pale, tapering legs. Little puddles formed around her toes. She bit her soft lower lip as a handful of towel buried itself up between her thighs, roughly drying the satin skin of the soft, inner flesh and dragging abrasively against the labial folds. Miranda suppressed a squeak of protest and suffered the attentions of the supple, ruthless hands.

Matron stepped slowly around her, coming to a stop immediately in front of her. Miranda automatically inched back. Matron took an intimate half-step forwards, her face, now a mere six inches from Miranda's, seemed to be glazed with a playful half-smile mixed with a preoccupied frown of intense concentration.

Miranda saw the look of remote, unfocused attentiveness in her tormentor's pale, colourless eyes, which were now dilated by lust. It was as if Matron had cast her mind back to some remote moment in her life, trying to recollect if it had rained on her twelfth birthday. Something half remembered, elusive and yet unimportant seemed to be distracting her.

The moments ticked by. The fingers within the thick towelling worked busily, worrying the tingling pink folds of flesh that partly sealed Miranda's tender opening. Miranda stood, her bottom annoyed by the wet plastic shower curtain that clung lovingly to her nakedness. Her damp feet were splayed apart, her inner thighs receptively submitting to Matron's towelled hands. A full eight minutes later, just as the first scent of Miranda's excited fragrance tinged the air, Matron seemed to snap out of her trance and hurriedly gathered up the soft towelling into her capable arms.

'Onto the examination table, girl. Up. Hurry. I haven't got all day.' This time the tone was slightly less harsh. Brisk but almost amiable.

Miranda, conscious and resentful of the sticky moistness oozing where Matron's devilish hands had been so busy, stumbled numbly up onto a long, low examination couch which had been prepared with a paper sheet. Matron, deft and professional, checked Miranda's eyes and ears and then monitored her heart and lungs. After taking her blood pressure and pulse, she pronounced herself to be satisfied.

'On your tummy. Over.'

Miranda rolled over obediently, squashing her generous, naked breasts beneath her as she lay face down. Matron's broad, firm hand came to rest gently, pink palm down, across the swell of the upturned bottom.

'Such a pert, pretty bottom. Such a naughty girl. You have been very naughty, haven't you? Hmm?' Matron asked in a bright tone, as if discussing some more pleasant, lighter topic. One could have discussed the seasonable weather in exactly that politely interested tone.

Miranda remained silent.

'You have been naughty, haven't you?' Matron persisted, her voice darkening a shade.

Miranda murmured something about there having been a misunderstanding.

'Such a pretty bottom. A pleasure to punish, I'm sure,' Matron crooned, massaging the soft pillows of pliant flesh with a gentle vigour. 'Are you regular?'

Miranda was nonplussed.

'I am a firm believer in regularity. Laxatives and roughage are all very well in their way, I suppose, but I find an enema much the best thing. Shall we have an enema? Yes, I do believe we shall. Stay still, my dear.'

Patting Miranda's naked rump tenderly, Matron turned to open a cupboard and took down a large plastic jug, a length of rubber hose, some gloves and a small tube of clear lubricant. Miranda's toes turned up in a tight curl of anxious anticipation, as if Matron were wielding the strap once more. She gritted her teeth. Should she resist? Could she resist? Any disobedience and this monster could, and undoubtedly would, summon help with the touch of a bell press. With painful consequences for Miranda. The First Position, or perhaps the more shameful and painful Second Position.

The white tiled room started to spin around. Miranda's troubled brain swirled. Was there to be no end to this nightmare? Would her naturally fierce pride snap as it was prone to do, earning her even more humiliation and pain?

At the sink, Matron filled the plastic jug with warm water, then returned to the examination couch. Attaching a funnel to one end of the rubber hose, she dabbed the snout of the other end with the lubricant jelly.

'On your side, please. Knees up to your tummy. That's the way.'

As if in a dreadful dream, Miranda obeyed. The watching, wakeful part of her brain knew that to resist would incur an instant caning. Or worse. Shuddering, eyes very close to unbidden, bitter tears, she lay passively awaiting the horror and indignity that was to overtake her. The cold, slippery snub nose of the rubber tubing tickled the lower part of the dark cleft between her clenched buttocks.

'Relax.' The tone was firm, brooking no denial of the command. The nozzle poked and probed inquisitively, finally finding the tight rosebud of the sphincter's whorl. Imperceptibly, at first, it worried the pale pink muscle and then, with infinite slowness, slipped inside and wormed its way upward.

Miranda clenched her fists, trying desperately to deny the indignity. A wave of self-disgust broke over her as the length of cold rubber inched up inside her bottom. Then a strange, unfamiliar sensation swept over her, starting in the remote distance of her consciousness and growing stronger and clearer like an approaching light. Falling a considerable way short of delight or pleasure, it was more of a tickling anticipation. Horrified at even the merest glimpse of this unbidden emotion on her inner horizon, Miranda struggled to fight down the subtle, seductive twinge. She could not, as yet, define or name the curious, disturbing sensation.

The warm water trickled down the funnel, along the length of the rubber tube and into her innermost parts. Soon, it was flooding the anal canal and surging into her colon. The warmth burgeoned within her, and the sensations were decidedly pleasing, if the circumstances were unpleasant.

Miranda felt utterly helpless. The absoluteness of Matron's power over her became a palpable thing.

To her horror and shameful surprise, the earlier feelings swam into crisp focus: she wished that her vague feelings of helplessness were more concrete. If only her hands were rendered immobile, or Matron would pin her down firmly. Perhaps her ankles could be bound.

The notion was fleeting but intense. Miranda, now fully aware of what her yearnings truly were, was filled with self-disgust and banished the lurid images away almost immediately. Almost. They lingered, leaving a trace of their presence on her mind. Nevertheless, Miranda smarted at the recognition of these urges as she would smart if lashed on the naked buttocks by a strap or supple cane.

The enema completed, Miranda shuddered as the nozzle was gently eased out from her bottom. She shivered as it left her with a faint 'plop'. Fighting down the rising tide of humiliation that surged up within her, Miranda lay back, her eyes tightly shut.

'Slip into that cubicle over there, my girl. It should take effect shortly.'

Miranda, still naked and blushing furiously, walked gingerly over to the WC. She clenched her buttocks tightly, terrified of the consequences of relaxing her inner muscles. Burning with the unaccustomed flame of raw shame and humiliation, she sat down on the gleaming white porcelain bowl and, moments later, having passed wind furiously, submitted to nature as it took its violent course.

'There. That's much better, I'm sure. We must do this every morning, my girl. Now get dressed. Come along,' Matron barked sternly. 'Quickly, girl. Mrs Boydd-Black awaits.'

Miranda, trembling, and weak after her experience, hastily wriggled into her tight, white shorts and figure hugging cotton vest. Out of the corner of a wary eye she saw the examination table on which she had so recently undergone such indignities. Her face flushed as a dark thought clouded her mind. Had she really, at some imprecise point in the ordeal, actually wanted to submit utterly and completely to that improbable monster? Her eyes sparkled. She blinked. Had she really nurtured, or even harboured somewhere deep down in her remote subconscious, the desire to be totally dominated by Matron – submitting to the fierce delights of being rendered helpless by the cruel strictures of bondage? Miranda shook her head as one would shake disbelief, or the dregs of sleep out of one's eyes.

'Thank you, Miranda. Tomorrow morning. Be prompt,' Matron grinned.

'Thank you, Matron,' Miranda murmured in her daze of confusion.

'You will work in the kitchen for a settling-in period. Simple, menial tasks. But important. Cleanliness is vitally important, so attend to your tasks with care and probity. We are a sizeable community here at the Academy. Six members of staff and nineteen naughty girls.'

Mrs Boydd-Black was warming to her theme. It was her favourite topic of conversation. The Academy. The structure, the rules, the regulations and the punishments.

'As a greenband, or reception girl, you will have to earn lots and lots of merits before we can consider promoting you up to the next grade. It is, I believe, a long and frequently painful journey. After green, red. Then up to blue, where there is the extra responsibility of administering punishments to the lower grades. And finally gold, or leavers as we like to call them. Clarissa is a blue band. She will be both mentor and monitor to you. Understand?'

Miranda, hands at her side, blonde head downcast, nodded.

'Clarissa has absolute control over you. Listen to her and obey. We believe in delegating our duties here at the Academy. It is both character building and character forming. And remember. One day, in time, you may well become a mentor to a new girl. You will, through judicial discipline and control, exercise supreme authority over some new greenband reception girl. Prepare yourself to undertake those duties carefully. Listen. Learn. Obey.'

The headmistress paused, finished the thimble of dry sherry she had been sipping, and placed the tiny cut glass down on an occasional table. Head tilted back, chin jutting out, she turned, calling back, 'Come along, girl. Don't dawdle. This way to the kitchen.'

Down in the warm basements, where dry, warm flagstones kissed the naked soles of her feet, Miranda was put to work alongside the large-eyed Asian girl who had smiled encouragingly at her earlier that morning. The task was simple. Scrubbing pots and greasy pans. They worked in the obligatory silence for a quarter of an hour, under the ever vigilant, sharp eye of the stern woman with the braided hair who had read to the community at breakfast. A leather strap dangled from a loop stitched into her tightly-waisted skirt.

Miranda studied her fellow sufferer obliquely. A slim, willowy girl, whose pale gold skin was delicious against the crisp white vest and shorts. A

57

leaver, Miranda noticed. The golden armband was almost invisible set against the honey-hued forearm. Why was a leaver, the most senior rank, doing something so menial as washing up? Miranda frowned.

Soft footsteps padded up the stone steps. Their supervisor had departed.

'Jaya,' whispered the Asian beauty, her smile broad and warm.

Miranda replied, giving her own name.

The thick coil of lush, dark hair worked itself loose from Jaya's head and tumbled down her pale nape. Her arms deep in warm suds, Jaya was unable to rescue and capture it. Miranda shrugged, grinned, wiped her hands and gathered up the gorgeous tresses. The spontaneous intimacy of the act drew the girls together.

'It is all very alarming at first. But do not be very afraid. You will soon learn. I could tell. At breakfast. You are strong.'

'Not very,' Miranda admitted. 'How long have you been here?'

Jaya frowned.

'It is strange you ask me that,' she replied.

'Strange?' Miranda echoed.

'Most girls simply ask when am I going.'

Miranda nodded.

'Of course. The gold band. You should be going soon.'

Jaya drooped her head.

'I am not sure,' she said sadly. 'I have displeased Matron. That is why I am back here scrubbing pots like a greenband.'

'Matron is strange,' Miranda said, 'not a woman to upset.'

'I have been here seven months and already I have eighty-seven merits.'

'Only thirteen to go,' Miranda said enthusiastically.

'Yes, but Matron is displeased with me. It is difficult. I have not been whipped or caned for a week, but my luck may not hold.'

Miranda shuddered. A brooding silence settled over them. Then Jaya spoke. Softly. 'Miranda?'

'Mmm?'

'Did you see Matron this morning?'

Miranda blushed as she nodded.

'Did she give you an enema?'

Miranda's blush deepened.

'Do not be shy. We all suffer under her hands. Some more than others. She is not kind. The other staff have to punish but they are kind. Matron is not. And she has a way of touching . . .'

Miranda nodded again.

'She makes you feel strange. Makes you think things.'

Miranda wrestled with a large, heavy black-bottomed frying pan and placed it on the shelf.

'That's true, Jaya,' she said. 'I felt exactly the same. I couldn't believe the thoughts I was having. Ugh.' Miranda shivered.

'Be careful. Matron has the evil touch. I am full of shame when her hands have found me out.'

Miranda gazed directly into Jaya's large, dark eyes.

'That is so true. I felt just like that myself. I couldn't believe it. Oh, Jaya. This place terrifies me. I feel as though I am in a nightmare. I wish I could just wake up.'

Miranda felt a sudden surge of close friendship,

59

companionship and affection for this gentle, honest Asian girl. She needed a trusty friend and felt that she had probably found one.

'Do not worry,' Jaya said sympathetically. 'You will feel frightened and confused. But it will pass. All will get better in time. Slowly, at first. But better, in time. Believe me. And I will look after you if you will let me.'

Miranda, normally so proud and aloof, nodded her willing assent. Then, stung by a sudden curiosity, asked, 'Why are you . . . I mean, what did you . . .?'

Jaya laughed.

'I am Indian,' she replied, 'born just outside Ascot, actually. Daddy is very strict. He wanted that I marry a banker from Bihar state.'

'Bihar? Which part?' Among Miranda's ancestors she counted a District Governor or two who had propped up the Empire.

'Most of it. The family are very, very rich. Almost as rich as Daddy,' Jaya shrugged. 'I wanted to go up to Cambridge. To read Law. There was so much trouble. I ran away. They had me snatched and dragged back. Daddy knew a man, a business acquaintance. A solicitor. I hate that solicitor. He brought me to this evil place. I can leave when I agree to marry the Bihar banker.'

'Will you?' Miranda asked breathlessly, both fascinated and appalled by the story she had just heard. 'It is simply dreadful for you, Jaya. You must go up to Cambridge. And read Law. And marry who you like. I mean, love. Oh, Jaya, what will you do?'

'Exactly what she is told,' crackled an angry voice behind them.

Miranda spun around and saw the stern faced

woman. She had returned silently and overheard their rebellious talk.

'You are not making a very good beginning, are you Miranda? First Position, girl. Shorts down, please.'

Slowly, deliberately, as if pausing to savour the moment, the stern white fingers gathered up the supple leather belt from her waist and flexed it, sensuously.

Shorts around her white-stockinged ankles, blonde hair hanging down freely, Miranda placed her pale hands behind her knees and gripped hard as she had been carefully instructed. The warm air of the kitchen played almost affectionately on her naked buttocks. The soft leather strap tapped her fully exposed, upturned bottom.

'Feet together, girl,' came the crisp command.

Miranda obeyed, clenching her teeth and squeezing her eyes shut tight. The leather quickened and flickered into life, whistled through the air and snapped down with a loud crack on her soft, satin flesh. A cruel swipe of dead flesh on living skin. Miranda squealed as her beautiful bottom took the first of five stinging lashes.

Chapter Three

Fat wood pigeons, swollen by their success in the surrounding harvest fields, murmured dreamily in the denuded branches of trees that had slowly begun to disrobe their leaves some weeks since in strict obedience to autumn's stern command. Their muted notes stole softly into Miranda's dreams. She opened her eyes, blinked, then remembered. It was Saturday morning. Of that much she was sure. She had been at the Academy exactly one week and one day.

Suddenly, the quick pulse of anxiety that was never fully dormant fluttered through her brain. Had first bell been sounded? Had second bell been rung? She jumped out of her bed and ran to the door of the small, forlorn dormitory. Outside, in the empty passageways and along the cold landings, all was silent and still. Her heart slowed down from its sudden surge of beating and she breathed a little more calmly.

Shivering slightly as the early morning chill caressed her soft nakedness, she returned to her narrow bed. What time was it? Six-thirty? Seven-forty-five? She simply had no idea. The Academy had no clocks visible, and all the girls incarcerated there were denied the privilege of wearing a watch. All activities were tightly timetabled, and whether it was to supper or to punishment, the girls were summoned by bells.

Punishment. Miranda stretched out luxuriously, enjoying her stolen moments of peaceful solitude. The narrow bed was warm where her soft body had curled and slept, but the furthest parts of the taut linen remained deliciously, sensuously cool. Her warm, naked feet sought out and relished these virginal corners of her bed.

Punishment. As she lay on her back, her legs stretched wide apart, Miranda's brain produced a fast forward mental video of the events she had experienced or witnessed over the past eight days.

Pause. Rewind. Clarissa caning her, with a reluctant severity, before her first breakfast. *Pause. Fastforward.* The daily ordeal with Matron. The cold nozzle of the rubber tubing inching up inside her bottom. *Forward. Pause.* The silly little redhead with the large, green eyes being spanked resoundingly. Spanked so severely for merely running down the sweeping staircase and laughing. *Hold.* The girlish redhead being spanked.

Miranda's cool fingertips fluttered below the gentle swell of her taut belly, tenderly exploring and rustling the fringe of her pubic down. Eyes screwed up tightly, she sharpened the focus of the mental imagery. The redhead, pinned firmly over the knees of the dominant headmistress, Mrs Boydd-Black, her naked, golden bottom squirming as it writhed under the punishing hail of stinging slaps. Miranda's fingers strummed her soft, sensitive folds of secret flesh. They moistened and parted like a rosebud annointed by sunbeams.

Hold. Rewind. Pause. The image was fixed. It

burned like a shimmering, dancing flame. The muscles around Miranda's belly tightened.

The redhead. Naked, pinioned and punished. Fluttering feet threshing the empty air as the spanking commenced. Squeals punctuating the loud smacks. Miranda's fingers quickened as they scrabbled at the tingling, honey-dewed lips of flesh centred within her firm, splayed thighs.

The redhead's tiny white shorts pathetically abandoned on the deep crimson carpet at the foot of the sweeping staircase, like a flag of surrender, were etched behind her eyelids. *Smack.* The reddening cheeks. *Smack. Smack.* A thin squeal. Miranda conjured up the sounds of the punishment.

Rewind. Search. Pause. The images of the Academy became fluid once more as they spilled like quicksilver through her brain. She scanned her molten memory banks for more. More vivid memories to fuel the throbbing engine at the base of her glistening belly. Feeding her vortex of excitement, she glimpsed with her inner eye a myriad of freeze-frames showing snatches of the punishments seen and heard.

Punishments. The swishing strokes of a cane thrumming in the air. The harsh barking snap of a searing strap. The ruthless crack of a supple leather belt stinging naked buttocks. The white blur of a firm hand on soft, pink cheeks.

Miranda's finger plucked and punished her own wetness rhythmically, her frenzy fed by the lava flow of hot, liquid imagery. Breathing heavily through her nose, her throat and neck muscles spasmed and tightened like knotted cord. Her full hips rose up as her arched spine shuddered and quivered. A warm rush suffused her loins.

64

It was coming. About to break over her like a violent thunder storm in summer. Soon. Soon. Her brain blazed, frantic to explode from her inner tumult into the ravishing climax.

Suddenly, to her confusion and alarm, the dominant image was of Matron. Matron pinning Miranda's naked body down on the examination table in the white-tiled san and inserting the enema tubing up into her vulnerable, exposed bottom.

Yes. Miranda surrendered to the powerfully overwhelming image, suddenly yearning for a taste of bondage. She manipulated the image, adding the picture of Matron binding her wrists and ankles. *Yes.*

Miranda ground the palm of her hand down into the pulsing wetness between her thighs, gyrating flesh upon flesh until the surging climax broke. With a low, feral groan that melted into a deep, protracted sigh, the orgasms fluttered and rippled belly-outwards until every nerve and muscle shivered and tingled as she was scorched by the lambent flames of fulfilment.

Turning over in her narrow bed, she buried her face into the single, hard pillow. Her eyes were tightly shut, her mouth slack and open with drained passions. Flooded and almost drowning in the sensations of submission and utter surrender to dominant forces, Miranda unconsciously raised her naked bottom up, as if offering it willingly for savage punishment. A punishment she found herself keenly wanting and curiously welcoming. The last waves of the ebbing orgasm licked and lapped within her sweat-soaked thighs. She had surrendered to the new-found delight completely.

Later, sitting up in the bed, her chin resting

pensively on her hunched knees, Miranda wrestled with the troublesome thoughts that worried and confused her. Haunted by the burning image of her surrender to domination and control in her fantasy, her wish for bondage and humiliation at the hands of the capable Matron, Miranda was brooding and feeling distinctly uneasy. From what depths had it peeped out into the crimson and golden explosions in her brain?

The climax had been her most powerful, most delicious and most ravishing ever, but the images that had fuelled it were alien to her. A naturally confident, strong-willed and headstrong girl, fully used to giving and not taking orders, she could make no sense of her capitulation, just on the brink of the paroxysm of climax, to deep desires for subjugation and self-surrender. True, she was discovering new sensations, unsuspected and strange delights and undiscovered yearnings since her arrival at the Academy.

The aged, mellow Queen Anne building was a heavenly façade housing a physical and psychological hell within. And within those deceptively sober walls, walls so solid they deadened the shrieks of those punished inside, Miranda had become exposed to a range of new sensations and privations. Cold lino under naked feet, feet familiar only with the deepest pile. The taut stretch of her brief, white uniform over her voluptuous body, a body more accustomed to the kiss of silk and the caress of satin. New scents and smells. Girls freshly scrubbed with carbolic soap and corridors where boiled cabbage lingered. The smell of chalk dust in the sunbeams and of waxed and polished wooden floors.

Perhaps these, and many other, strange aspects of her spartan life under the strict regime at the Academy had kindled dark desires. Or could they be the result of the emotional and psychological turmoil she had undergone? She was certainly wrestling with many forms of inner conflict. Always fiercely proud, she was quickly and painfully learning to curb and bridle herself, and where once she would have spoken out brusquely in her kitten-quick-tempered manner, she was restraining herself for fear of the sharp lash of discipline. Logic and control, fear and restraint were now beating down and subduing her former volatility. And the luxuries she had once demanded were now replaced by privations she detested.

Gone were her expensive perfumes, designer lingerie, chilled champagne and blinis. Sheer silk was now rough cotton. Cocktails and canapés were now milk and halibut oil vitamin pills. These and other, more distressing, experiences were slowly but surely peeling away her outer layers of custom, habit and at a deeper level, personality and character. Exposed were new aspects, unfathomed desires and unsuspected yearnings.

First bell sounded. The startled wood pigeons fluttered and flew down from the branches of the gaunt tree outside Miranda's dormitory window, applauding the new day with wings that clapped the autumnal chill of dawn. Miranda snapped out of her reverie and scrambled out of her bed. She struggled into her tight, white vest and brief, thigh-hugging shorts, flinching slightly as the elasticated waistband bit into her soft flesh. Quickly tidying her bedclothes, she suddenly remembered the green armband. To appear at breakfast downstairs without it

67

would earn her buttocks the instant punishment of three withering strokes across their splendid swell.

The only greenband reception girl currently at the Academy, Miranda felt slightly self-conscious as she joined the headmistress, Matron, four other members of staff and eighteen other girls for breakfast. It had never bothered her before. Being slightly conspicuous. Indeed, she was used to having Special Branch shadowing her when attending a reception. She only had to smile instead of fiddling with cheque books and credit cards when on a Knightsbridge spree. But here, within the strict and severe confines of the Academy, the green armband marked her out as different. Different and conspicuous. Conspicuous and therefore vulnerable. Especially to the predatory attentions of canes and straps.

As usual, the stern staff were tucking into crisp bacon and fluffy heaps of scrambled eggs, dark oyster mushrooms and plump, pink sausages from gleaming silverware. A large, cold, breaded ham, dishes of poached haddock and a silver salver winking with buttered kippers sat patiently on the fumed oak sideboard behind them. At their lower tables, the dejected girls nibbled hungrily at their ration of crispbread.

The potent aroma of strong coffee stabbed Miranda's memory as she sipped at her weak herbal tea. The refectory was unusually tense. None of the girls spoke, keeping their sorrowful eyes down on their unappetising breakfasts. Mrs Boydd-Black wiped her mouth delicately with her white napkin and rang the little hand bell which always held pride of place at her elbow. Instantly, the girls stopped eating and drinking. All sat in silent attentiveness.

'Girls. I regret to inform you that there has been

a quite dreadful transgression committed by one of your number. There will therefore be a Chair before lunch. A Chair with a Quarter Exercise. That is all.'

The frisson of fear rippling through the breakfasting girls was tangible. Miranda looked cautiously around. Jaya looked unperturbed. Good. So did Jane, another girl Miranda had befriended in a furtive way. Then Miranda caught a glimpse of Clarissa, who had been so kind to her when trying to protect her from suffering during her first caning all those punishments ago. Clarissa had turned deadly pale, and Miranda instinctively knew that it was this girl who was to undergo a Chair and Quarter Exercise later on that morning.

The girls rose and departed in silence. Matron summoned Miranda up to the san for her morning enema.

'Shorts off, girl. Up you get,' she said in her no-nonsense tone that defied reply or protest.

Miranda slipped her hands down inside the tight elastic waistband and slowly eased the white cotton shorts down, revealing ivory hips and shadowed, golden thighs.

'Come along, girl. Busy morning. A Chair and Quarter Exercise before lunch,' Matron chuckled grimly. 'I'm having jugged hare with a spot of claret. Very toothsome.'

Matron, it seemed, was devoted to both food and punishment, finding each quite delightful. Miranda stepped out of her shorts, peeled off her vest and climbed up onto the examination table.

'Come along, quickly now. Don't tarry,' Matron said crisply, snapping on her rubber gloves.

'I don't need these enemas. I am quite regular,' Miranda replied, slowly and mechanically.

Smack. The firm, rubber-gloved hand slapped Miranda's naked bottom harshly as she lay on her side, knees drawn up and squashing her soft, shuddering bosom.

'I'll be the better judge of that, girl. Now unclench those cheeks. Come along. Open wide.'

Once more, the nozzle of the rubber tubing, winking with its blob of lubricant, worried the ultra sensitive whorl of Miranda's pink rosebud sphincter. She shivered. Her belly tightened. Almost at once the sensations she both relished and abhorred kindled within her body and her mind. Without thinking, she dropped her hand down to her side, grazing her plump thigh negligently.

It was an unwitting, unconscious gesture of futile self-protection, an abject token of resistance to safeguard her vulnerable bottom. Her trembling fingertips brushed the warm, rubber tubing, sweeping it aside. As it slithered out silently, warm water spilled all over the couch.

'Stupid little fool. Get up at once.' Matron was livid.

Miranda jumped down immediately, fearful of the hand of wrath that might seek out and find her naked buttocks.

'Sorry,' she mumbled in her confusion and dismay.

'You certainly will be, girl,' came the menacing response.

The spillage wiped up and fresh paper spread across the soft, dark leather surface, Miranda was briskly ordered back up onto the examination table. As she lay on her side, waiting passively for the length of rubber tubing to invade her vulnerable softness, she suddenly felt her hands being gathered together and pinioned firmly at the wrists in Matron's fierce clasp.

'We don't want any more nonsense, do we?' Matron rasped, gripping the wrists of the naked girl who lay curled up before her. With one strong hand pinioning Miranda tightly, she plied the supple rubber tubing in between the clenched cheeks of the fully rounded buttocks.

'Relax. Open up,' she ordered.

Miranda, dizzily delighting in the delicious yet vaguely perturbing vortex of new sensations, instantly obeyed, relaxing her bottom to allow the questing rubber tubing to explore her innermost softness. Soon, the warm rush of water filled her, and that sensation, combined with the thrill of being pinioned down into utter helplessness, caused a silvery liquid bubble to peep out shyly between her slightly parted thighs. Hot shame burned redly in Miranda's face as she felt the wetness saturate her pubic fringe. Sniffing the odour of her victim's unbidden excitement like a shark sensing its prey, Matron bent over to examine her supine charge.

'Responding to the treatment, I see,' she chuckled with malevolent glee. The tone of approval mixed with indulgent understanding sickened Miranda, who squirmed with pure shame.

The enema tubing was briskly removed. A rubber-sheathed fingertip and firm thumb found and held Miranda's left nipple. The peaking strawberry of flesh was tweaked and teased in an expert pincer. The right nipple responded with alacrity. Soon, both nipples strained achingly as they rose up, an angry shade of crimson, from their smooth, creamy burgeoning mounds of flesh. Miranda clamped her thighs together tightly. It was a gesture of both defiance and resistance.

71

'Over onto your tummy,' rasped Matron.

'Why? I haven't –'

Smack. The soft buttocks joggled under the firm slap.

'Silence,' Matron thundered. 'Obey without question. Over.'

Miranda rolled over, presenting her naked bottom up to her tormentor. Inside her, the enema was taking effect. She pressed her legs together anxiously, welding them at ankle, knee and inner thigh. A shiver ran down her dimpled spine as a length of the rubber tubing brushed her rounded buttocks, coming to rest across the swell of their softly swelling mounds.

'I am going to break you, my girl. Spoiled little bitch. All those chances. Wasted. Thrown away. Look at you. Pretty. Rich. Titled. I never had those assets.'

The tone was one of controlled anger. Chillingly vehement. Miranda tasted the sour tang of fear in her mouth.

'You will learn, bitch. And make a good pupil. I've seen the signs. I shall relish tutoring you.'

Miranda panicked. The monster had detected her unwilling response to the domination and was now set to ruthlessly exploit this at both her leisure and will.

'But look who is on top? Eh?'

The sadistic tone had an edge of rising triumph in it that startled Miranda. The rubber tubing lay dangerously still across her skin.

'Me. And you will quickly learn that I . . .'

A telephone rang shrilly. Matron paused in mid-sentence, fumed impatiently and, turning savagely on her heel, strode across the san to a locked cupboard. Selecting a key from the large bunch on her leather belt, she unlocked and opened the cupboard door.

All telephones in the Academy were locked out of sight and reach of the girls. As an extra precaution, the phone number had been erased from every dial.

Miranda lay, seething with indignation yet cowed into fearful submission, naked and face down on the examination couch. The length of rubber tubing remained draped over the soft contours of her generous buttocks, resting on her taut, satin smooth skin, potent yet inert, full of the delicious threat it both posed and promised. The Matron grunted into the phone, replaced the receiver and locked it away in the cupboard. She turned to Miranda, fingering the key in her strong fingers.

'Go to the toilet. Then get dressed. I will attend to you later. In fact,' she pondered aloud as Miranda ran across to squat down with relief on the toilet, 'I will see you . . .' Matron paused, savouring the tension her delay created. The awful moments stretched to a full minute until Miranda almost screamed. 'I will need to see you twice a day from now on. Come back just before supper. I will deal with you more thoroughly then.'

Miranda pulled up her brief white shorts and struggled into the tight cotton vest. It both moulded and squashed her full bosom as the taut fabric embraced her.

She left the san deep in thought. It was not just her immediate fate, the imminent pain and humiliation that awaited her, which troubled her. It was the vigorous sense of injustice. Matron was emerging as a sadistic bully with a terrific chip on her shoulder. The powerful inferiority complex she had just unintentionally revealed fuelled her hunger for discipline and thirst for punishment. Miranda reflected upon the fact that the regime at the Academy was strict and severe enough. To be so ruthlessly abused was, to her sense of fair play, abhorrent. Something would have to be done, a small voice inside her insisted.

Miranda drew upon twelve generations of noble birth, and her chivalrous flame flickered, as did her fierce pride. She suddenly knew that she had the courage, the right and indeed the duty to challenge and curtail Matron's nasty bullying. Bullying which went far beyond the admittedly bizarre punishment schedules of the Academy.

'My goodness, Miranda. We are looking thoughtful.' Miss Frobisher smiled warmly.

Miranda looked up guiltily and smiled, flushing heavily. She had almost walked straight past Miss Frobisher, the poetry and art tutor with the exquisite hands, without offering the required courtesy of a polite greeting.

'I'm sorry, Miss Frobisher. Good morning,' Miranda said hastily, anxious not to give offence to this pleasant woman.

'And a very good morning to you, my dear,' replied Miss Frobisher, smiling to show that she had overlooked the unintentional lapse of good manners. 'Not planning or plotting naughty deeds, I trust?' she added gently, fluttering her shapely, slender hands gracefully.

'Oh, no, Miss Frobisher.' Miranda blushed.

Miranda had taken a very strong liking to this fey, winsome 34-year-old tutor. Delicately beautiful, she taught the girls in an inspired way, encouraging them and rewarding their efforts with praise.

74

Miranda had been informed by many of the girls that Miss Frobisher, though an art tutor, helped everyone with maths and other hateful subjects they struggled to master. But like all the other members of staff, the beautiful Miss Frobisher administered discipline when it was necessary to do so, never flinching from her duties to chastise the naughty, the disobedient or the wayward. Appropriately, she put her beautiful hands to effective purpose. The girls often whispered that a spanking from Miss Frobisher was a memorable one.

'Down to your chores and allotted duties, my dear. Don't be late,' the pleasant woman said, smiling warmly.

Miranda turned to watch her stride off down along the corridor, her soft cashmere dress clinging lovingly to her shapely hips and thighs. Miss Frobisher had a subtle charm, Miranda suddenly realised, and a quiet, understated beauty.

Down in the kitchen she joined Jaya at the pots and pans. Neither spoke as the supervisor prowled by continuously, strap at the ready. The arduous morning dragged on slowly, the brooding cloud of the impending Chair and Quarter Exercise casting a dark shadow over their minds.

'What is this Chair, exactly?' Miranda whispered at length, breaking the oppressive silence.

'Of course, you don't know. Didn't Mrs Boydd-Black explain?' Jaya sighed.

'No. She only explained the coloured band system. You know. Green for newcomers. Then red, and finally gold.'

'When you were in her study, didn't you see that ugly old chair?'

'Yes, I think I did.'

'That's the brute. And a Quarter Exercise means . . .'

Jaya was ordered to stop talking by the supervisor who fingered her strap menacingly. Obediently, both girls bent down and resumed their tasks, elbows deep in the frothy, warm suds.

At roughly eleven o'clock, Miranda had to go to her singing lesson. There were five other girls in the class, one blueband and four redbands. Their tutor, Madame Nina, was in an impatient, tetchy mood. The impending Chair and Quarter Exercise seemed to be unsettling everyone, Miranda reasoned. In the airy drawing room, gathered around the piano, Madame Nina hurried the six assembled girls through their *chansons*.

Singing in French was held by Mrs Boydd-Black to improve the girls' accents. Singing in French was held by the girls to be a bore. Madame Nina had her work cut out for her, but proved equal to the task.

Miranda thought the singing lessons trivial, but wisely kept her views to herself. France to her meant going to the races at Saint-Cloud, or attending exclusive and expensive Parisian night spots . . .

'*Non, non, non!*' snapped Madame Nina. 'C-sharp.'

One of the redbands steadied herself at the piano and tried the elusive note again. Her efforts were unsuccessful.

'*Encore*,' said Madame Nina impatiently.

'Lah,' sang the girl, again missing her key.

Madame Nina tut-tutted petulantly, rose from her seat at the piano and stood directly behind the nervous girl. Pulling down the anxious redband's white shorts with a single jerk, the music teacher gazed at the top half of the naked bottom her action had

76

revealed. Miranda noticed how the taut elastic waistband bit into the double hemisphere of pillowy flesh as it tightly encircled and embraced the pliant softness of the half-exposed rump.

Smack. The small, firm hand of the music tutor spanked the bunched cheeks of the luckless redband.

'Lah,' the timorous girl quavered.

Smack. The ivory orbs pinked.

'Lah.' Too high, Miranda mused. Too high.

Smack. Reddish crimson stole across the superb buttocks like a spreading flame.

'Lah.' It was C-sharp at last.

Miranda watched the punished cheeks disappear behind their veil of white cotton as Madame Nina roughly pulled the shorts back up over the freshly spanked bottom. She did so with a sigh of exasperation, then resumed her seat before the piano.

Three short, shrill bells sounded. They seemed to reverberate around the bright, airy drawing room.

'*Vite, vite!*' Madame Nina hissed, chivvying her charges out into the cool corridor.

It was time, Miranda realised, for the Chair and the Quarter Exercise.

When Winston Churchill spoke of the 'welcome sparkle brought by Providence into a time of bleakness' on 2 June, 1953, Coronation Day, he was heard to add, 'In these times when the present is hard and the future veiled.'

Miranda's Uncle Teddy had been within earshot of the grand old man and the words were often repeated by Uncle Teddy on subsequent visits to Sandstones. Miranda, a mere elf as Uncle Teddy achieved his anecdotage, would often sit at his knees during nuts and port and overhear the famous

77

phrase. Now, as she walked towards the Chair, she was to come to know the full meaning of the great man's remarks.

For the first time in her gilded eighteen years, her present was hard. Very hard. And her future was veiled. Before the Quarter Exercise was over, a corner of that veil would have been lifted. What chilling possibilities would be glimpsed, she brooded anxiously as she walked in solemn single file towards Mrs Boydd-Black's study. Pulse aflutter, she entered the room.

With the entire community of the expectant staff and subdued girls fully assembled, the double doors were silently but firmly closed. On a square of pale blue carpet woven with a thin but intricate silver leaf pattern, the beast of a seventeenth-century, hand-carved, mahogany chair stood gleaming in a shaft of shimmering gold autumnal sunshine. A splendid polished sheen managed to wink with a dull, evil malignancy from the dark wood.

Head bent in shame, an anxious Clarissa presented the picture of penitence. The headmistress, in a loud check, stood with her back turned to the gathered women and girls. She remained silent, continuing to stare out wistfully across the breadth of shaven swards of lawns and prinked terraces.

Miranda, relieved to see that Clarissa was fully dressed, or at least as fully dressed as her regulation uniform of brief vest and white shorts permitted, breathed a quiet sigh of relief. Whatever this Chair business, and the Quarter Exercise meant, it clearly wasn't going to involve any physical chastisement.

Miranda felt a pang of disappointment and a sense of relief. The pang came from a sense of loss. Watching Clarissa being whipped would have given her a curious and satisfying thrill. The sudden sense of relief came from the realisation that she was not to have her darker desires met. Such was the state of turmoil, confusion and uncertainty within Miranda that in her disappointment lay her relief. Clarissa was to receive nothing more than a tongue lashing, a verbal reprimand. Thus it was that Miranda was consoling herself when Mrs Boydd-Black turned to address all present.

'I do thank you for coming along so promptly. Punctuality is a virtue the Academy places something of a premium on.'

Innocuous enough, thought Miranda.

'There are many virtues to aspire to just as there are many vices to avoid.'

Miranda relaxed a little more. Goodness, she sighed to herself silently. She's just going to talk and talk for ages. All this hype over a public ticking off for Clarissa. How bogus.

'One of your number has lapsed. I will spare you the squalid details and I forbid any further speculation as to the exact nature of the gross transgression. The wretched girl involved . . .'

All eyes fixed on Clarissa, who sought refuge in staring down at the carpet. Miranda saw the small, white-stockinged foot trace the silver leaf pattern with the delicacy of a ballerina.

'Head up, Clarissa. That's better,' the headmistress barked. 'I repeat, the wretched girl has confessed promptly and so I will not insist on the Half Exercise which the nature of her lapse fully warrants. A Chair with Quarter Exercise will suffice,' she concluded grimly.

Imperceptibly, the girls shuffled in their white socks.

'To the Chair, Clarissa,' came the command.

Clarissa hesitated, then stooped and plucked off her white ankle socks. As she wriggled out of her white shorts, a knot of fearful expectation tightened in Miranda's belly. Clarissa's plump, rounded bosoms bounced free as the vest came up over her shoulders and off over her mane of thick, tousled hair. Her pale face was flushed after the sudden exertion of stripping off. Utterly naked now and trembling slightly, Clarissa approached the Chair.

Miranda felt her palms turning clammy and damp. Her lips felt dry and her tongue felt thick in her suddenly sour mouth. Clarissa clambered into an ungaily kneeling position on the wide seat of the Chair, presenting her back, buttocks and small pink heels to the assembled throng. Then, stretching up, she leaned right up and over the tall backpiece of the wooden Chair, disappearing behind the slab of carved wood so that her head, shoulders and arms were completely hidden from view. Miranda saw that Clarissa's beautiful naked buttocks were now completely exposed as they remained high up in the air, presented fully for whatever chastisement they were destined to suffer. The unhappy girl supported herself on her knees and straining thighs. The position was both uncomfortable and very, very humiliating. And how unpleasant and insupportable, Miranda shuddered, to have one's head, arms, shoulders and breasts – one's whole upper torso – stretched over the hard wooden edge of the horrendous Chair.

'A Quarter Exercise. As we are approximately twenty-five, that makes a team of six. But I think five will suffice for the punishment squad.'

So that's what a Quarter Exercise means,

Miranda thought. Gosh! Imagine having the entire assembly line up to thrash you!

The headmistress called out five names. Miranda, her horror tinged with curiosity and a vague delight, heard her name among them. The three other girls, together with Matron and Miranda, were invited to approach the large, leather-topped desk and pick up table tennis bats.

In her slightly trembling hand, Miranda's felt heavy and somewhat cumbersome. It was of average size, covered on both sides with a thin coating of soft, dimpled latex. The bat had a short, stubby handle. Suddenly, Miranda found herself trying to calculate the surface area of her bat. Was it two times pi times the radius or pi times the radius squared? Avoiding the imminent horrors, her mind sought refuge in trying to focus on the problem of multiplying twenty-two over seven times the radius of her bat. But her eyes were drawn inexorably towards Clarissa's beautifully rounded, pale bottom that bulged generously, invitingly, as it awaited its punishment.

'Approach the Chair,' boomed Mrs Boydd-Black in a businesslike tone that failed to conceal her thickening excitement.

The appointed five obeyed, bearing down in silent menace upon the soft, exposed nakedness of the doomed girl.

'Position One. Two strokes each. Punish her soundly,' came the grim admonishment.

Miranda watched breathlessly as a blue armband, a slim girl with whom she had not yet actually spoken, stepped up, stood square to the Chair, raised her bat up – paused – and brought it down vigorously once, twice, quickly and sharply across the perfectly rounded bare cheeks. Clarissa hissed. The slim girl then held the bat out behind the back of the Chair, an inch away from Clarissa's lips. Miranda thrilled inwardly as she both saw and heard the punished girl meekly kiss the instrument of her torment.

The second member of the punishment squad stepped forward. Again, a girl with whom Miranda had exchanged few, if any words. Weighing the bat momentarily, she paused, then raised it up again to swipe it down in a vicious twinkling. *Crack. Crack.*

A faint, pinkish blush now tinged the deep, ivory cream of Clarissa's velvet flesh. Miranda winced as the soft, pliant skin momentarily flattened, squashed down into cruel submission as it yielded to the ruthless blows. Again, the striking surface of the bat was thrust behind the tall back of the Chair. Again, Miranda heard and saw Clarissa submit to it with a soft, reluctant kiss.

The third in line was Matron. She strode forward briskly and brought her table tennis bat down with two unerring, resounding splats. The reddening cheeks wobbled under the stinging onslaught, and as Clarissa kissed the dimpled latex with her dry, parted lips, Miranda stepped up and assumed her position.

Gazing down, she saw Clarissa's white toes curled up in fearful expectation. How unseemly and how ungaily it must be to sustain such a humiliating posture, she thought sorrowfully. The strain of maintaining the awkward stance was beginning to tell, she noticed, in the taut sinews of the smooth, curved thighs.

Poor, poor Clarissa. The repeated strokes of the table tennis bats were leaving pink blotches to commemorate their brief, stinging visits to the large, naked buttocks. Miranda gulped as she saw the dimpled imprints of the cruel latex. Swallowing hard, and trying desperately to ignore the flicker of excitement that unfurled in her belly and between her thighs, she judged the distance between herself and the half-kneeling, half-squatting miscreant.

Raising up her heavy bat, she cracked it down, loudly but lightly, across the wobbling left buttock. The firm bat almost bounced off the rounded cheek of springy, spongey flesh. Clarissa sighed. Again, the bat was drawn up, only to fall quickly to crack four-square against the luscious cheek. *Splat.* The tiny white toes curled and uncurled in a pathetic reflex spasm. Miranda blushed. She had intended it to be a light, glancing swipe but the peculiarly intense excitement of the moment had high-jacked her sense of timing and clouded her judgement. The stroke had been a stinger.

She offered up the striking side of the bat to Clarissa's trembling lips. A single teardrop glistened, welled up in Clarissa's eye and spilled down with a liquid splash onto the hot, dimpled latex. Miranda shivered slightly as she resumed her place among the punishment squad. Not a tear shed in pain, she consoled her miserable conscience, but a tear spilled in shame. Miranda was fond of Clarissa, the girl who had gallantly tried to protect her on that dreadful first morning at the Academy.

Crack. Crack. The fifth girl, a redband, administered her two strokes of the bat without pause or apparent pity. Clarissa mewed like a rain-soaked kitten. Miranda sighed deeply with relief. It was over.

'Position Two,' snapped Mrs Boydd-Black harshly.

To her horror, Miranda watched as Clarissa slowly eased herself down from the awkward posture across the high back of the Chair, stood back briefly and then reapproached the cruel throne. This time she insinuated her head and shoulders underneath one arm rest, crawled belly down across the broad seat and emerged, head, shoulders and outstretched arms, beneath the other arm rest. She now lay, breasts squashed down into the polished wood, glowing buttocks upturned for punishment, effectively pinioned by the twin arm rests beneath which her supine body lay stretched out at full length.

'Proceed,' instructed the headmistress.

The first girl, the blue armband, approached the Chair. Her buttocks bulged as she knelt down on both knees, steadying herself by gripping on to the left arm rest. Raising the bat up she swiped it down, twice, in rapid succession. *Splat. Thwat.*

It was a slightly duller, less sharp sound as the latex seared the passive, joggling cheeks. Clarissa bucked and writhed, but trapped in the almost cage-like structure of the Chair, she could not escape the searching blows. The bat was presented for the kiss, then withdrawn.

Crack. Splat. Again, the exposed cheeks bounced under the double strokes. Again, Clarissa's sensuous lips were pressed unwillingly against the warm latex skin that sheathed the cruel wood.

Matron approached. She knelt down on one knee, unlike the first two punishers, and cracked her bat down right across the twin orbs of the double dome. Miranda watched wide-eyed and dry-mouthed as the dark cleft between the buttocks widened and deepened as it spread under the impact of the harsh strokes.

Miranda swallowed to lubricate her throat. It was her turn once more. She approached the Chair. The two cheeks of Clarissa's bottom were now ablaze, a fierce scarlet blush spreading across the tender, ravished globes. Suddenly, as she knelt down closer to the beautiful, but punished, bottom, Miranda was gripped by an intense desire. She yearned to place the cool palm of her hand on the hot, curved flesh. Just gently ease the heat with her soothing hand. Perhaps spread a little cold cream on the scalded, satin hillocks. Unconsciously, she found herself rubbing the tip of her index finger against her thumb as if a blob of cold cream lay in between them.

Or kiss them. Yes! Miranda surrendered to the brief but overwhelming desire as it transfixed her. To kiss the scalded, quivering bottom slowly, tenderly and lingeringly, feeling her full, moist lips pressing into the scorched satin skin and then slowly peeling away.

'Proceed,' barked the headmistress harshly.

In a flurry of panic, Miranda raised the bat up high and cracked it down vehemently on the exposed bottom. She again unwittingly succumbed to the sheer momentum and overpowering impulse of the occasion, thrilling to the dark, unbidden pleasure of being given licence – indeed, being commanded – to punish this beautiful young woman's adorable, naked rump. At the same time, a part of Miranda's turbulent thoughts recognised the sense of regret at the suffering and humiliation Clarissa must be enduring.

A distinct and growing tingle developed in Miranda's moistening labial folds as she greedily took in the sight of Clarissa's tousled hair spilling down over her pale, slender shoulders onto the surface of the proffered bat as she strained to kiss the dimpled latex yet again. In a delicious yet confused daze, Miranda retreated to her appointed spot and heard the final flurry of strokes being delivered vertically down onto the horizontal buttocks.

'Position Three. Final position,' Mrs Boydd-Black barked.

Miranda nearly swooned. Was there no end to this delirious nightmare? This dark nightmare with the inner core of scarlet, seductive light that beckoned Miranda onto the shores of wicked wantonness.

Clarissa wriggled her body out from beneath the arm rests, her buttocks now as shiny red as polished apples. She scampered, tearfully, around to the back of the Chair. The final position clearly required her to adopt a posture which left her facing the room, belly and breasts squashed up against the hard wooden back of the grisly Chair, hands gripping the upper head rest, legs and feet splayed out behind. It was as provocative as it was perfect for perusing, appreciating and punishing the delectable bottom left so fully exposed and nakedly vulnerable. Forming a precise geometrical hemisphere, the twin rounded globes of her red bottom hung in passive suspension as they awaited further torment from the swooping wood.

'Continue.' The command crackled crisply.

Crack. Crack. Kiss. *Crack. Splat.* Kiss. *Thwack. Splat.* Kiss.

The litany of discipline rose and fell sonorously as the chastising inexorably unfolded. Then it was Miranda's turn once more. Stumbling slightly in a mesmerised trance, she approached the Chair for the third time. As she neared, she saw the muscles on

Clarissa's forearms spasm as they tensed to absorb the punishment. Miranda suddenly knew how fiendish this humiliating punishment truly was.

What was the history of this Chair? Fashioned by some devilish hand hundreds of years ago, what brute lusts and shameful passions had it witnessed? Surely no ease or comfort could be found on its hard seat, rigid back or spindling arm rests. And just as surely, she thought, nothing but shame and sorrow could be enjoyed by anyone directed to it by Mrs Boydd-Black. The complete and utter exposure, the humiliation, the scalding pain.

Miranda had never seen a naked, properly punished bottom in such close proximity before. Never had she actively participated in the beguilingly and seductively pleasurable process of administering punishment. Her pulse raced fiercely and she physically buckled under the burden of the temptation to squash her cool breasts down onto the blazing cheeks. She steadied herself and then applied the bat.

Once. Again. Then came the delicious moment when Clarissa, tears sparkling in her large, sorrowful eyes, was forced to press her lips in penitent submission against the hot, dimpled latex.

Miranda, to her shameful joy, her dread and delight, was quite wet by the end of the Quarter Exercise.

Outside in the cool, dry autumnal air, Miranda sought the privacy of a quiet, secluded spot in the thick bushes bordering the edge of the kitchen gardens. She strode past a pile of golden leaves. The heap was speckled with orange, tawny, green and brown, all neatly stacked into a nearly perfect pyramid. A thin plume of yellowish white, pungent smoke curled up into the air to hang like a spreading veil in the still calm of the late morning. Little gold and crimson tongues flickered hungrily at the outer leaves. The fire had taken. Soon it would be ablaze.

Miranda strode on, hurriedly. Between her thighs an invisible flame licked hungrily up into her belly. A fire she knew she must quench, a fire kindled by the punishment she had just witnessed and ignited by the pain she had just dispensed. Soon she was in amongst the heavy, waxy screen of shoulder high rhododendrons.

Within their cool, dense thickness she squatted down, her bare knees pressed into the cold clay. Her trembling hands eased down her tight white shorts and then paused, the tips of her forefingers searching blindly, finding, and then delicately parting her sticky labial folds. A fragrance, the perfume of excitation, bewitched her flaring nostrils. The cool autumn air played like a healing zephyr on her hot, turbulent membranes, but not even crushed ice could quench the fierce, inner heat. A probing fingertip found the delicious spot within the sticky folds of tender flesh. It probed and found that tiny pink sliver of shining tissue that sheathed such potent delight when unleashed.

Slowly, savouring the unhurried moment, Miranda dragged her fingertip up and across her quivering clitoris. It responded immediately. With increasing pressure, her eyes now clenched shut, she pressed down, harder and harder, slowly tracing small, concentric circles on the tiny stub of delicious tissue. A flood of exquisite tingling washed over her, thrilled her, illuminating her inner being with an electric charge. Almost unsupportable in its intensity. Never before had it been quite like this. Never, never before.

She paused, gulped for air, then fluttered her sticky fingertips up to her taut nipples that burgeoned beneath their tight sheath of stretched white cotton. Impromptu pincers of finger and thumb teased the hardening buds, causing waves of sheer delight to break in her belly and between her glistening thighs, from where liquid warmth oozed from her open wound like nectar from a split plum on summer's hottest day in some secret, bee-tormented orchard in paradise.

Sharp, vivid snapshots of the Chair suddenly flickered into focus against the retina of her inner eye. The dimpled latex bats. Clarissa undressing. Bending. Assuming the demeaning postures. Exposing. No, she thought, trying to deny the pleasurable images. No. Not that. Please, not that!

Her purblind fingers returned to her semi-erect clitoris, teasing out the tiny morsel and tweaking it. The fierce joy threatened to spill over into molten cascades of joy at any moment now. She was close. Almost there. No! No! Not that. No, she moaned softly, now only half resisting the sudden recognition that Clarissa's punishment was both fuelling and inflaming her tumescent excitement.

Yes! Clarissa's white bottom, pitifully bared for the pitiless strokes.

Yes! The softly rounded buttocks, now pink, soon red, squirming and writhing as the strokes rained down. Yes! The pliant flesh and its fulsome beauty enhanced by the wriggling and bouncing caused by cruel bat-kissing, suffering skin. Yes!

Her fingers were now strumming her innermost secret flesh like a frenetic flamenco guitarist possessed by the music. Yes! Clarissa kissing the hot latex. Yes! Miranda's scrabbling, sticky fingers were now a mere blur, webbed and heavy with her own wet dew. *Yes! Yes!*

Clarissa. The strokes. The punishment. Yes. The striped and blotched glowing, bouncing buttocks, the writhing, the squirming. Yes. The wide, sorrowful eyes. Teardrops. Yes. The naked bottom. The bottom. Those beautiful, rounded cheeks . . .

Miranda cried out softly as a sudden surge of heat, liquid and pulsating, flared up inside her loins and scalded the smooth flanks of her thighs. Never before had she buckled beneath such a molten paroxysm, such a tremendous, tumultuous orgasm. Again and again the warm pulsations coursed like quicksilver through her entire being, pushing her to the utter limits of consciousness. She collapsed, her face pressed down into the cool, damp moss. Her body arched up, held in a frozen shudder of delight. Her splayed buttocks were thrust up behind her in a feral, purely animal exhibition of total abandonment. From her gaping mouth came the soft moans of a wounded vixen.

'Miranda? Are you ill?'

The concerned voice of Jaya whispered fiercely from the nearby bushes.

'Huh?' Miranda replied in a distant voice thickened with lust.

'What is wrong? Are you unwell? I watched you coming into these bushes. What is wrong with you?' Jaya insisted anxiously.

'Nothing,' Miranda replied almost dreamily. 'I'm not ill.'

'Then what is the . . . Oh!' Jaya had stepped into the small clearing between the dense rhododendrons. She saw all. She understood everything. 'Sorry. I didn't realise . . .' she whispered shyly.

Miranda felt no shame. No embarrassment. At last she had faced and discovered the true nature and identity of her inner feelings and desires. She looked up into the wide eyes of the Asian girl and smiled.

'I had to come here. I had to . . . I can't explain.' Miranda said in a still, clear voice.

Jaya shrugged.

'This place. The Academy. It opens up our eyes and minds to strange emotions, new feelings, hidden desires. I too . . .' Jaya faltered, tugging her long, beautiful hair nervously.

'Clarissa?' Miranda whispered hoarsely.

The small dormitory was dark and still. Miranda could just make out a narrow bed in the gloom. On it, naked and face down, lay the recently chastised girl. Miranda stole softly across the cold lino and gingerly sat down on the side of the narrow bed. Clarissa, her face pressed into the pillow, turned her tear-stained face up towards her visitor.

'You shouldn't be here, Miranda. If they catch you they'll . . .'

'Sh. Don't worry, nobody will catch me. I had to come. Are you . . . are you . . .?' Miranda hesitated, unable to finish her question.

'Yes. I'll survive. I hated it, though.'

In the darkness, Miranda blushed. She had enjoyed it.

'Not the bat. The shame,' Clarissa said slowly. 'I felt so ashamed.'

'Is there anything you want? Anything I can do?'

'No, but stay a few minutes if you can. I am so

lonely, so empty. You don't happen to have a cigarette?'

Miranda raised her eyebrows in surprise.

'No, I don't,' she said, shaking her head apolo-
getically.

'Never mind. Just a long shot,' Clarissa sighed
wearily.

Miranda climbed gently onto the bed and pressed
her soft warmth along the length of Clarissa's
nakedness. Tenderly, she rested her hand on
Clarissa's hair, then slowly began to stroke the sad-
ness away. Soon the fingertips were straying down
along the furrow of the passive girl's cool spine,
pausing at the base of the gently swelling curves of
the recently ravaged bottom. Palm down, Miranda
slowly massaged the scalded cheeks, soothing their
tormented flesh with a healing touch.

'Mmm,' purred Clarissa. 'Yummy. Yes, please.'

'Nice?' whispered Miranda.

'Nice,' echoed the ecstatic girl. 'Not 'arf, mate,'
she added in her street-Cockney joke voice. 'One
fing missin', int there?'

'Wassat, me old mucker?' Miranda took up the
game.

'Couldn't arf go a fag, girl.'

They both giggled and hugged one another,
melting sublimely into the ensuing embrace. Kisses
followed.

'Well, well, well. I'm not altogether sure that this
is the sort of behaviour I approve of, girls.'

Miss Frobisher was standing in the doorway.
How long had she been watching them? Miranda
wondered anxiously.

'Long enough to see enough,' the fey, gentle art
tutor answered the unspoken question.

Miranda, blushing deeply, sprang guiltily up from the bed. Clarissa scrabbled down under her bedclothes, peeping out from them with large, frightened eyes.

'I'm sorry, Miss Frobisher. I only meant to see if Clarissa was all right . . .' Miranda murmured.

Miss Frobisher, who seemed to be engrossed with her leather belt, looked up.

'After a Chair and Quarter Exercise I'm sure the poor girl is far from all right,' she replied. She returned to concentrate on her slim waist. From her belt a supple leather strap dangled, tapping her slender thigh whenever she moved her svelte hips. Her eyes fixed on the length of cruel leather, Miranda felt cold fear crawl up into her stomach.

'Stupid belt. Keeps working loose,' Miss Frobisher frowned. 'I must get it fixed. There. That'll do for now,' she beamed, adjusting the belt with her beautiful hands.

Miranda relaxed immediately, sensing that the threat had passed.

'You'd better scoot, Miranda. I'll close my eyes and when I open them I expect to find you've gone for your lunch.'

'Thank you, Miss Frobisher,' Miranda said, smiling warmly before scuttling out of the forbidden dormitory with a huge sigh of grateful relief.

As she left she heard Miss Frobisher say, 'As for you, young lady, how goes it with that poor little bottom of yours? I've brought you a cigarette. And some chocolate. Is it very sore? Let me see . . .'

Chapter Four

Miranda knew that Miss Frobisher smoked. She had seen the distinctive packets of Camels buried deep inside the bursting hessian shoulder bag which accompanied the fey, affectionate art teacher wherever she went. Miranda also knew that Clarissa really needed a few cigarettes after her ordeal on the Chair. It was a typically headstrong, generous though very dangerous impulse but Miranda weighed the odds and thought them in her favour. All she had to do, she reasoned, was to watch and wait for the opportunity. She knew where Miss Frobisher's room was located, and resolved to slip into it and pinch a handful of Camels when the coast was clear. All it needed was common sense, split second timing and a firm resolve.

Miss Frobisher had a bright yellow ankle length coat. She often donned it when taking her customary meditative afternoon stroll in the secluded grounds that surrounded the Academy. When Miranda had completed her washing up duties, she slipped away from the hot kitchens and sprinted up to the first floor bathroom at the back of the mansion and opened the small window. To her delight, she saw in the distance a figure, draped in the long yellow coat, pacing slowly among the dismal blackcurrant bushes. Good. Miranda calculated that she had at least eight minutes. Plenty of time.

Quickly and stealthily, she walked towards the furthest part of the West wing, into forbidden territory, up another flight of stairs and along a carpeted landing. Miss Frobisher's room, her private quarters, lay beyond a green baize door. It was a perfectly proportioned, high-ceilinged, square room. Shining black coals were waiting patiently in the Adam fireplace, dormant until a flaring match brought them to vivid life. Two Renoir prints, of nubile bathers sporting playfully by their sun-dazzled pool, graced the cool, buttermilk walls.

The soft-piled, deep oyster carpet was littered with paperbacks, tissues, unopened letters, single shoes, a hat, gloves, a small jade cat with his ear missing and a pile of assorted polished stones. Brightly illustrated art magazines, tubes of oil paint and sharp black and white studies, in loving close-up, of the female form were strewn everywhere.

A writing desk enjoyed the late autumn, pale, golden light by a large sash window. On it, almost buried under even more debris, betraying Miss Frobisher's random, artistic nature, Miranda spied her goal. A red and yellow carton crammed with packets of Camels. Several loose cigarettes lay strewn around the desktop. She skipped over into the sunlight and reached out her hand.

'Can I help you, Miranda?' said the cool, calm, quizzical voice of Miss Frobisher as she shut the door firmly behind her.

Miranda spun around, startled. She flushed deeply. Four cigarettes dropped silently from her frozen fingers.

'I thought you were . . . I mean . . .' she stammered

guiltily, feeling frightened and ashamed. She noticed that the art teacher was wearing a soft, grey cashmere jumper and pale blue jeans that tightened at the crotch.

'Didn't know you smoked. A stupid habit. I'd like to stop of course and I dare say I could if I really tried to but they do help me relax when I'm working.'

'I don't. I was going to give them . . .' Miranda started to speak, then bit her bottom lip. So much for the nerves of steel and a firm resolve. She really was making a thorough muck up of this little escapade, she thought ruefully.

'To give them to whom? Jane, perhaps? Certainly not Jaya. Or were they for poor Clarissa?'

'Yes. No. I'm sorry. Please don't . . .'

A sharp knock sounded on the green baize door. It opened. Mrs Boydd-Black entered. Miranda froze.

'Miss Frobisher, I wonder if . . . oh, I see you are engaged. Is anything the matter? Has this girl been giving trouble?'

A cold fist of steel clenched and unclenched its sinewy talons deep inside Miranda's soft, white belly. It squeezed her entrails hard. She held her breath.

'Trouble? Good gracious, no. Miranda has a "free" this afternoon and has very sweetly volunteered to help me sort out all of this,' said Miss Frobisher warmly, spreading her arms vaguely towards the chaos on the oyster carpet. 'I really must get sorted out.'

Miranda could see that the Headmistress was far from convinced. She felt the dominant gaze directly upon her, drinking in her penitent stance, bowed head and downcast eyes. Surely this was enough to tell Mrs Boydd-Black the true story.

'I'm sure that you will pass the time profitably, Miss Frobisher,' came the terse, ironic reply through pursed lips. 'It is so very important to get things . . . sorted out,' she added drily. 'I came to see if you would do the floral centre-piece for the staff dinner this evening.'

'Delighted,' gushed Miss Frobisher.

'Jolly good. Carry on . . . sorting things out.'

The door closed behind the headmistress and as it shut firmly, Miranda knew that the distinct possibility of at the very least a Chair and Quarter Exercise, possibly a Half Exercise, had receded.

'Phew. That was close,' Miss Frobisher giggled.

Miranda looked up, an uncertain grin of relief mixed with disbelief spreading like melting cheese on a baked potato across her wide mouth.

'She would have skinned your bottom raw, my dear. Sherry?'

Miranda could hardly believe her ears. She nodded quickly.

'Mm. Please,' she murmured.

'Dry? Or something a little sweeter, perhaps?'

'An Oloroso would be perfectly divine.'

'Sweet and sticky is your weakness. Me too.'

The art teacher turned to a tantalus and poured out their drinks. How tight her pale blue jeans were, Miranda marvelled. How closely the stretch of fabric hugged the plump cheeks of her firmly rounded bottom.

'The old trout is OK actually. Firm, as they say, but fair. My God, can she be firm. Well,' she said, returning to a spot just before the unlit fire and passing Miranda a generous measure of golden sherry, 'here's to illicit pleasure. Tact forbids me from saying "Bottoms up". I think you'll understand. Hardly the right expression here at the Academy, don't you think?' she said with a wicked grin.

Miranda snorted into her glass. The sweet liquid slivered down her chin. She wiped it away with the back of her hand, and then licked her fingers. Miss Frobisher watched the gesture just as a hungry cat would a carefree sparrow. Squatting down, the teacher motioned the pupil to join her, patting a space on the carpet beside her denimed thigh. As Miranda sat, Miss Frobisher peeled off her shoes and tossed them across the room. Miranda was instantly self-conscious of her flimsy white cotton uniform which rendered her little more than a gauche schoolgirl beside the sophisticated woman next to her on the carpet.

'It's getting chilly. I must keep you warm. Shall we light the fire. Hm?'

'Please.'

'The matches are over there on the desk. Next to my cigarettes.'

Miranda, rising elegantly, blushed furiously. The teacher laughed gently.

'Just teasing. Help yourself to a Camel if you like. Light one for me.' Miranda did so, thrilling slightly as the dry filter tip went from her lips to her teacher's.

'You took a bit of a risk, my girl.'

'I thought you were down in the gardens. I'm sure I saw you.'

'Really?' frowned Miss Frobisher, perplexed.

'In your yellow coat . . .'

Miss Frobisher laughed.

'Silly girl,' she chuckled. 'That was Madame Nina. Always worried about catching a chill. Neurotic about her voice. I lent her my coat.'

Miranda bent forward and, half-kneeling, put a match to the paper and kindling. The white smoke curled and soon tiny orange flames were licking and lapping the shiny black coals. A comfortable silence settled between them as they sat before the glowing blaze, sipping their delicious sherry.

'I'm sorry,' whispered Miranda. 'I could have dished you with Mrs Boydd-Black.'

'Our headmistress is no fool. Wise as an owl. Knew something was in the wind, but trusts me to sort it all out.'

'And I'm sorry for stealing. Stealing's rotten.'

'My. Quite the little penitent, aren't we? Had you down as one of our tougher eggs. But I'm glad to hear you say that, Miranda. It strongly suggests that I should take a much more lenient view of things when determining your punishment.'

A prickle of anticipation flickered through Miranda's veins. Not quite excitement. Yet. But certainly a pleasurable apprehension.

'Punishment?' she echoed.

'Yes. Punishment. But we will discuss that in more detail a little later. And remember, my dear. Punishment need not always be harsh. Sometimes, punishment can be sweet.'

Miranda felt a pulse fluttering in her throat. This mildly perfumed, peach-skinned, cool goddess would be dealing with her bottom within the hour. The thought took hold of her and kindled her imagination just as her flaring match had brought the dark black coals to glowing life.

'Come here. Closer.' It was a gentle command.

Miranda shuffled over and snuggled up close to her tutor. Thigh brushed thigh. The movement immediately bridged the gap – physical and emotional

– that had up to that instant crackled between them. Miranda, squeezing her softness against the warmth of the more mature woman, felt at once both secure and safe. But it was a security laced with excitement, a safety tinged with tingling expectation.

Miss Frobisher took Miranda's head between her elegant hands and laid it gently down in her lap. Miranda surrendered willingly, curling up like a sleepy cat before the flickering coal fire. Thrilled by the touch of her teacher, she succumbed utterly to the mildly dominant embrace. As her wide eyes reflected the leaping flames, she became docile, supine and passive, suffused with a liquid joy of delicate tremulousness.

'Tell me your story. Everyone here has a story,' invited the golden voice of her tutor. 'Tell me,' she coaxed, her tone dropping a full octave to a mere honied purr. Silken fingers stroked the pupil's blonde hair. Miranda, accustomed to the terse, secretive world of the titled and the rich, found it remarkably easy to talk. With absentee parents, no brothers or sisters, and few close friends among her circle of brittle sirens and vain studs, she had never had access to this emotional candour and sense of intimacy. She shared many long pent up sentiments and feelings.

For a full hour they remained in close union, the teacher cradling the pupil as she listened attentively, never querying or questioning, simply encouraging and accepting. They drifted into a gentle, tender silence, united by their body heat and rhythmic breathing. The red coals settled, briefly disturbing their shared silence. Miranda, like a sleepy cat awakening, looked up and gazed into the large, serene eyes of Miss Frobisher. She studied their liquid depths in which the reds and orange golds of the coal fire were reflected. The neatly trimmed eyebrows. The luminous, porcelain skin. The slightly stub nose with the small, dark nostrils. And the mouth.

Miranda closed her eyes and imagined Miss Frobisher's plum-dark lips grazing her own. A tingling sensation teased her nipples. And the mouth. Miranda willed the imagined lips down onto her soft, white throat, pausing to suck before tracing a warm path down into the deep valley between her pulsing breasts.

And the mouth.

The thick lips, having paid full and lingering homage to her breasts, tormented nipples and curved belly, were now being willed down to Miranda's pubic fringe. In her inner vision, Miranda saw herself naked except for a pair of white, tarty fishnet stockings. Miss Frobisher was taking them down, slowly, one by one, with her mouth. Now the tip of the silvery pink tongue was longingly licking her legs back up to the sensitive inner thighs, back up to that shadowed delta where her scented softness awaited . . . She shivered.

'Chilly?' murmured Miss Frobisher with a mild note of concern. She too had been running the silent film of fantasy behind her dreamy eyes. In it, she was pencil sketching a naked Miranda in postures of which she knew all too well the Royal Academy would strongly disapprove of, were the work ever to be unveiled and submitted to their feverish gaze.

'No,' Miranda sighed, opening her eyes and staring up hungrily at the beautiful mouth hovering a mere tantalizing twelve inches above her own.

'I will build our fire,' the teacher whispered.

Our fire. Miranda almost hugged herself with delight. Our fire.

'And we shall have music.'

Miss Frobisher, after placing several generous pieces of coal together with a dry apple log onto the fire, padded softly over to her desk. She clicked on her old Bush portable. It had a mellow bass tone. Miranda expected the room to be filled with the austere strains of Radio Three. A shivering, tinkling piano recital. Scriabin, possibly. To her delight, Lou Reed whispered his carnal, curdling lyrics, as if sharing his dark secrets with them. The Bush belted out a selection of seventies pop records. Old favourites for the sophisticated teacher. New delights for her younger pupil.

The mood exploded. Bowie's 'Drive In Saturday' squealed, the notes wrapping around their brains like silk. The log crackled and blazed up, scenting the room with its balmy aroma of plums and custard. They ate dried apricots, nibbling the fruits and feeding one another. They fraggle-danced to Jagger's 'Brown Sugar', bottoms gyrating lubriciously and then, belly to belly, slow-smooched to Elton John's 'Rocket Man'. Miss Frobisher cupped Miranda's buttocks with a fierce tenderness.

'Better tidy up,' she laughed, releasing her willing captive. 'Mrs Boydd-Black will no doubt be back. Any excuse.'

They set to their task playfully. Both flushed and panting. They stacked the magazines, tidied up and shelved the strewn paperbacks, re-boxed pastel crayons and sticks of charcoal and put away the small tubes of oil paint according to size and colour. Miranda paused, holding a small tube with no label on it between her fingers. She gently unscrewed the top and peered in.

'What colour is it?' Miss Frobisher asked gaily.

'Red,' came the enraptured reply.

'Red? Scarlet as in woman or vermilion as in sin?'

'Red. Just like your lips,' Miranda whispered audibly.

The art teacher paused, carelessly scattering an armful of notes she had just painstakingly assembled, and strode softly across to Miranda. She took her by the hand.

'Come,' she commanded firmly.

'Yes,' her pupil meekly obeyed.

They passed through into the bedroom next door. It was a much smaller room, much more intimate. It was warm. And dark. Miss Frobisher positioned Miranda next to a low divan bed, steadying her with a strong hand.

'Skin the bunny?' She smiled, her voice just under control.

Miranda blinked, puzzled.

'That's what my granny used to say to me. At bedtime.'

Undress. Miranda shivered pleasurably and surrendered herself up completely, passively allowing the older woman to ease her vest up over her breasts, shoulders and head. As the taut cotton sheath left her soft body, her breasts swung freely in their satin, heavy weight. The undressing left her blonde hair in tousled disarray. Then two cool thumbs worked their persistent way inside the elastic waistband of the tight, white, bottom-hugging shorts. Sinuous fingers.

'Let's skin the bunny,' whispered the teacher in a low, urgent voice.

She gently slid her cool, sensitive hands over the outer swell of her captive's hips, peeling off the taut second skin of cotton in a single, sweeping gesture. They came to rest just above Miranda's tremulous knees, leaving the shorts there to imprison the legs together. The creative, imaginative hands fluttered like two silent doves back up across Miranda's soft buttocks and along her furrowed spine, coming to rest once more on the satin skin of her white shoulders.

Soon the firm thumbs were exploring the upper slopes of the naked, perfectly formed, pendulous breasts. Miranda surrendered her aching, peaking nipples to the plucking, searching fingers. A delicate pincer of finger and thumb teased their tiny pinkness into thickening buds of quivering ecstasy.

At length, the twin breasts lay cupped, weighed and squashed within the expert, knowing hands. Such creative, such intelligent, such vibrant hands. Time congealed. As her soft mounds thrilled beneath the pressure, Miranda signalled her compliance and delight with a trickle of secret silver from her tightly wedged thighs.

Miss Frobisher slowly knelt, sinking to both knees in a languid genuflection. As her head lowered, her thickened, moist tongue traced a wet track down along Miranda's white belly into the valley beneath. Miranda's breath fluttered in her throat. On both knees, the art teacher pressed her face against the curve of the soft belly before her. It was a cameo of enthralled submission and dominant adoration.

Miranda gazed down to see her swollen, ravished breasts bob lightly as they nuzzled Miss Frobisher's hair. The warmth of her teacher's breath against her naked belly sent little static thrills searing up and down the length of her vulnerable, exposed nakedness. Soon the warmth announced itself a little further down, and Miss Frobisher's mouth came to rest as it closed softly over her opening flower.

A faint rustling crackled as fine, small white teeth crunched and mouthed the frizz of golden pubic hair. Miranda shuddered and gripped the soft, cashmere-sheathed shoulders that pressed against her waist. Steadying herself, she tried to follow the impulse of nature to open her legs and part her throbbing thighs a little wider but the tight shorts remained at her knees, a fiercely tender bondage. Her long legs quivered. An urgency, hot and delicious, coursed through her scorching veins like liquid fire.

Now the thick lips were working busily against her moist, sensitive flesh folds, dragging, sucking and deeply kissing her wetness with a dedicated feverishness. Miranda's knees fluttered and spasmed. She swayed slightly. Miss Frobisher reached up behind and steadied her pupil by placing a firm, cool hand on the tremulous buttocks. Miranda almost swooned, so delicious was the sensation of the palm against her swollen, satin skin. Soon both cheeks were held and steadied, giving the inquisitive, adoring hands full opportunity to squeeze, mould, grip and enjoy the pliant, captive flesh. The fingers encompassed the heavy globes and tightened their grip, dragging outwards slightly, causing the cleft between the cheeks to widen. Soon those very fingertips were drumming along the innermost sensitive membrane of tingling flesh, lightly skimming the shadowed depths until Miranda almost slipped away into a complete, delirious abandon.

'Punish me,' she heard herself imploring hoarsely, beseechingly.

Keeping her thick muscle of tongue pressed tightly into the labial folds that had parted as smoothly as velvet curtains, Miss Frobisher flickered her large, inquiring eyes upwards.

Miranda gazed down, the hungry urgency in her own eyes meeting the soft, penetrating gaze of those below.

'Punish me,' she pleaded, her voice a mere feral whimper. She jerked her buttocks back, pressing them into her teacher's firm palms. 'Punish me for stealing. I must be severely punished.'

'No,' murmured Miss Frobisher, mouthing the word deliciously into Miranda's wetness. 'No harsh punishment for stealing. I have forgiven you for that. But tender, sweet discipline . . . yes. The discipline of love. That you shall have.'

With one, easy, graceful movement she rose and sat on the edge of the bed, placing her hands on the swell of Miranda's hips. In another delicious movement, as fluid as it was fluent, she twirled Miranda around, presenting the naked bottom a mere four inches from her parted lips. She planted a firm, lingering kiss on each supple globe of heavy, luminous flesh before nipping the joggling buttocks with her tiny white teeth. Miranda squealed out in sweet agony. Miss Frobisher mouthed the creamy flesh drunkenly, taking in folds of the passive, naked cheeks into her own warm wetness one by one. She gorged on the flesh as a leopard would feast on an antelope still warm from the kill.

Burying her face deep into the saliva-silvered bottom, Miss Frobisher worshipped fully the rounded splendour, her tongue flickering to catch the warm, clear honey that spilled freely from the flesh below. Miranda cried out in sheer ecstasy, a primitive paean to pure pleasure. Gathering Miranda by her slender waist with her left arm, she eased the trembling girl down across her denimed lap.

Miranda lay helpless and supine, bottom up, over Miss Frobisher's knees. The teacher placed her white hand down onto the pupil's nape and pinioned the girl in the punishment position, parting her thighs a fraction in order to take the weight more comfortably. Eager for the chastisement, Miranda raised her rounded bottom up, signalling her impatient desire for the spanking to commence. Her teacher was not to be hurried. Such moments were to be fully savoured. Each fleeting moment should be spun into eternity.

She carefully steadied and positioned the naked girl to her supreme satisfaction before attending to the legs and feet, which she trapped firmly beneath her own arched foot. The tight white shorts, still binding Miranda's knees together in sweet bondage, ensured that the buttocks were roundly bunched together in a geometry of perfection, fully and passively prepared for their ravishment. Miss Frobisher placed her right hand down lightly on the double domes of vulnerable, naked flesh. The bare buttocks shuddered and jerked responsively, as Miranda shivered with pleasurable expectation. The palm of the steady hand depressed one soft bottom cheek, then the strong fingers splayed out, pushing away the opposite dome of trembling flesh. The dark cleft between was forced open a fraction. Then wider still. Miss Frobisher flexed her fingers out to their full extent. The valley between the creamy hills yawned.

With at first her thumb, then following with fingertips, the teacher strummed the pupil's sensitive flesh until Miranda bleated like a lamb. Ripples of immeasurable delight radiated outwards until her belly and breasts were ablaze. A determined thumbnail scratched gently into the very depths of the dark cleft. Miranda squealed and bucked in a paroxysm of pleasure. Her mind and body were now capitulating in sweet surrender, her wet delta weeping freely into the taut, powder-blue denim that stretched across her teacher's warm, fragrant lap.

'Please! Please, now,' she moaned silently as she neared the delicious brink.

Miss Frobisher seemed to sense the mute supplications and conceded to their demands. She slapped the full bottom tenderly. Then spanked it again. And then again. The punished girl sighed blissfully and settled down for the assault of skin on skin. She thrust her buttocks upwards in her eagerness for the fiery joy to come. Miss Frobisher knew full well that discipline, like music, was enhanced by strict observance of timing, by obedience to the dictates of rhythm and beat. She deliberately paused after the first four stinging slaps, and gently rubbed the glowing, rounded cheeks of punished flesh. And then she spanked again. A sharp flurry of harsh smacks cracking like pistol shots as they exploded across the firm domes of ivory. Miranda moaned sweetly, her sheer delight curdling in her throat.

Spank. Pause. The punishing hand hovered, stayed for a moment in its delicious threat. *Spank.* Pause. Again the hand hung motionless over the quivering, blushing cheeks. *Spank. Spank.*

Miranda, in her swimming delirium, found the delightful delays as intensely pleasurable as the spirited slaps and solid smacks of hard hand on pliant, vulnerable flesh. She turned her head eagerly, trying to look up over her left shoulder at the beautiful tormentress under whose spell and in whose thrall she was utterly helpless.

Miss Frobisher, totally absorbed in the magic she was weaving, merely placed a single, dominant finger on Miranda's parted lips in a gesture for absolute silence, then, turning Miranda's head face down once more, gathered up a loose handful of her blonde hair and re-established the desired, subjugated position. A trembling thrill coursed through the entire length of Miranda's nakedness. She spilled her hot silver freely from between her clamped thighs.

Smack. Smack. She jerked, squeezing her weeping, sticky thighs even tighter together. *Smack.* Her tiny white toes scrabbled half an inch above the carpet. *Smack.* Miss Frobisher tightened her controlling grip on Miranda's hair, and, inclining her tightly denimed leg in against Miranda's soft, naked lower thighs and swelling calves, pinioned her completely. A touch of severity introduced itself into the rhythmically paced and strictly controlled spanking.

Smack. Smack. Miranda squirmed, twisting from side to side as she attempted to roll free from the fiercely tender punishment that scalded her bare bottom so searchingly. Her little hands fluttered pathetically in their bid to ward off the burning joy.

'Hands down,' came the crisp admonishment.

Miranda obeyed instantly. Fresh slaps scorched the crown of her superb rump, then, as Miranda twisted and writhed, the left cheek and the twin right cheek. The spanking hand left the throbbing globes fully ablaze. Both satin-skinned hillocks of pliant flesh were now completely rubescent with a scarlet glow. The teacher sensed her pupil's approaching climax. The arching spine and rigid thighs spoke their own words of imminent carnal liquifaction.

The first paroxysms of spasmodic delight caused Miranda's hips to jerk and shudder as she hovered perilously on the very brink of abandonment. Quickly wrenching away the restricting bondage of the white shorts, the punisher turned the punished over onto her scorched bottom across the edge of the divan bed and knelt down before her, burying her lust-slackened features deeply into the gaping, splayed wetness that beckoned.

Miss Frobisher's tongue licked and flickered, darted and probed until Miranda, with her white knuckles gripping the eiderdown, tumbled headlong into the spinning vortex of orgasm. As her soft, silken shrieks split the air, the teacher gripped her pupil's buttocks in a fierce, controlling grasp of desire, sinking her dominant fingers into the lambent fleshy orbs.

Miranda bucked and gyrated like a wild pony under the first taste of the whip that would tame. Slipping down onto the soft carpet, her reddened rump corrugated against the edge of the bed as she slithered, the delirious girl hugged the triumphant teacher with open arms and wet thighs. She encircled the denim clad hips with her own hot, sticky thighs and, firm bosom to firm bosom, squeezed with all her might. They melted into paradisical fusion for timeless moments until brought savagely back to dull reality by the stern voice calling from beyond the outer door.

'Miss Frobisher? Are you there?'

It was the headmistress. Miss Frobisher suppressed a giggle and bundled Miranda's naked body under the bed, throwing socks, vest and white shorts after her.

'In here, headmistress,' she called, in a voice as neutral and even-toned as her recent excitement would allow.

'About the floral centre piece, my dear,' boomed Mrs Boydd-Black striding into the bedroom without ceremony. 'I do think white roses so very becoming, don't you?'

The headmistress took in the scene at a glance. Especially Miranda's empty sherry glass tossed drunkenly next to Miss Frobisher's own. And the greenband curled up on the floor by the foot of the bed.

'Dark in here. Headache?'

'No. Yes. Just taking a little nap.'

'Jolly good,' came the noncommittal reply. Mrs Boydd-Black chose to say little, but her eyes swept the rumpled bed.

Under the bed, sniffling a little dust, Miranda sneezed.

'Got a stray in here?' Not a good idea that, encouraging strays. Jolly good.' Mrs Boydd-Black departed.

The art teacher sighed. The headmistress knew something was afoot. That last remark had nothing to do with the nearby farmyard kittens that plagued the Academy.

'Has she gone?' came the whisper from beneath the bed.

'Yes,' replied Miss Frobisher. 'Time for you to go, as well.'

Miranda held out her hand. Miss Frobisher gathered it up and planted a heavy kiss, first on the palm and then onto the back.

'Here, don't forget your greenband.' She passed it across to Miranda who had just hastily dressed, sheathing her ripe softness in the cool taut white cotton.

'Thanks.'

In the larger drawing room, the fire still blazed brightly. So did the curiously fierce sparkle in the tutor's eyes.

'Here, for Clarissa.' She dropped half a dozen Camels into Miranda's open palm.

'Thank you, Miss Frobisher.'

'Wait. You have blanket fluff in your hair. Let me ... and you must call me Emily, when we are alone.'

'May I call you Emily soon? Tonight? Oh, please ...' Miranda, only a few weeks ago so cool and aloof, whimpered frantically.

'Impatient girl. We shall see. We shall see,' the beautiful teacher smiled, her exquisite hands, so light and yet so capable, aflutter.

Miranda stole out of the room and softly paced along the carpeted corridor leading from the west wing.

'You have a visitor, Miranda,' the headmistress said, stepping out suddenly from a shadowed alcove.

Miranda gasped, dropping the Camels in her alarm. They lay at her feet like accusing white fingers pointing out her guilt.

'Pick them up quickly, girl. I did not think that you succumbed to that particular vice.'

Blushing, Miranda stooped and scrabbled at the cigarettes with anxious fingers. The headmistress took two steps forward, standing dominantly, legs astride, looming large over the bending blonde. One polished brogue rested inches from Miranda's fingertips, trapping a stray cigarette.

'Miss Frobisher can be very kind to her special little friends. Did you get sherry?'

Miranda remained silent. She held her breath in anxious anticipation. The brogue moved, the polished toecap arching up to release the slightly squashed Camel.

'Are they for Jane?'

How the hell does she know everything? Well, almost everything, Miranda wondered as she regained her upright stance, trying to avoid the penetrating, shrewd gaze of the headmistress.

'Or are they perhaps for Clarissa? Yes. No doubt they are. A kindly gesture, my girl. Clarissa probably needs a little treat after the rigours of her Chair.'

She *does* know everything, Miranda swore to herself silently.

'It is no bad thing that our Miss Frobisher has apparently taken an . . . interest in you my dear. It will, I trust, help you settle in here at the Academy. I'm rather afraid you have made something of a poor start here. But Emily will guide you. Does she let you call her Emily yet?'

Miranda, puzzled by the identity of her visitor, nodded her head absently.

'Jolly good. Come along, then. But first, I think, you may pop in briefly to say hello to Clarissa. Be sure to tell her to open her window while smoking.'

Miranda smiled, in spite of herself. Mrs Boydd-Black really was amazing. She seemed to be quite human underneath it all. Tolerant, even. As long as she knew everything, that is. And total knowledge in itself, Miranda suddenly realised, was exactly the same as total control.

'Your visitor awaits you in my private office.

Knock before you enter. You must not ask any questions and, most importantly, discuss any aspect of life here at the Academy. Normally, visitors are not allowed.' Neither are letters or phone calls thought Miranda ruefully. 'Nor must you disclose any of our methods, customs or practices. On this point as on all others I am adamant. Do you understand?'

Miranda nodded hastily.

'Jolly good.'

Clarissa received the handful of Camels with wide-eyed delight. She hugged and kissed Miranda and, in answer to Miranda's solicitude, peeled off her shorts and displayed her generous, gorgeously honey-hued rump.

'Look. No nasty bruises. Bit sore, though,' she smiled.

'Good,' Miranda grinned. 'I hope I didn't hurt your poor bum.'

'Liar. You loved every minute of it. Who doesn't?' Clarissa laughed good-naturedly. 'Where the hell did you get these?'

'Secret,' Miranda shrugged enigmatically.

'Miss Frobisher?' Clarissa countered in a teasing tone.

Miranda struggled to conceal her surprise. Nevertheless, she blushed.

'Thought so. Did Emily give Miranda a little . . . treat, then?' Clarissa laughed, lit a Camel and exhaled luxuriously, expelling the blue smoke out through the narrow opening of her fortified window.

'Don't tell Jane,' Clarissa warned, wiping a fleck of wet tobacco from her thick lower lip with her fingernail.

114

Miranda was immediately surprised – and later uneasy – at the remark.

Mr Porteous was just finishing his last forkful of heavily creamed strawberry gateau when Miranda knocked dutifully and then entered into what she assumed to be Mrs Boydd-Black's private office. To her utter amazement, the office was sumptuously furnished and opulently decorated. Powder pink flock wallpaper was edged with a gold gilt dado trim. Heavy Victorian-looking glasses shimmered in the intense glare of a huge candelabra. Decorative Adam chairs encircled an imposing High Dutch period desk. It was an effete, decadent room. Miranda frowned. How unlike the Mrs Boydd-Black she thought she knew.

At the grotesque desk, clearly reflected in its polished depths, she glimpsed the piggy face of the loathsome family solicitor swallowing the last of his glutinous gateau. Wiping his soiled snout with an exaggerated flourish of his starched white napkin, Porteous nodded to a chair. Incongruously, a state-of-the-art lap-top computer blinked at his elbow. He had evidently just been using it. Columns of figures winked from the screen. Financial spread-sheets, Miranda hazarded. Porteous pocketed two discs and put what looked like a video cassette into his yawning briefcase. Miranda's frown deepened.

'Good afternoon, Lady Miranda,' he almost purred.

Miranda had been unable to mask her disappointment. She had expected to see Aunt Emma. Uncle Peter. Possibly one of her parents. Indeed, anyone would have been more welcome than this obnoxious little toad.

115

'I trust I find you well?'

Miranda remained silent, hating his open perusal of her youthful fulsomeness which her Academy uniform both accentuated and revealed.

'I am told that you have not settled in as quickly as expected. Not made your mark, I am given to understand.'

Miranda turned these words over in her mind. They were not without a certain irony. The Academy had certainly made its mark – frequently – on her. Usually faint red stripes or crimson handprints.

'I was merely passing through the area and thought it fitting to call in. Normally, visitors are discouraged. But Mrs Boydd-Black agreed to make an exception. A delightful woman.'

But why? Miranda puzzled. What was this toad really doing here? Making free use of her headmistress's office. Using a computer. Eating gateau as though he almost owned the place . . .

'The Academy has a splendid reputation,' the solicitor's voice droned on, like a bullish chairman at a floatation launch for prospective investors, 'quite splendid.'

With a flush suffusing his pink, piggy face, the solicitor sat back, palms pressed together, and gazed up at three naked cherubs wrestling in a distinctly uncherubic tussle on the ceiling. His voice droned on and on. Miranda watched him with gathering loathing. At last he paused.

'You seem to me to be remarkably quiet. Nothing at all to say?'

No, thought the furious girl. Nothing to say. Porteous must know nothing of her humiliation and suffering here. That would be too much for her to bear. But she could send out a written SOS using this jackanapes as her messenger. Yes. Of course, that was it. A brief note to Aunt Emma, full of contrite promises, begging her to come and remove Miranda from the Academy.

As Miranda weighed up the possibilities of this course of action – pen and paper sat waiting for her on the desk – the solicitor commenced on a bland, innocuous catechism of meaningless questions. Miranda remained monosyllabic in her terse, grudging answers. She gave nothing away at all. She certainly would not give him the satisfaction of letting him, of all people, know how miserable she was.

As he continued to twitter away pompously, she leaned forward, took paper and pen in hand and hastily scribbled a brief but telling note to her aunt. She folded the piece of paper carefully, placed it in a large white envelope and addressed it to her aunt. Did Porteous know that all forms of communication with the outside world were strictly forbidden? Mustering up as casual a tone as her beating heart would allow, she handed the note across the desk.

'You are very kind to call in and see me, Mr Porteous.'

He bowed his greasy head, acknowledging and accepting the compliment.

'Be so kind as to pass that to Auntie. Just my best wishes to her and Uncle Peter,' she said guilesssly. Her thin smile hid a trembling heart.

'Certainly,' replied the solicitor, pocketing the envelope. He beamed with a sudden sense of his own vital self-importance. His almost lidless eyes flickered like a lizard's.

The brief interview concluded, Miranda shook his limp, soft hand mechanically and returned to her bleak little dormitory. She gave little thought now

117

to the real purpose of his visit. Suffice that he had arrived, seen her and agreed to pass on her message. A sudden rush of relief swept over her. How fortunate she was to have this sudden opportunity to arrange her release from the Academy. Aunt Emma, she felt sure, would not let her down.

As the time for her appointment with Matron neared, Miranda concentrated hard. She had, she knew, to find some way of resisting this tormenting monster. But how? Direct disobedience would only bring down harsher punishments onto her defenceless buttocks. Matron wielded a fierce and unerring strap and seemed to be deaf to squeals for mercy. Indeed, pleas for pity only seemed to inflame her all the more. There must be a way. There must.

Outside the san door, Miranda hesitated. From within came the sound of stifled sobs. Miranda grew pale, her hand fluttering anxiously as it paused before knocking to seek admission. Matron's stern voice rose above the bitter weeping. Miranda shuddered and tapped twice on the door.

'Come,' commanded Matron.

Stepping into the brightly lit, white-tiled room, Miranda was horrified to see Jaya, sitting on a stool, her hands tied behind her back, head bowed down and weeping openly. Around her feet lay her once crowning glory of luxurious, rich, dark hair. Matron, a glinting pair of scissors in one hand, stood behind Jaya. With her free hand Matron was roughly massaging the recently shorn, stubbled head of the heart-broken girl.

'This stupid girl defied me. See the result? Look and learn, my dear,' she snarled triumphantly. 'Resistance is futile and the consequences . . .' she

118

squeezed Jaya's soft cheeks between her out-stretched hand. Jaya shook her head but could not release it from the vice-like hold. 'I repeat, the consequences are quite dire. Do you understand?'

Miranda, wide-eyed with both shock and concern, nodded dumbly.

'Good. Get undressed and prepare yourself. You,' she returned to Jaya, 'I want you to consider our little discussion and come back here tomorrow morning. You may have changed your mind by then. If you are sensible, you will have.'

What evil act had Matron attempted upon Jaya, causing the gentle young Asian beauty to resist and thus merit such a savage punishment? With her severe crop, Jaya looked like a pathetic little duckling just in from a storm. Wiping away her copious tears, the shorn girl took up a brush and slowly, resentfully, swept up the remains of her glorious hair.

Miranda turned away from the scene, it was too painful to witness. With tears of pity now pricking and glistening in her own eyes, she turned to mount the dreaded examination table. A surging tide of fear and loathing, shame and resentment welled up inside her. Being at the ruthless whim and scant mercy of this overbearing demon numbed her sensibilities almost completely. Almost. Not completely. There were still enough quivering apprehensions kindling within her to feed and fuel her flames of dread. And Miranda knew that those shadowy flames would soon have flickering substance as her punished buttocks were set ablaze once more in scarlet suffering.

'Hurry up girl. Get ready,' Matron snapped.

Miranda, utterly naked, shivered before slipping up onto the examination table as instructed. She lay on her side, drawing her knees up until they nestled into and squashed her passive bosom. Jaya, having completed the heartbreaking task of sweeping up her own hair from the floor, was ordered out of the san.

'Over. Onto your tummy, my girl. Face down. Full stretch.'

Miranda, puzzled, obeyed.

Matron picked up the short length of rubber tubing and flexed it menacingly in her hand. A hand that remained gloveless. Miranda frowned. And where was the customary jug of warm water? The cold lubricant? The cruel funnel?

'No enema for you tonight, my girl. I am far too busy for all that. Staff dinner. Brace of pheasant with bread sauce. So I'll be brief.'

Miranda closed her eyes, remembering the gentleness of Emily, the art teacher. She tried to picture Emily, head bowed, her beautiful fluttering hands like butterflies as they shaped white roses for the floral centre-piece.

'Brief, but effective.'

Miranda opened her eyes in alarm. Matron was flexing the rubber tubing with a tenderness close to affection.

'You are failing badly, my girl. It has been noticed. I do not tolerate failures. Not at the Academy. It is clearly time your independence of spirit was truly broken. You need several harsh lessons and a firm teacher.'

The flesh on Miranda's rounded soft cheeks crawled. She clenched her buttocks anxiously.

'Only total and absolute obedience will suffice. I am sure that strict discipline will secure that obedience. This, my girl, will be the first of very many lessons.'

Crack. The length of rubber tubing kissed the up-turned, satin cheeks with a savage adoration. The snap of the whippy rubber on taut flesh exploded in Miranda's brain along with a searing flash of red pain. She winced, gasping audibly. *Crack.* Again, with unerring accuracy, the length of supple rubber whipped down across her rounded buttocks, striping the soft, creamy domes with a lustful caress of violent intimacy. *Crack.*

The searing lash burned into the blazing, exposed bottom, causing it to buck and bounce in contorted pain.

'Get it up, my girl. Up. Higher.'

Miranda dipped her belly obediently and offered her scalding rump up for the next stroke. *Crack.* Matron gave a carnal grunt as the rubber tubing hugged the convex contours of the supine buttocks. Faint pink and red stripes were emerging across the sheath of simmering flesh.

Crack. The tingling tongue of fire licked deeply, ardently, across the taut expanse of defenceless skin. Miranda struggled, but failed, to suppress the squeal that flew from her parted lips. She gripped the edge of the examination table, her knuckles whitening. *Crack.* Her fingers splayed out, registering her pain. Resentment rose like hot bile in her tightening throat.

Crack. The fire fanned out, spreading the swathe of its hot dominion. She whimpered, burying her face down into the hard leather surface of the bed of suffering. *Crack. Crack.* A vicious double swipe that left her buttocks almost molten.

Matron sighed with deep satisfaction. Coiling up the supple instrument of punishment in her left hand, she strode across to the prone girl and placed the cool palm of her hand down on the hot flesh of the punished bottom. A good session of severe discipline. How many strokes? Eight? Less? Or more? Matron counted the nine thin red stripes. Excellent. Tomorrow she would make it a dozen. And the girl would be bound, wrists and ankles. But tonight, nine would suffice. There was an excellent dinner of game bird and claret soon. Her mind wandered to the promise of another sort of hot flesh. Roughly thumbing the pliant, scalded cheeks, now emblazoned with the pinkish red stripes, she chuckled as she examined her handiwork.

'And that, my girl, will be your daily diet henceforth.'

Miranda climbed down and thanked Matron through gritted teeth.

'Get dressed. I will see you first thing after breakfast tomorrow morning.'

Jaya was weeping a little more gently when Miranda found her just before daybreak. They were both assigned to early breakfast duties, a rare occasion for snatching a few moments' conversation as they sliced platefuls of bread, boiled vast kettles on the Aga and scurried about preparing the food for the community. Miranda took the sniffling girl gently in her arms and softly kissed her tear-stained cheeks. Bosom to gently heaving bosom, they remained cradled in their mutual embrace.

'That was a cruel and wicked thing to do. The bitch. How could she? You had beautiful hair. And will have again, in time. She must have been jealous of you.'

'She scorned me for refusing to marry. She said no man had ever asked her for her hand. Who was

I to refuse such an offer. Then she threatened to . . . to . . .'

Jaya was overcome by shame. Miranda could only hazard a guess at the miserable suffering threatened.

'But you are right. She always pulled my hair. Said I did not deserve it.' The tears returned.

'We have to do something. We have to do . . . something.' Miranda put her hands out in an unconscious gesture of despair.

'What can we do? We are utterly powerless,' Jaya chided gently.

Miranda felt a stab of anguish as she recognised the truth in the Asian girl's words. Never before in her cosseted, pampered life had she met the feeling before. It rode uncomfortably with her, but she came from a strong breed. A breed of achievers, a lineage of arrant nobility.

'Then it must be an all or nothing venture. Are you game?'

The timid Asian beauty, painfully shorn of her crowning glory, nodded vigorously. The fierce light of vengeance flashed in her normally gentle eyes.

'Good,' Miranda smiled grimly. 'What do you usually think of when Matron comes to mind?'

Jaya shrugged before replying.

'Pain. And shame. Fear . . .'

'No. Well yes, of course there is always that. But what else?'

'She is fat,' Jaya said simply. 'She always talks about food and eating.'

'Exactly,' triumphed Miranda. 'Always talking about food. Come on. Breakfast will be served in twenty minutes. Let's give them something of a surprise on the menu today.'

* * *

123

Up in the san Miranda and Jaya worked quickly and stealthily. All they had to do, Miranda argued, was slip a pillowcase over Matron's head. Split second timing was of the essence. If Matron caught the merest glimpse of either of the two girls, all would be lost and their suffering would be great.

Their silent entry into the san safely accomplished, the pillowcase was slipped over Matron's completely unsuspecting head in a twinkling. She roared like a bullock but was deftly gagged with a towel within a twinkling. The next stage of the impromptu plan – always the best thought Miranda fleetingly – was to bundle their quarry down to the large refectory where breakfast was due to be served. Getting there before the rest of the community was paramount. Jaya, quivering with anxiety, acted as look-out as Miranda propelled the struggling captive down the two flights of stairs. The coast remained clear. Scuttling silently across the hall, the two girls jostled and shoved their burly captive into the deserted dining room and up towards the top table.

They quickly stripped the fat bully's clothing off and bundled it out of sight, keeping the bound and gagged, hooded and helpless Matron under strict restraint. The naked woman was forced to lie at full stretch – how Miranda grimaced at the memory of that phrase – beneath the length of the top table where the headmistress and her staff would shortly be taking their appointed places.

Miranda skipped into the kitchen and returned from its busy bustle unobserved. She grinned wickedly as she brandished a small glass of cooking sherry and a cucumber from the salad box. Stooping, she carefully poured the contents of the cup over the pillow case, taking care to dribble the pungent sherry over Matron's face and hair. Stifled outrage greeted this action. Already the heady fumes of strong drink spread like a miasma around the top table. Miranda nodded her satisfaction. Jaya grinned her delight. The cucumber, annointed with soft butter, was slowly but surely inserted in between their victim's pale, flabby buttocks. Jaya, shocked and delighted, stopped her squeals and giggles just in time. The ample cleft parted to receive and accept four inches of the probing cucumber. Matron groaned.

Four minutes to go. Four minutes before the large brass gong would boom out its summons to the community. Like the discipline and the punishments at the Academy, breakfast was always prompt.

Three minutes to spare . . . Miranda stretched up and grabbed a little Georgian silver mustard pot. Applying the tiny little spoon deftly, she annointed Matron's nipples with freshly made, yellow mustard paste. The fat bully, more accustomed to having her mustard spread on rashers of crispy bacon and moist, plump sausages, writhed.

Two minutes to go . . . Already the serving girls in the kitchen were bustling under their laden trays and salvers. Noises of preparation spurred the two girls to their task. Miranda untied Matron's hands, which immediately flew to ease her puckering, inflamed nipples. The gong boomed harshly with a reverberating echo. Miranda, still pinioning the Matron face-down into the carpet by her shoulders, looked directly into Jaya's eyes. They had remained absolutely silent throughout the entire escapade, but the tension between them now was almost unbearable.

125

Soft footsteps of stockinged girls approached. Miranda, giving the cucumber a final twist, whipped off the pillow case and threw it away into a far corner. She nodded to Jaya and in a silent twinkling they both melted into the shadows of the early morning dining room. The Academy assembled in its entirety within seconds. Last to enter, striding majestically in, was Mrs Boydd-Black. From her customary seat, Miranda distinctly noticed the headmistress sniffing the air. Good. She had smelt the sherry. Miranda smiled.

'Be seated,' came the command all were used to hearing and obeying.

All assembled sat, and from her lectern the thin, reedy voice of Madame Nina started the reading, taken from Samuel Butler's *Erewhon*, a dry, dull text.

A mounting sense of excitement gripped the air. From their vantage point, several of the girls could see Matron's naked legs and thighs spread out under the top table, at which the headmistress and staff sat unconcerned as they wolfed delicious hot breakfasts. Matron's absence was only remarked upon by a casual glance at her watch by Mrs Boydd-Black. But the drama was too much for a little dark-eyed redband to bear. She giggled, clapped her hands over her mouth guiltily, then scampered from the room. Amazed, the headmistress scanned the room for an explanation. She was met by a sea of strained, amused, giggling and undisciplined faces gazing back. Not back, exactly. Down at her feet. She looked down and scanned the carpet, staggering up from her chair in stunned astonishment at the discovery of Matron, naked, obviously the worse for strong drink, clutching her bare breasts in a frenzy of delicious torment.

'Matron. Can you explain?' the headmistress thundered.

The fat, naked woman rolled, scampered and staggered out from her partial concealment into the full view of all assembled. Several girls, seeing the obscene cucumber, shrieked. Some with horror, more with delight. Matron, having soothed her ravaged breasts, pawed the empty air behind her, found the cucumber and removed it. Miranda could not suppress her joy as pandemonium broke loose as Matron brandished the cucumber, gazing at it in bewildered horror.

For the first and only time, breakfast at the Academy dissolved into ungovernable mayhem. It took the headmistress a full eight minutes to restore a semblance of order and impose the customary regime of disciplined obedience.

It took her only six minutes to relieve Matron of her duties, position and presence there.

Chapter Five

The day after Matron's departure, Miranda was instructed to visit Mrs Boydd-Black in her smaller,
private office. As soon as Miranda saw the full white
blouse of the generously bosomed headmistress reflected in the polished black surface of the Japanese
lacquered bureau desk, she remembered Porteous
and her SOS. Was Aunt Emma coming to rescue
her? Had her discharge and release been secured?
Why else would she be ordered to this inner sanctum, instead of chopping cabbages, scrubbing floors
or wrestling with trigonometry under the vigilant,
stern gaze of the indominatible Miss Eaddes.

Maths had always beeen something of a mystery
for Miranda. Cosines and the cane were her present
horror. Miss Eaddes seemed to think that all
answers rested in the length of her whippy cane. But
no mention of any communication from Sandstones, or indeed any suggestion of an impending
visit from Aunt Emma, was made. Mrs Boydd-
Black referred briefly to Matron's debacle.

'You did not laugh along with the other wretches.
Neither did that minx, Jaya. I watched you both,
carefully.'

'Jaya had nothing to do with . . .' Miranda replied
with spirit, eager to protect the buttocks of her

dusky friend from the lash of retribution, trailing off as she realised she had given herself away. Mrs Boydd-Black smiled. How typically loyal and decent of this well-bred girl to do the right thing.

'Logic dictates that your answer strongly suggests that you have certain knowledge. If you know who was not responsible, you must know who was. Hm?'

Miranda, in her headlong rush to Jaya's defence, had not anticipated this cruel trap. She did not reply, choosing instead to tread carefully along the path of silence.

'An absolute outrage. Chair and Full Exercise for the culprits, of course. That goes without saying. And believe me, I'll see to it personally that the tennis table bats are laid on good and hard.' Mrs Boydd-Black enunciated the words with a distinct relish. Miranda grew pale, her palms pricking with sweat.

'But I suppose that we shall never get to the . . . dare I say bottom of the matter,' Mrs Boydd-Black said, chuckling.

The wry humour was intended as a truce offering. Miranda's quick mind picked it up. She took a deep breath.

'The Academy was not her true home, Ma'am,' she volunteered.

The headmistress looked at her shrewdly.

'An interesting observation, my dear. Continue,' she invited.

Gathering up her courage, but not wishing to sound like a gushing toady, Miranda spoke freely. She felt that she could confide in this intelligent woman, whose magnetic personality would drag her thoughts out in any case. The Academy, she said, had a positive purpose. It imposed discipline and instilled self-discipline in those who both needed and deserved it. But Matron was a bully. She broke the rules and went too far.

Silence. Miranda trembled. Had she said too much?

The headmistress rose from her seat and walked slowly around the impressive, ornate desk. Coming to a rest behind Miranda, she placed her hands lightly on her shoulders.

'You are a brave, and a sensible girl, Miranda. I have great hopes for you. And yes, I agree. As you say, Matron had not found her true home with us at the Academy. But your attitude to the spirit of the Academy and the difficult work we undertake here interests me.'

Aunt Emma will have me out of here before long, Miranda thought smugly, not really listening to what the headmistress was saying. Mrs Boydd-Black mistook Miranda's secret reverie for rapt attention. She spoke at some length. At first, Miranda did not bother to pay much attention. All she half heard was an intense homily outlining the work, and success, of the Academy. Then Mrs Boydd-Black's tone changed, taking on a softer, more reflective note. She spoke of her own daughter, killed on the Swiss ski slopes six years ago. She would, Miranda learned, had she survived the fatal avalanche, be almost exactly Miranda's age.

'But I have something of a proposition to make to you. Having the advantage of privilege, the ability to command and lead others comes instinctively and naturally to one of your pedigree. Six green-bands are due in this evening. There was something of a minor rebellion, if not an actual revolution, at a distinguished public school in Dorset. Subsequent investigations uncovered the presence of a vicious element. Bullying, smoking, sherry parties and general misconduct. The usual story,' the headmistress sighed. 'The Academy has been approached through an intermediary . . .'

Miranda noticed the sour grimace that accompanied the word.

'I have agreed to take them for a spell of discipline and character moulding. They will be subjected to a particularly rigorous regime. We will commence with a very firm approach. And you, Miranda, as a newly appointed redband, will take three to induct and mentor. Jane, already a redband, but showing marked signs of promise, will assume responsibility for the other three. Whoever does the best job will be awarded the rank of blueband.'

'Look,' said Miranda, proudly tapping her redband – as though it were a priceless Cartier.

Jaya smiled, unconsciously fingering her own gold band. Clarissa, a blueband, pouted.

'All that sucking up is paying off, it would seem. First, you have sweet Emily eating out of your hands . . .'

'If not actually eating you out,' said Jane, dangerously.

'And now ma'am herself is promoting you up to redband.'

'I've got three sprogs to sort out. So have you, Jane. And whoever does the best job gets to be a blueband.'

'I'll soon lick them into shape,' Jane remarked, coolly.

'Better stick to simple discipline, if I were you,' Clarissa said, chortling.

A pillow fight, as friendly as it was frantic, erupted. Jaya did not participate, merely remaining aloof while shaking her head and tut-tutting in her detached way. In the maelstrom of writhing limbs and soft, contorted bodies, Jane somehow ended up at the bottom of a heap which also involved a breathless Clarissa and an aroused Miranda.

At nineteen, but looking younger, Jane was slightly taller than her friends. But much more heavily breasted. Her tight vest was never quite able to conceal the delightful, burgeoning bosom that often threatened to burst through the stretched cotton sheath. Her generous bust, a beautifully rounded 38 inches, a C-cup when last intimately measured by a severe Swedish dressmaker in Wimpole Street, aroused affectionate regard, spiteful resentment and darker passions in equal proportion amongst all who knew her. Clarissa found her face happily pillowed in Jane's soft valley, resting between the gentle mountain slopes.

'Hold her down,' she cried to Miranda.

Jane threshed like a gaffed pike but it was a useless, futile struggle. Quick as a cat's paw, Miranda had gripped the pinioned girl's wrists in one hand and then pulled up the white vest with the other. Extricating herself a little from the mixture of assorted limbs, she lay out at fully stretched length alongside Jane, clamping the hips of the struggling girl between her own scissored thighs.

'Mmm,' purred Clarissa, easing herself up to sit astride the helpless, spread-eagled Jane, whose naked, satin, gleaming pillows of swollen, ripe flesh joggled softly.

'What was all that talk about licking things into shape,' said Miranda, giggling.

132

'Bloody beasts,' squealed Jane, clearly enjoying every minute of her present predicament together with the promise held by her immediate future under Clarissa's soft, warm thighs.

'I'll teach you the meaning of a good licking,' Clarissa threatened in tones of pure velvet.

Slowly, with consummate self-control, she lowered her head, inch by breathtaking inch until she sank her face over the vulnerable left breast. She parted wide, then closed, her sweet, sticky lips over the dormant pink nipple. It responded at once to her warm flesh, stiffening and peaking with a delicious ache. Jane moaned a drunken, lust-dizzy groan. Taking the darkening nipple up between her firm, expert lips, Clarissa commenced to suck deeply.

Jaya shook her head in disbelief, but feasted on the scene with clouded, opaque eyes that narrowed with avid curiosity. Soon, Clarissa's tiny white teeth replaced her full red lips around the tingling, throbbing nipple. Jane screamed softly but lay perfectly still in a posture of utter submission. A trickle of wet silver glistened down onto the nipple as Clarissa's mouth worked busily. Tongue tip having punished the captured nipple for several timeless moments, Clarissa's mouth withdrew, leaving it stiff, erect and almost trebled in size.

'Wait,' squealed Miranda. 'Get her shorts off. Let's see if she passes the Whore of Babylon test.'

'What test is that?' cried Jaya, now wide-eyed as Clarissa pulled the tight, white shorts down to Jane's threshing ankles. The taut cotton became enmeshed in her struggling feet, taming and subduing them completely.

'Nope. She's still dry,' said Miranda, holding up her dry index finger whose length she had just dragged between Jane's thighs. 'Try the other one.'

Jaya shook her head, mildly shocked but secretly thrilled as Clarissa bent down once more, her soft buttocks grinding into Jane's splayed thighs. Obeying Miranda's command, she took up the nipple of the right breast between her lips, sucked fiercely, then encircled it with her tiny perfect teeth. Once more the stubby pink tongue did sterling service, eliciting several squeals of sweet torment from the pinioned, helpless victim.

'Slightly sticky,' triumphed Miranda, holding aloft the glistening finger she had just extracted from Jane's moistening thighs. 'Give the bitch the full treatment.'

Clarissa, who by this time had taken the full breast into her mouth and was almost gagging on its fulsomeness, drew back her head and applied a searching finger-thumb pincer to the left nipple, working it furiously. Freeing her hand from beneath the soft weight of Jane's heavy buttocks, she repeated the divine torture to the left nipple. Jane's squealing threatened to draw down the wrath – and instant chastisement – of any staff member within reasonable earshot.

'Gag her,' Clarissa ordered, laughing.

Jaya threw her hands out wide, arms akimbo. Miranda looked up impatiently.

'Use her shorts. Quick.'

The svelte Asian girl was galvanised into action. Entering fully into the orgy of delicious naughtiness, she scooped up the loose white shorts and silenced Jane's cries into muffled whimperings. Jane's eyes bulged as, now gagged and helpless, she wriggled and writhed within the merciless thrall of her loving tormentors. Clarissa, concentrating hard, massaged both breasts vigorously, cupping and squashing the beautiful mounds of pliant, supple flesh.

'There she blows,' cried Miranda exultantly, extracting a wet finger from the depths of the happy victim's liquid thighs. 'Jane, you are, without doubt, the Whore of Babylon!'

'This is very naughty business. How you say? Disgrace. *Très mauvais.*' It was the clipped, heavily accented voice of Madame Nina. She had slipped into Jane's dormitory unobserved by the frolicsome girls. 'Shorts down at once, Clarissa. *Et vous*, Miranda. Give to me your bare bottom. *Alors. Quelle infâme!* All of you. Face down across the bed.'

Beneath the comic accent, the tone was one of brooding severity. French or English did not matter. Punishment spoke in universal tones.

Flushed and panting, the three girls obeyed with alacrity. Three gorgeous, mouth-watering bottoms appeared, naked and passive, as the girls lay belly down, lengthways across the single bed.

'Jaya. It is the moment for you to prove you have, how do you say it, won your spurs. The right to wear a goldband. The *bande d'or* carries responsibilities. Take my strap. Ten strokes each.'

'Oh, Madame. I do not –' Jaya murmured.

'Do it, girl. No, no, no. Don't stand there. Get up to the bed. Closer. That's better. Begin.'

The ox hide strap was nineteen inches long. Jaya's dark burnished hand covered the first five inches of it as her fingers tightened their grip. This left fourteen inches of the supple leather, some three inches wide, to punish the waiting buttocks. Jaya, flexing the strap, planted her white-stockinged feet comfortably apart and curled her toes expectantly. She approached her task conscientiously and with a sense of curiosity kindled with a flicker of mounting excitement.

Jane had the largest bottom. The fully rounded cheeks wobbled slightly under the impact of the first four carefully aimed strokes. *Snap. Snap. Crack. Snap.* The length of leather whizzed through the air with a crisp hiss each time before splatting down to flatten and squash the curved surfaces of both meaty globes. After seven severe swipes, Jaya paused, panting slightly as she inspected her handiwork. Then she turned her attention, along with the potent strap, to Miranda's twin golden, rounded domes. Firmer and trimmer, the flesh seemed tighter under the silken sheath of taut skin.

Crack. Crack. The leather sang its stinging song. The passive buttocks clenched and shuddered responsively as she applied the broad strap with a shy eagerness. Red marks appeared almost immediately on the softly moulded, perfectly symmetrical curves after each treacherous Judas kiss. *Crack. Splat.* The sixth and seventh strokes snapped out aloud in the massive silence of the dormitory. Again, Jaya paused after administering the first seven lashes, noting how the pale golden flesh soon burned deeply with the reddening blush of shame.

'*Bien*,' commented Madame Nina appreciatively, inclining her head sideways slightly. 'You must try to get the strokes right across both cheeks of the bare bottom, *n'est-ce pas*? Maximum punishment for minimum effort. Make each blow with the little strap count, girl. That is, how you say it ... the ideal to strive for.'

'*Oui, bien sûr*, Madame,' Jaya replied in faultless French. Clarissa's small bottom was a veritable peach. Even the dark velvet shadowed cleft was tempting to the eye, fingers and mouth. The superbly moulded creamy cheeks demanded to be addressed by hand, cane or strap. It was a bottom born, and destined, for the pleasures of punishment, like lips that deserve to be kissed, and nipples that yearn to be licked and sucked. As nectar attracts the browsing bee, Clarissa's derriere demanded discipline.

Jaya took a short pace to the side of the bed and planted the strap straight down across the broadest curved quarters of the bunched cheeks. *Crack. Snap. Thwack. Crack.* Jaya thrilled as both buttocks shivered, reddened and slowly glowed. She suddenly decided to give Clarissa her full ten strokes all in one sharp, searing staccato of lashes. The punished beauty's protesting heels drummed mutely in the empty air. Two shrill squeals were snatched from her parted, red lips.

Returning her concentrated focus to deliver the concluding three swipes to Jane, Jaya flexed her aching arm. Madame Nina noticed the flagging gesture.

'*Courage, ma brave fille.* Carry on. Three apiece. Three more for each naughty little bottom,' she urged.

Jane clenched the bedclothes into which her soft breasts were buried. *Crack.* The leather lashed the utterly exposed, defenceless buttocks, flattening their convex swell under its impact. *Crack.* A scorching swipe which left her creamy cheeks ablaze as they blushed from cherry pink to lustrous scarlet. *Crack.* The last stroke snapped down with venomous accuracy, scalding the juddering hillocks of naked flesh with a blast of livid fire.

'Give me that. *Bien.* I will give the final three strokes to Miranda. Your arm is tired with the fatigue, I think. *N'est-ce pas?*'

Jaya had hoped for the chance to let Miranda off

lightly, in gratitude for all her kindness. Miranda had been hoping for something like that too. She groaned inwardly when she realised that Madame Nina was going to intervene. The petite French mistress with the chignon of lambent auburn hair took the leather strap, snapped it twice in the empty air and then approached the bed with a soft, menacing padding of feet on lino, sending a tingle straight up Miranda's naked spine. Her tightly bloused breasts bulged and her full cleavage yawned invitingly as she bent down over Miranda's bare bottom and swung the length of harsh leather down.

Snap. Thwack. Crack. The three fierce strokes swept the golden domes of tender flesh with scalding flames of brutal fire. Miranda yelped like a puppy in the vortex of surprised pain.

'And let there be no more of the, how you say, "horse's play", *n'est-ce pas*? Behave yourselves, girls. You know the penalty full well if you do not. It is harsh. Such naughtiness will be dealt with. *Toujours la punition.*'

Rolling up the leather strap between her capable, strong white fingers, Madame Nina strode out of the dormitory with a toss of her auburn chignon as swiftly and as silently as she had entered.

The three girls on the bed rose up slowly, in subdued silence. In continuing silence, they ruefully examined each other's bottoms, gleefully thumbing the scarlet weals. Jane comforted Clarissa with soothing strokes of her cool palms. Jaya gingerly swept her trembling fingertips across the heavy swell of Miranda's hot globes, her touch as timorous as that of a butterfly alighting on a sun-ripened rose. Miranda closed her eyes, keenly savouring the gentle, tender care. A full three minutes later, she

138

opened them. Jaya was standing against the wall, shorts off, legs splayed lewdly apart, her thighs wide awake to her fluttering fingers.

'Look at her,' Miranda hissed, her eyes stretched with wonder. Jaya, head tossed back and eyes mere slits of fierce concentration, was fingering her silvery wetness slowly, lingeringly.

'Sh. Don't interrupt her. Let her be,' Jane cautioned. 'I feel a bit like that myself.'

Clarissa moaned, her left hand now buried up to her wrist between her pulsing thighs. Miranda, inflamed by the scenes before her, sniffed the fragrance of the group excitement that hung in the heavy air like a perfumed miasma. Jaya groaned in sweet distress, clearly approaching the heights of her self-generated ecstasy. Jane, frantically fingering herself, echoed the deep, velvety groan. Clarissa tapped Miranda's warm, naked shoulder with her sticky fingers, by now webbed with her own wetness.

'Swops?' she pleaded in a tone of urgent, shy pleading.

Miranda nodded gleefully. They squatted closer together, thighs brushing, buttocks plumply splayed and squashed down on their heels. Inquisitively, they dipped their fingers into each other's hot wetness, probing with feverish delight. Jane opened her eyes.

'Hey, that's not fair. Look, Jaya. They're frigging each other off.'

Jaya opened her eyes, which were bleary as though she were drunk, and staggered over to Jane. Kneeling down, she silently took Jane's hand and placed the pale, thin glistening fingers down between her own plump, dark-skinned thighs. In a simple, graceful gesture, her brown fingers sought out Jane's milky softness. Silently, the idea spread like a flickering flame between them all, the unspoken urge communicating itself mutely. Lust does not need the gift of tongues, just consenting silence.

Jane took the initative, shuffling inwards to form a closer circle. She reached down and covered Jaya's pleasuring hand with her own, and slipped her free hand in between Clarissa's pouting labia. Clarissa echoed both the posture and the gesture, forcing Jane's fingers in deeper with her left hand, and commencing to pleasure Miranda with her right. Miranda secured Clarissa and stretched out to finger Jaya's sticky flesh. The four naked, sweating girls, now with faces almost touching, leaned into their tight circle of forbidden joy. Each carefully controlled and guided the welcome intrusion of fingers between splayed thighs while working busily at the nearby wetness their other hand had breached. Soon, surrendering to the shuddering delight, they were merely ciphers, fused links in a ring of liquid lust.

The intense silence was broken only by their rasping breathing and the slippery sounds of flesh exciting wet flesh. Jane, who had the lowest boiling point, bubbled over from her threatening simmer into a foaming surge. A shrill squeal signalled her imploding climax. Her spine arched and her thighs shuddered. Clarissa followed quickly afterwards, mewing responsively as the high waves of pleasure crashed down and broke over her, triggering off Miranda, who spilled her hot quicksilver and hooted like a faraway owl on a foggy night. A haunting, shivering hymn of pleasure.

Then Jaya came. Her three companions did not realise it but the strict truth of the matter was that

140

Jaya had never climaxed before. Ever. Cultural restrictions and personal inhibitions had up to that moment prevented Jaya from exploring herself beyond some furtive nipple play, botton fondling and timid pussy rubbing. Her clitoris and its potent delights were as unknown to her up till then as the atmosphere on Jupiter. It was her first full, reverberating orgasm.

She held on to Miranda firmly as, belly tight and mouth slack with the tension of her climax, she screamed softly, hot tears of sheer joy blistering her sallow, plump little cheeks. Miranda placed her hands on Jaya's breasts and squeezed. Jaya convulsed into a threshing frenzy, her naked buttocks squirming in her own pool of wetness. Miranda slowly pushed the glistening Asian beauty backwards until she lay supine on the cold, hard lino. Her mouth sought and found the dusky-thighed beauty's inner sweetness. Jaya screamed a responsive, thrilling squeal and clamped her honey-dark limbs in shivering ecstasy.

Later, they collapsed into each other in a panting heap of spent lust. And later still, when the dormitory was deserted, the only tell-tale trace of the intimacies that had taken place there were four, tiny distinct pools of slippery wetness shimmering on the cold lino. Into one of these puddles of delicious quicksilver, Mrs Boydd-Black dipped her finger and, raising it up fastidiously just beneath her nostrils, sniffed. She smiled a grim, knowing smile.

Miranda decided to bring her three reception greenbands down to the gym in the converted cellars that evening. An hour or two in that cool, remote room with the polished wooden floor and walls covered in

141

climbing bars would, she reflected, be ideal for breaking them in. She knew that she must stamp her absolute authority and total will on them if she were to be successful in managing their induction period.

The forlorn trio, Susie, Zoe and Clare, who had been consigned into Miranda's stern care and controlling tutelage, had been led blindfold from the large blue Volvo estate car that delivered them to the Academy that afternoon. Showered, suppered and spanked, they had been stripped of their school uniforms – white blouse, green tie, green jumper and black mini-skirt, pale green ankle socks – and ordered into the regulation white vests, tight shorts and little socks.

Mrs Boydd-Black, the odour of the other four girls' wetness still stabbing her memory, had supervised the initial reception vigorously. Now these stood, chastened and subdued, under the harsh neon lighting of the windowless gym. Miranda promptly ordered them to kneel, with their hands on their heads. They looked quite a tough proposition. To establish her dominance, she decided to be very, very firm.

'Clare,' she almost whispered, tapping the cane against her thigh.

'Yes?' gulped the girl anxiously, shifting from buttock to buttock.

'Come here, Clare.'

Miranda tapped the scuffed leather vaulting horse with the tip of her clouded yellow cane. Clare rose up unsteadily onto one knee, wobbled, then stood up. Reluctantly, she approached the leather bound horse.

'Up,' commanded Miranda. 'Face down, toes just touching the floor.'

Clare assumed the position as instructed, fully aware that it left her beautiful bottom exposed to anything Miranda might choose to do with it or to it. She eyed the cane fearfully over her shoulder as she wrapped her arms around the cold, shining belly of the vaulting horse, her toes scrabbling to touch the polished wooden floor.

'This time, you will keep your shorts on. All future interviews or subsequent punishments will be conducted with your shorts off. First,' Miranda continued imperiously to establish her supremacy, 'I will be brief. Simply answer my questions and your discomfort will not be too great. Second, do not plead for pity. I will show you little mercy. I know why you are here and propose to make sure that you fully benefit from your visit to the Academy. Although you do not think so now, one day you will thank me for being so strict.'

Approaching the horse she rested the gleaming length of bamboo across Clare's tightly rounded buttocks. They flinched and clenched in a reflex of fearful anticipation. The cane lay patiently, full of potent malice, across the tightly bunched cheeks sheathed in their taut cotton. Clare squirmed noticeably beneath the tender threat of the inert wood.

'Tomorrow, we shall have an intensive tutorial. I will go over all the rules and regulations, disciplines and punishments that operate here. Tonight, I merely wish to get to know you. Informally.'

She raised the cane 26 inches up above the trembling bottom.

'Name?'

Clare answered, giving the name of a bullion speculator often featured in the financial press. Recent money, Miranda thought. A tough, brash breed.

'Age?'

'Eighteen . . . nineteen next month.'

'Virgin?'

Clare remained silent. *Swipe.* The cane flickered down across her tight, white shorts, cutting deep into the fleshy double domes. The pale arms hugged the belly of the apparatus. On the floor, the punished girl's toes scrabbled in surprised pain.

'Virgin?' repeated Miranda laconically.

'N . . . N . . . No,' whispered the anxious, fearful girl.

'Reasons for attending this place of correction? Why were you sent here?'

'I'm not sure –'

Swipe. The bamboo cane swished down once more across Clare's plump, rounded rump. She squealed, wriggling her buttocks deliciously.

'Fighting, swearing and bullying . . .' she spluttered.

Swish. Another cutting swipe of supple wood on cotton-sheathed flesh.

'Smoking . . . drinking sherry . . . breaking the rules . . .'

'That's better,' murmured Miranda. 'You will find it easier to confess. All questions must be answered. Never try to conceal anything from me. Ever. I shall and will find out. I need to know everything. I am in complete charge and control of you for the next few weeks at least.'

Clare rubbed her feet together, toes curling. She shook her golden curls as she tried to wipe a tear which had escaped her green eyes against the scuffed leather surface of the horse.

'Get down, Clare. But remember. Listen, learn and obey. Next. You, Zoe. Up on the horse.'

144

Miranda tapped the worn leather with the tip of the cane. Zoe shivered and clambered up, babbling loudly as she did so.

'My name is Zoe Winterman and I'm just eighteen and I'm not a virgin and I was sent down from my last school for the same things as Clare and please oh please don't –'

Swish. The cane sliced the raven-haired girl's spreadeagled bottom with a crisp, incisive lash which, falling exactly across the middle of her cleft, quartered the bucking orbs with mathematical exactitude. She squealed.

Swish. Swish. Her anguish was redoubled as she squirmed under the cruel bamboo that kissed her flesh so insistently.

'Silence. Speak only when spoken to. Understand?' Miranda said menacingly.

Zoe nodded, her mane of raven hair tumbling over her white shoulders in sweet disorder. In the massive silence, her stifled sniffling sounded all the more pathetic.

'Now. Answer me slowly and properly. Do you intend to reform and behave yourself while at the Academy?'

Zoe nodded her reply. *Swish.* The cane spoke once more. Zoe's bottom bounced, the deep cleft of her rounded cheeks accentuated by the tight, white cotton shorts that moulded and pertly defined each buttock. She squealed.

'Answer my questions, Zoe,' Miranda hissed.

'Sorry, yes . . . I mean no, I mean I will be good . . .' Zoe whimpered, frightened and confused.

Swish. Again, a lethal swipe across her generous buttocks, cracking down onto the swelling domes of luminous flesh.

145

'Silence. Get down. Next.'

Susie scampered to the horse, her blonde hair swinging impishly behind her. She had an elfin tread and the gait of a naughty pixie. Miranda immediately felt herself drawn to this impertinent little minx, drawn to punish and to dominate – and later, perhaps, to enjoy.

Susie, being petite, struggled to mount the leather horse. She slithered twice from the slippery mount which loomed up over her on its tall wooden legs. Miranda raised the cane and swished it against Susie's plump little bottom. The startled girl turned, glared and then redoubled her efforts. Miranda watched the buttocks squirming provocatively as Susie eventually wriggled up and sat astride her mount in triumph.

'Down on your tummy, Susie. Bottom up,' Miranda chided the minx sternly, managing to suppress a smile.

The petite greenband obeyed, straddling the gym apparatus sensuously.

'Name?'

Susie, not without a flicker of rebellious pride, gave the surname of one of the current leading television game-show personalities.

'Age?'

'Seventeen.'

'Virgin?'

'Yes,' came the soft response.

Swish. The cane whispered even more softly. Susie whimpered slightly as the bamboo cut across her perfect bottom. She slithered down from the vaulting horse, her belly dragging against it during the ungainly descent.

'Bloody bully,' she hissed as she rubbed her rump.

'Don't hit me with that cane anymore, OK? I'll not stand for it. Just you wait until my dad gets hold of you . . .'

'Silence.'

Miranda did not shout the command – such a slip would have suggested loss of control. She simply dropped her voice down to a deadly whisper.

'Shorts off. Now.'

'You can't do this. Who the hell do you think –' Susie wailed.

In a vicious twinkling, Miranda yanked the tight white shorts down to the protesting girl's ankles then scythed Susie down onto the rough, prickly coconut matting. The diminutive rebel squealed as her sensitive skin sank into the abrasive, wiry prickles. Miranda pounced, positioned her foot firmly in the small of Susie's squirming, wriggling back and flicked the cane down four times. The whippy bamboo licked the writhing rump with savage affection. Susie, firmly pinioned, bucked and threshed as the searing swipes kissed her naked bottom, striping it with discernable pinkish strokes. The punished girl buried her face in her quivering hands and sobbed hot tears of vexation and shame.

Spoiled little madam, Miranda thought. No breeding, no backbone. Just easy money. The type who could afford anything but knew the value of nothing. And a virgin? With the showbiz connections she found that very strange. Daddy's little princess? Decidedly. Daddy probably kept her well away from men backstage. Lesbian potential? Possibly. Perhaps the girl underfoot needed awakening . . . Miranda made a mental note to the effect that Susie would prove the most interesting of this penitent trio.

147

'Back over there with the other two. On your knees, hands on head,' she commanded.

'Get lost, fat bitch,' Susie muttered, sniffling as she stomped back to where Clare and Zoe knelt, pale and trembling.

'Susie,' Miranda called softly, her tone dangerously controlled.

'Oh what now?' The sulking girl pouted, pulling her shorts up over her scalded rump and flouncing around, hands on hips, to stare directly back at her imperious tormentress.

'I want you to do something for me, Susie, and do it at once. I want you to go over to the wall bars and climb up about four or five bars. Can you do that for me, please?'

'Suppose so,' answered Susie, tossing her hair and shrugging her shoulders petulantly.

'Thank you,' Miranda whispered, her tone saccharine sweet and carefully modulated.

Susie padded over towards the wall bars, her pert bottom swaying gently in a lazy, provocative manner. Miranda's hand tightened around the cane, almost as if in anticipation. Susie approached and then mounted the bars, scrambling up until her little feet were at least six feet clear of the floor. Miranda followed, climbed up alongside the clinging girl and swiftly bound her hands and wrists to the wooden spar with two lengths of thin rope. The knots were cruel and tight. Susie hung at full stretch, her hands tightly bound, her breasts squashed into the bars, her feet pointing downwards. Miranda removed her shorts down to her pathetic ankles and pulled Susie's vest up over the bulge of the bunched breasts, revealing the bare buttocks. Susie squirmed and squealed.

148

'You are here to do a few simple things, girl. Listen, learn and obey. Do you understand?'

'Pig,' howled Susie, her aching arms infuriating her.

Miranda placed the cane down gently, almost tenderly, onto the highly polished gym floor. It rattled slightly. A dry, eerie sound. Raising her hands up to shoulder height, Miranda placed them palm down over Susie's bare cheeks. The plump buttocks filled each cupped palm with warm, recently punished flesh. Miranda squeezed, gently but firmly, spreading the defenceless bottom apart, widening the cleft ruthlessly. Susie squealed. Without pity, and determinedly deaf to the frantic protestations from the penitent girl suspended by her tightly bound wrists, Miranda drew a thick fold of the imprisoned flesh between her splayed fingers and thumb pincers. And twisted.

The cheeks became mere wax within her cruel grip. Susie's tiny, white-stockinged feet, toes straight down, danced in the empty air. The arch of her instep spoke mutely of her pain. Miranda's hands worked the bare bottom like a potter works pliable clay. Squeezing and gripping, twisting and turning. A few hot tears splashed down from Susie's screwed up eyes as her liquid remorse moistened her naked bosom. Miranda's firm thumbs burrowed slowly, deeply, into the exposed, warm shadowed cleft between the soft cheeks, finding then rubbing the sensitive membrane therein with burning strokes.

'Sorry, sorry, sorry . . .' gasped the petite girl, her spine arched in exquisite torment.

'Silence. Face the wall,' commanded her punisher, stooping down and snatching up the cane. Miranda tapped Susie's bottom twice, and then took two steps back.

'No. Please . . .' whimpered the girl, straining to look down over her tear-stained shoulder, her eyes large and wide with fear.

'Listen, learn and obey. Do you understand?'

'Yes. I do. I promise to . . .'

'No, you don't. Not really. Not yet. But you will. Believe me.'

Miranda stood next to her suspended captive, raised the supple cane and swished it vertically up against the taut cheeks. Again. Then again. *Swish. Swish. Swish.* The thin wood sliced through the air and bit into the tight satin flesh. A long thin wail of distress filled the cavernous gym as Susie gave voice to her anguish.

'When you get back on your knees, consider. And consider this very carefully. You can do things two ways at the Academy. The painful way, or the very painful way. The choice, such as it is, is yours, girl.'

Reaching up, Miranda deftly undid the cords that bound the slender, white wrists. Susie slumped down onto her striped rump with a sudden bump. She snivelled, dried her eyes and watched the tip of the bamboo cane with a mixture of wary anxiety and grudging respect. Susie scampered back to her allotted place between the two awestruck girls, wriggled into her shorts and sank to her trembling knees. The cool white crisp cotton that kissed her hot flesh was soothing. Bliss.

Miranda turned and surveyed the penitent trio. The three girls, kneeling, gazed up at her sorrowfully. Miranda suddenly felt the meaning of power. Power and control. It broke over her like a delicious surge. She had, of course, exercised considerable power and influence in her life before the Academy. Gossip columnists stalked her. Head waiters had

150

fawned. Acquaintances had imitated. Her name, her money and her privileged status had opened many doors, turned many heads. But this new-found, intimate power was almost intoxicating.

To be so close, so palpably close to the freshly washed, soap-scented skin of a naked bottom. To exercise sovereign control, domination even, over a tear-stained girl's bare buttocks – ruling the tender flesh with cane, strap or naked hand. To feel the pliant flesh sink and yield to her own touch. These were all exotic, hothouse fruits new to her palate, new to the tongue. Fruits she had not tasted until her arrival at the Academy, and none more intensely than this evening in the gym. And the flesh of this fruit was luscious. And the flavour of this fruit was sweet.

'Time for bed. Follow me in silence to your rooms. In the morning, first bell will sound. Be up, dressed and ready to come down to breakfast by second bell. I will collect and supervise you. Tardiness will not be tolerated. Latecomers will be publicly thrashed. Up. In silence,' Miranda commanded sternly.

The quartet of skimpily uniformed girls, one erect and confident, three muted and subdued, trod the carpeted passageways through the Academy in silence. Miranda, cane in hand, wrist loose and supple, drove her greenbands as a goosegirl, wand in hand, once drove geese. Zoe's was the first dormitory they arrived at, and so, leaving Clare and Susie standing, heads bowed, outside, Miranda ordered her in.

'Strip, and into bed,' she commanded crisply.

Zoe dawdled as she shyly unvested her milky bosom. Miranda flicked the cane impatiently. The humming bamboo caused Zoe to shiver and peel off her shorts in haste. Miranda noted the dark pubic delta at the soft, seamless junction of the naked girl's thighs. Not a virgin, she suddenly remembered. The thought thrilled. Miranda quenched it, focusing on her duties.

'Bed,' she instructed.

But despite her determination to remain coolly clinical and in command, Miranda's heart fluttered with an unexpected urgency as she watched the naked girl turn, raise one knee and bend her golden suppleness down over the stark white sheet. Zoe's bottom bulged fulsomely as she clambered into the bed. Miranda savoured the audible shiver as the cold linen kissed the warm flesh. The bare buttocks were beautiful. Quite superb. Spankable.

I hope she is a bad girl. A very bad girl, Miranda suddenly thought. I want to spank her. Have her all to myself, warm and softly naked, bare-bottomed over my lap. My hand resting gently on her swelling curves, her rising mounds of pliant flesh. Then, the intimate punishment. My hand holding her down by the soft white nape of her neck. Or gripping her protesting hands by the wrists. Her hot tears on my bare thighs. The kiss of palm on cheek. Hot, hard palm on soft, juddering buttocks.

Miranda sighed and snapped out of her intense reverie. All in good time. There would be tomorrow. And many more tomorrows after that. Tomorrows full of such sweet sorrows. Zoe's head lay sideways on the single, hard pillow. Her eyes were still open.

'Are you a bad girl, Zoe?'

'Sometimes,' whispered the girl.

'Good,' whispered Miranda, then suddenly corrected herself. 'I mean, goodnight.'

152

Minutes later, Clare shook her golden curls and closed her large, green eyes as her tight vest came off. Interesting breasts, Miranda mused. I will soap them in the shower, and dry them with a warm, white towel. Very slowly and very, very thoroughly.

Shadows played along the length of Clare's dimpled spine as she stooped and stepped out of her tiny tight shorts. Between her exposed thighs, her pubic fuzz sparkled like spun gold. Miranda caught her breath. She shuddered as the desire to touch, to delicately fingertip the spun gold seized her. To trace a quivering fingertip through the matted web of tiny golden curls. 'Get into bed,' she commanded, her throat tightening.

Clare obeyed, her breasts bobbing as she bent and climbed in between the spartan covers which she drew up modestly to her chin. Miranda approached the bed. Reaching down, she slowly picked up the covers between her trembling fingers and eased them back. Over the soft, pale shoulders. Further back, down over the milky, rounded breasts. Further, to reveal the swell of the taut, flat belly. Further, to allow the swell of the hips to emerge. Miranda gazed steadily into Clare's shy but untroubled gaze.

The splendid breasts wobbled, the dark nipples suddenly and briefly mobile. Miranda steadied the pillowy flesh until it calmed into delicious stillness. Clare returned her steady gaze unflinchingly. A tacit communion trembled between them. Miranda swept her hand, knuckles against the silky flesh, down over the flat belly to the golden curls between the softly parted thighs. Slightly nervous, yet thrilled with her sheer wanton audacity, Miranda gathered a wisp of the golden pubic hair between her finger and thumb, and tugged gently.

Clare blinked and gasped softly through parted lips. Miranda tweaked the captive curl of slightly wiry, oily pubic hair. Clare winced and silently mouthed a muted protest. Miranda arched her eyebrow, challenging the tremor of protest. Clare closed her wet lips, firmly crushing any flicker of rebellion. Miranda smiled a soft, secret smile of triumph. With her curled little finger, Miranda teased up fronds of the golden downy fuzz. Delicious. Bliss. This was what power meant. Power and absolute dominion. But she would not abuse it. Not wickedly, like Matron. No. Not like that.

Notions of decent behaviour, of fair play and doing the correct thing were suddenly banished by the raw, carnal desire to tie and bind Clare with ropes and cords that bit into her passive, pale flesh. Miranda suddenly bubbled with a silver trickle of sheer wet excitement. Yes. Yes, she would rope this filly in and then, when Clare was utterly at her mercy . . .

Susie refused to strip. But she was careful.

'I never sleep in the raw. Please may I keep these things on? Please?'

Miranda's first impulse was to soften and relent. There was, after all, something about this spoiled little bitch that struck a deep chord. What was it? What could it be? Why did she feel so drawn to this little minx? A wilful, pert little beauty accustomed to getting her own way. Ungovernable and undisciplined. It came to Miranda in a flash. Of course . . . the insight was as complete as it was unsettling. She saw herself in Susie, and Susie in herself. Both spoiled, monied little bitches. Miranda chuckled softly.

'No. You must take them off now. Be quick about it,' she urged.

'Shan't. Want to be warm,' Susie sulked. 'Let me keep them on,' she wheedled.

Miranda took a firm hand in the matter. She stripped the girl briskly and then bent her over the edge of the bed. Susie struggled but Miranda held her in a capable grip.

'I will make sure that you go to bed warm, my girl.'

'Pig,' yelled Susie over her shoulder, her soft buttocks joggling as they shivered in expectation of the spanking to come.

'If I don't punish you, be sure that someone else will. And believe me, Susie, it won't be pleasant.'

Smack. Smack. Smack. The firm, spanking hand sang out sweetly and loudly on the fully rounded bottom, stinging it sharply with each crisp slap. Susie writhed, her thin waist, swelling hips and shapely bottom sensuous and provocatively knowing in their sinuous squirming. Miranda noticed the cleft between the gorgeous little pert cheeks widening slightly as the delectable Susie wriggled and writhed under the discipline.

Smack. Smack. Smack. The spanks exploded as hot hand kissed hotter cheeks. Miranda found herself growing deliciously sticky. Soon she was deliriously wet. Susie lay, subdued and naked, across her lap.

'Susie, I want your spell at the Academy to be misery free. Believe me. I do not want you to suffer. Not more than you deserve. Trust me. I mean to curb and bridle your spirit. Crush the demon in you. You will thank me when you understand.'

Miranda stood up, picked up the cane and addressed Susie's scalded buttocks, tapping the reddening cheeks with the tip of the cruel wood.

155

Swish. Swipe. Susie squealed, clenching her cheeks and drumming her little heels.

'You will quickly come to understand that what I am doing is for your own good.'

Swish. Swipe. Another slicing stroke that bit the double domes savagely. Susie sobbed a dry sob. Her fingers flexed as they gripped the bedclothes. Her little, punished nectarine-shaped rump bucked and bounced.

'Susie. You must remain still. You must accept any and every punishment I, or any other empowered to thrash you, decide to administer. Do you understand?'

Silence. *Swish. Swipe.*

'Yes, yes ... I understand.'

'Good.'

The cane came to rest lightly on the upper quadrant of the left buttock.

'Now get into bed.'

Susie turned and buried herself into Miranda's full bosom.

'Daddy never spanked me,' she sobbed. 'Never.'

She curled up like a kitten in Miranda's lap, her hot bottom pressed against Miranda's naked thigh. Miranda's fluttering fingertips traced the taut curves of the punished girl's flesh. Susie snuggled into Miranda, pressing her soft breasts into Miranda's firmer flesh. The punisher's warm hand cupped and cradled the punished's hot bottom, holding and keeping it in an embrace of dominant affection, of tough tenderness. Miranda felt the sniffling girl's head settle gently on her shoulder. Teardrops splashed down, wetting her white cotton vest.

'Bedtime,' Miranda whispered gently.

'OK,' Susie snuffled, planting a shy, wet kiss full onto Miranda's surprised, half parted lips.

Miranda tucked the girl snugly into bed, patting the crisp sheet down into the soft, warm body of the passive girl, her eager fingers seeking and finding unresisting clefts of shadowed warmth. Bending down closely, Miranda kissed Susie, now acquiescently submissive, tenderly on her rosebud mouth. Susie smiled a wide, happy smile and rolled over sleepily. A tiny voice inside Miranda's head thrilled. These were the joys of being in charge, in control. A redband had pleasures she had not dreamed of ever experiencing. A redband . . . damn. She had left her band down in the gym.

Miranda didn't bother with the light. She remembered taking off her badge of authority and leaving it across the top of the leather vaulting horse before chastising the rebellious Susie's bottom against the wall bars. Yes. There is was.

In the darkness of the gym, she rolled the redband up in her right hand, reflecting dreamily on the pleasures that lay before her. Zoe's breasts, Clare's bottom, Susie's will. All hers to relish, enjoy and dominate. Yes. Dominate. For true pleasure had its deep roots in control as well as sensuous experiences of flesh directly on flesh.

Arranging the redband on her upper arm, she was about to leave the dark, deserted gym when voices, deep in conversation, approached. Looking around for somewhere to hide – as escape was impossible – Miranda slunk back into the recess where the gym equipment was stored. There, shrouded in darkness heavy with the smell of dust and girlish sweat, she cowered behind a heap of prickly matting.

The door squeaked and yawned wide. A click. The harsh strip of neon flickered and blazed.

Miranda crouched painfully down, her breasts punished as they squashed into the wiry mats. The harsh light flooded every corner of the gym. Into the swathe of brilliance stepped Mrs Boydd-Black, followed by the termagant maths teacher, Miss Eaddes.

The fearsome maths teacher wore a loose pale blue track suit unzipped casually to her navel. Her full breasts, creamy and shiny, bounced freely. The cleavage caused Miranda's mouth to water as it once would to roast duckling with a tossed green salad after an hour or two in the paddock on a brisk spring morning.

Whatever they had been talking about, the discussion was over. In absolute silence they took up what seemed to be well rehearsed positions. A familiar routine. Miranda watched in amazement as the headmistress shook off and stepped out of her silk dressing gown. It fell into a pool on the floor. Underneath, Miranda saw the firm, full breasts held in the tight clasp of a front fastening black brassière. So heavy were the breasts that the two black shoulder straps bit into the flesh of Mrs Boydd-Black's shoulders. Wispy, black lace panties stretched across her supple hips. The panties were high-waisted, the fabric taut, adding a touch of surprising severity to the erotic femininity.

Miranda focused back on her headmistress's breasts. A little over-ripe, perhaps? But what a choice bosom to submit to. Miranda fleetingly imagined herself being breastfed by the dominant Mrs Boydd-Black. Forced to accept and suck the pendulous breasts. Sucking them with eagerness before being spun over in the ample lap to have her bottom smacked soundly by those large, white hands.

Highly charged from her disciplining of Clare, Zoe and Susie – yes, especially Susie – Miranda was almost at fever pitch. A slow volcano slumbered and stirred within her. A volcano that emitted little tongues of liquid fire between her glistening thighs. Her mind too was molten, hot and fluid with delicious fancies.

Miranda held her breath as she crouched and saw Miss Eaddes unpocket several lengths of thin rope together with a thick white bandage. Wordlessly, the headmistress walked over to the wall bars and stood up against them facing the deserted gym. Miss Eaddes followed her, hands full of the wherewithall for the bondage and domination session.

First, the austerely beautiful Mrs Boydd-Black submitted to the roll of bandage which, when deftly applied, deprived her totally of both sight and speech. Then each spreadeagled wrist and ankle was offered up in turn to be tied tightly to the polished wall bars. Trussed and immobile, the headmistress was rendered utterly helpless. Miss Eaddes eased down the panties with her slim fingers as far as the naked, splayed legs before her would allow. Those same slim fingers pinched a tuft of the exposed pubic hair and tweaked it gently, gave it a twist that caused her vulnerable, willing victim to gasp and then pulled the fuzz ruthlessly.

Miranda's hand flew up to her wide open mouth. More sweet, punishing abuse was dealt to the helpless headmistress who moaned softly under the exploring hands and tenderly cruel fingers which pinched and probed, slapped and caressed her passive nakedness. Stepping back as if to survey her victim, Miss Eaddes scrutinised every knot carefully, checking the security and severity of her handiwork

159

– then promptly left the gym. In her taut bondage, the headmistress endured her sweet suffering. Miranda blinked, almost disbelievingly. She paused in her hiding place for several seconds then decided to make her escape.

She rose carefully and started to creep, with a feline stealth, towards the gym door. In the darkness – for Miss Eaddes had snapped off the harsh neon light – Miranda's toe stubbed on the dull weight of a medicine ball. The pain flashed crimson across her eyes. The medicine ball rolled silently towards a group of four green and yellow skittles, scattering them on impact. The noise filled the gym like a reverberating thunderclap as the skittles rolled across the hard wooden floor.

'Hmmm?' grunted the naked, trussed Mrs Boydd-Black, startled and alarmed, 'Hnnghh?'

Miranda, breathing deeply to calm her frazzled nerves, steadied herself and made for the gym door.

'Who's there? Who are you?' mumbled the headmistress thickly. In her urgent anxiety, she had clearly managed to work a corner of the bandage from her mouth.

'Speak up. Come here. Undo this blindfold. At once. Do you hear me?'

Despite her obvious predicament, the headmistress spoke in her usual imperious tone that brooked no gainsay or denial. Miranda paused. On the brink of flight, she was suddenly swept by a surge of pity and tenderness for this strong, determined, charismatic woman. This lonely woman. Yes, Miranda suddenly realised. Lonely. Lonely enough to seek these furtive pleasures alone. A peculiarly solo joy, down in the gym after hours, with no partner to pleasure her further. Burdened by the heavy and onerous duties and responsibilities of office, she sought scant release in this way. A widow, with no apparent attachments. And still a young woman. A strikingly beautiful young woman.

Miranda hesitated by the door, turned around and padded softly over to where Mrs Boydd-Black stood arraigned in the disciplining ropes and knots of bondage. Approaching the naked woman, Miranda placed a soothing hand on the soft, gleaming shoulder, patting it reassuringly.

Mrs Boydd-Black jerked her face up, inquiringly. Miranda placed a single raised finger against the slightly parted lips that lay red and wet beneath the loosened bandage gag. The tense muscles of Mrs Boydd-Black's arched back slackened and relaxed immediately at Miranda's touch. Even more so as Miranda's flattened palm swept down across the plump breasts, squashing them fleetingly before resting gently against the taut belly. The cool palm returned to the breasts, to stroke and tease the ripening nipples before cupping and weighing the taut, warm bosoms.

'Please ... please ...' the headmistress almost whimpered.

Miranda suddenly resolved to give her anxious, expectant captive a delicious treat. A treat the lone, neglected woman would never forget. Into each life a little thigh-moistening ecstasy must fall, she mused as she stretched up to firmly re-tie the bandage that gagged the full, sensuous mouth. A mouth more accustomed to barking commands and ordering swift punishments. Punishments that scorched quivering, naked buttocks bending before the magisterial presence.

Now Miranda had tamed that mouth, a delicious

thrill stole into her soul. She returned from the dusty recess moments later with trembling hands. In the grip of her fluttering fingers she caressed an inverted wooden juggling club. Grasping the club by the tapered base, she gently inserted the thick stubby end between the loose breasts that swung down before her. Slowly, lingeringly, she rolled the club from side to side, forcing down on the heavy wood to flatten and squash the pliant fleshy bosoms. Soon she was shafting the length of the club up and down the perspiring cleavage.

In her taut bondage, the captive writhed in unashamed delight. Miranda traced the belly, hips and thighs with the blunt nub of the club, delineating every swelling curve with tremulous delicacy before finally addressing the pubic delta and placing the tapered tip up between the parted thighs.

The wet, pink labia received the stubby shaft eagerly. The recipient groaned thickly. A deep, sweet groan. It made Miranda's fluttering belly curdle. Slowly, she inched the thin, smooth shaft up inside the spreadeagled, bound and helpless headmistress. Noting the clenching buttocks, the tautening belly, Miranda gave it a half turn, rotating the club between sweating palms. Then another twist. Her happy victim rose up in an arch of response. Another full inch upwards. Another deliberate half turn. The oiled shaft of wood grew warm with an oozing, sticky wetness. Miranda smiled with grim satisfaction, and gave the club another teasing half-turn twist. The headmistress shuddered and gasped. An oath escaped her tightly gagged lips. Miranda chuckled softly and continued to ply the devilish wooden shaft upwards.

When a full five inches were buried in the soft

warmth, Miranda slowly dragged it down until the tip nudged the quivering labia, then quickly reinserted it, dragging it slowly down again before plunging it back into its sheath of glistening muscles. With gathering rapidity and momentum, the shaft shot up and down within the headmistress. Behind her taut gag, her breathing became rapid and shallow. Miranda noticed the flared nostrils. *Now.*

Gripping the base of the juggling club, she plunged the dripping shaft up and down in a frenzied flurry, taking care to ensure that the smooth wood dragged itself against the tiny pink clitoris. Mrs Boydd-Black arched and stiffened, quivered for a full 30 seconds and then slumped and sagged within her tight cords of restraint. Smashed and pulverised by the orgasm that savaged her so sweetly, she hung in her crucified bondage in spent exhaustion. Miranda stretched up and planted three soft kisses on each outstretched palm before stealing out softly from the gym. Shaking with excitement and triumph, she padded swiftly and silently back towards her empty dormitory.

Chapter Six

Mr Porteous inserted the video cassette with trembling fingers. Outside, in the yellowing light of a dull November afternoon, the heavy Fulham Road traffic snarled up. Impatient taxis honked. Inside his office, the secretive solicitor arranged six darkly shining chocolate eclairs in a perfectly symmetrical pattern of radiating spokes on the wheel of his priceless Dresden china dish. In his ornate teapot of solid beaten gold, the amber leaves awaited the cascade of boiling water. In the corner, a vast square screen flickered and snapped into dazzling life.

The picture of a well-appointed drawing room, such as one would expect to find in any civilised country house, swam into sharp focus. The room seemed to be deserted. Mr Porteous flinched as the kettle began its shrill, rising whistle. With a tut-tut of annoyance at the interruption, he silenced the shrill noise and prepared his afternoon tea, keeping an avid eye on the large screen as he poured the boiling water. Despite his gathering excitement, he didn't spill a single drop.

The picture blinked with a zigzag of time-lapse distortion. It returned, now showing the capacious room filling up as a file of nubile girls entered, heads bowed, hands abjectly folded behind their backs. Mr

Porteous took an eclair between his trembling fingers and raised it to his mouth, guiding it blindly to the expectant, wet lips. Precise, rat like teeth sank into it. The movement was clinical. His jaws worked mechanically. Mouth distended with the chocolate eclair, his bulging eye fell onto his leather topped desk. Good. He nodded with satisfaction. In his wire tray, seven dossiers lay waiting for his careful perusal. In each dossier were reports from chauffeurs, housekeepers, under-gardeners and maids. His twitching web of domestic spies. Spies, in his pay, all working in the houses of the rich and influential, who could not afford their private problems to go public. Problems that needed to be dealt with in secrecy.

On the screen, a rather promising young beauty was being singled out and ordered to prepare for some sort of ceremony. Mr Porteous kept the volume mute. He knew what the ceremony was and what it entailed. He swallowed his eclair and sipped his tea. Weak. Heavily sugared. Perfect. Yes.

Seven dossiers. From seven households in each of which a crisis was unfolding. A crisis involving a rebellious girl. Porteous was extremely careful when targeting his potential prey. They had to be wealthy – preferably in the public eye – and currently blighted by the antics of naughty nubiles. Daughters, nieces or wards. Shoplifting, unsuitable boyfriends. A record of expulsions, perhaps.

On the screen, he watched as the beautiful girl knelt awkwardly within the cruel confines of a large wooden chair. Her bottom, naked, was caught by the camera in a lingering big close-up. A superb shot, he nodded. A clever touch. Indeed, perhaps a bonus for the eyes and hands behind the hidden lens, he thought. He swallowed the second bulging eclair greedily and noisily sipped his tea.

A trembling finger pushed the remote control. The sound welled up. *Crack. Crack.* Porteous giggled his delight, his eyes hard and glinting in their mesmeric gaze. Damn, he whispered. That should have been a tracking shot. A pan, at least, he mused with the annoyance of the feverish amateur with professional pretensions. He was instantly placated by a big close up of the beautiful buttocks bouncing under the impact of the punishment they were receiving and undoubtedly suffering. The reddening blotches attested to the suffering, as did the pitiful squeals. Porteous licked his cream-sweetened lips.

Much better, he nodded slowly. And the soundtrack delighted him. His flabby fingers drummed the leather desk top, counting out the merciless strokes. Yes. Again. He nodded. His fat finger stabbed the pause button. Hold. He felt his excitement slipping ahead of him too quickly. His throat tightened and the blood at his temples pounded. He must regain control. Savour every sweet moment. Control it all. Yes. He sipped his tea.

Looking down onto his desk he counted the seven dossiers which would mean his intervention into the private crises of seven notable families. And certain doom for seven, nubile, headstrong young girls. More business for Porteous. More clients for the Academy.

On the screen, in a freeze frame, Clarissa's tear-stained face was caught in a timeless moment of anguished shame as a blonde girl cracked a table tennis bat down across her exposed buttocks. That blonde, Porteous mused. Surely? Why of course. The Gordon-George bitch. The Right Honourable Lady

Miranda Davinia Gordon-George. Swallowing his third eclair he fished out a pigskin wallet. Unearthing Miranda's hastily scribbled SOS note to her Aunt Emma, he placed it down on the smooth leather surface of his desk and flattened the creases out. He would send the note, with a covering letter, to Mrs Boydd-Black in the evening post. That should certainly make things hot for the Right Honourable's little bottom, he chuckled grimly. He would make sure that the punishment was carefully recorded, like all the punishments at the Academy, on video tape.

He must send that marvellous Miss Eaddes a bonus. She really was becoming most adept with that video equipment he had installed. Excellent results. And such a profitable sideline, selling these videos of the girls being chastised. No simulations. This was all too clearly for real. No cheating lipstick made those faint pink stripes across those naked, glowing bottoms. Without question, they were the tell-tale marks of canes kissing and straps swiping. And those thin squeals. As genuine as the sparkling tears were salt.

He giggled, rubbed his fat hands and bit into another eclair before pressing the play button. Another pleasurable and profitable afternoon the evil genius smiled, greedily wolfing his eclair. Seven more for the Academy, grossing many thousands of pounds for him as its anonymous Director. And better still, a chance to have that blonde bitch whipped to order. What was her name? Ah yes. Miranda. Always treating him like some sort of species of slug. How he was going to relish seeing her having her arse reddened. Just like this quite excellent video, which he would copy and distribute among

167

his select network throughout the City. And, he sighed blissfully, a delicious tea of eclairs.

On screen, Clarissa squealed as her Chair and Quarter Exercise continued inexorably. Porteous narrowed his eyes. A perfect touch, insisting that the penitents kissed the bat. He had been right to over-rule Mrs Boydd-Black on that matter. A perfect touch. Clarissa, her bottom large and round, her spine dipped, hissed her torment as the cruel bat sliced through the air and cracked sharply across her scalded cheeks. The video captured every stroke, every sob, lovingly and intimately in a range of care-fully selected shots. Yes. Miss Eaddes was becoming quite expert. And, thought Porteous, these eclairs were simply quite delicious. As his tongue sank into the soft sweetness, Clarissa threshed and yelped once more . . .

The frosty glint of Mrs Boydd-Black's pince-nez sparkled in the red glow of the early setting Novem-ber sun. A lilac mist was gathering beyond the elms, bringing with it the chill of an autumn dusk. The glint was replaced by two orange orbs as she raised up a pair of field glasses to her narrowing eyes. The field glasses caught and reflected the setting sun as it sent its dying shafts almost horizontally through the stark elm trees. The hand that held them shivered as a sudden memory flickered through her mind.

The headmistress shuddered deliciously as those exquisite moments in the darkened gym returned to her. Who had found her there? Who had ap-proached her, so tenderly? So understandingly? Who had touched her, then pleasured her, so effec-tively, so efficiently?

Her nightly little indulgence with Miss Eaddes – who left her and returned an hour or so later to diligently undo those sweet, tormenting knots – had become something so much more rich, more resonant last night. But under whose hands had she melted into such sweet paroxysms of liquid delight? Who?

The question haunted the headmistress. She shook it away, trying to concentrate hard on the magnified images brought to her by her field glasses. Out in the grounds, in the shadows of the elms, the dark, lengthening shadows, Jane was disciplining her three charges. Through her study window, an original mullioned glass of historical importance, the headmistress could savour details of the four girls in sharp detail.

Jolly good, mused Mrs Boydd-Black, her lips pursed appreciatively. Jane, a paddle-like wooden butter pat from the old dairy clasped in her right hand, was rigorously supervising and, when necessary, chastising, the three greenbands in her care. She had just ordered them to cease running on the spot, hands on heads, taut bosoms protesting as they joggled within the cotton vests, and was now getting them to leap-frog over one another. As each girl vaulted over the back and rounded buttocks of the girl in front, the raised butter pat would come down swiftly and sharply across the crisp cotton shorts that strained and stretched across taut, plump buttocks.

Jane was proving to be very accomplished with her little wooden paddle. Despite the afternoon chill of the November sunset, her three girls must be feeling very warm indeed. The headmistress continued to watch as the rigorous workout proceeded and was suddenly struck by an idea. She would, she decided, instruct both Jane and Miranda to hold a cross-country race at the end of the week. Each team of three greenbands would compete along a carefully selected, punishing route within the grounds of the Academy and the winning team would earn their captain a number of merit points together with the promise of keeping the highly prized blueband. Yes. A jolly good idea, she smiled. That would certainly put a little pep into the disciplining of the new girls. Disciplining ... Mrs Boydd-Black's mind surrendered once more to the memories of the haunting sweetness of last night in the gym.

Jane closed the study door and looked at Miranda triumphantly.

'My little lot will win. I've already had them in training. Put them through their paces. That blueband is as good as on my arm. Hard luck, old thing.'

Miranda grinned.

'Don't be too sure. There's still time for me to get my angels into shape.'

'You're too soft with them. Especially Susie.'

Miranda flashed a look of troubled resentment at Jane. The taunt rankled. Jane laughed softly.

'Yes you are. You've got some peaches there, mind you. Susie. And Clare. I wish I had Clare's arse all to myself to control. Ooh. Lovely. But at least I've got my three up on their toes. They'll win. You'll see.'

Miranda frowned. Perhaps Jane was right. Maybe she had been a little bit too indulgent with her three greenbands. She left the study and sought out Jaya to discuss it with her. Jaya was a loyal friend. She would know what to do.

Jaya listened carefully, then shrugged.

'If they are to win the race for you they must be properly prepared. In two ways,' she observed.

'Two ways?' Miranda queried.

'They must run with fear in their minds and love in their hearts.'

Miranda could not conceal her puzzlement.

'Fear of your displeasure must spur them on,' Jaya explained. 'Just as loyalty and devotion to you must speed them towards the winning line.'

'One or the other, yes. But both?' Miranda said in a dubious tone.

'Yes. It is possible. Believe me. Let me come down to the gym with you and help you to prepare them for the race.'

Down in the gym Miranda and Jaya stood together, heads closed in whispered conference, as Susie, Clare and Zoe stripped off into goose-pimpling nakedness. Susie stood, legs slightly parted. Her eyes were dreamy. At her pubic delta, stray fingers absent-mindedly plucked at her wispy duckling down hair.

Clare, whose bottom both invited and demanded punishment, stared warily at the two senior girls. Only Jaya, she noticed, was holding an instrument of punishment – a loose length of four-ply, waxed and knotted rope – in her hands. The rope made Clare's cheeks clench in fearful expectation. Spiders of fear spun their silken webs over the taut skin of her swelling buttocks.

The rope appeared to be stiff and potent with the promise of pain, yet supple and lithe as it was tested in the empty air with a casual flick. As it snapped,

171

the three naked girls eyed it in mutual dismay. Working to a pre-determined plan, Miranda took up her position at one end of the gym while Jaya stood, feet slightly apart, at the other wall. The waxed rope dangled from her hand, gently brushing against the swell of her dusky thigh.

The cross-country race to be held in four days time, and its importance to Miranda, was announced. Zoe, Clare and Susie looked at one another. Before they could comment or speculate, Jaya sternly instructed them each to take up a medicine ball. One by one, the naked girls bent down to clasp the soft heavy leather spheres to their squashed breasts. Susie staggered slightly under the weight.

'Zoe first. Then you, Clare. Then Susie. Run to me first then down to Miranda. We want to see what sort of shape you're in. Go.'

Zoe gripped the medicine ball and held the awkward weight tightly to her own soft, warm spheres of heavy flesh. Her breasts bulged as her elbows angled sharply. Her knuckles whitened as her hands gripped the weight between them. She scampered bare-footed towards where Jaya waited, waxed rope swaying idly at her thigh.

'Touch the wall,' commanded Jaya.

Approaching the white-washed brick wall, Zoe stretched her arms outwards and upwards, pressing the heavy ball against the wall. As she did so, legs splayed, spine arched, Jaya flicked the waxed rope across the perfectly rounded naked buttocks. Zoe squealed as the lash sliced her curved cheeks.

'Move,' came Jaya's curt command.

Zoe's bare feet pattered down the length of the polished wooden floor. Reaching the far wall, she stretched up to press the ball against the gaunt brickwork, Miranda swept her hand down between the panting girl's parted thighs, brushing her fingertips delicately along the velvety labial crease. Zoe mewed with sheer delight. Her submissive sigh of pleasure was almost instantly drowned by the crack of the lash – and immediate squeak of pain torn from Clare's parted lips – as Jaya licked the length of cruel cord across the beautiful bottom. Clare skipped down the length of the gym, her rounded rump bearing a scarlet stripe which betrayed its submission to the tormenting rope.

Miranda was waiting for Clare, and as the full, recently whipped bottom spread itself before her when Clare raised up her medicine ball, Miranda bent down and kissed it, dragging her wet tongue across the red stripe emblazoned on its convex curves by Jaya's waxed rope.

At the other end of the gym, Susie's pert buttocks juddered as Jaya played the rope across them. She yelped, struggled to maintain her hold on the medicine ball and scampered down to where Miranda stood. As Susie strained to thrust the heavy ball up against the wall, Miranda slipped her arms around the waist of the quivering girl and gently squeezed her loose breasts, pinching the exposed nipples in a thrilling tweak with her questing finger and thumb. Susie, her bottom still scalding from Jaya's crisp lash, hissed her pleasure and surprise at Miranda's tender touch.

The three naked girls were commanded to complete ten full laps. Each time they raced down to Jaya, their bottoms were greeted and punished by a stinging swipe of the supple rope. Each time they reached Miranda, punishment was replaced with

173

pleasure as their soft nakedness surrendered to her probing fingers and tongue, dragging lips and fluttering caresses. Between pleasure and pain, ecstasy and anguish, the glistening girls romped, shuddering at the lash and shivering with pleasure as they alternated between the dusky punisher and the blonde who proffered delight.

Panting and perspiring, Zoe yelped as the rope hugged her rounded buttocks for the tenth tormenting time. Her bare feet, white toes curled, skipped down along the polished wooden floor for her tenth appointment with pleasure. Miranda received her with expansive arms which embraced her, crushing the soft bosom into her own starched white vest and cupping her scalded buttocks tenderly.

Miranda drew her hands around the supple hips of the breathless girl and eased them down between the opening thighs. Zoe dropped her medicine ball. It fell with a dull thud. Miranda joined her hands together, as if in prayer, palms pressed tightly, and rubbed them slowly along the curved flesh of Zoe's wet warmth. The naked girl moaned and buckled at the knees, almost fainting away into the exhilarating, trance-like swoon of submission. The searching hands rubbed her inner fleshfolds more vigorously. Moments later, Zoe orgasmed with a soft scream torn from her quivering, passion-contorted mouth. The bright neon light burned red and gold in the ink blackness of her tightly closed eyes.

Miranda stepped back, leaving her charge crumpled in spent ecstasy on the floor at her feet. A harsh cry split the air as Clare's beautiful bottom shuddered under the kiss of her tenth lash. The reddening rump joggled provocatively as Clare bounded down towards Miranda, completing her tenth punishing

174

lap. Miranda took Clare from behind as the sweating girl strained upwards to touch the wall. The punished bottom grew full and round as Clare stretched up on her toes. Sinking swiftly to her knees, Miranda clasped her arms around Clare's wide, glistening hips and sank her cool face into the hot flesh of the ravished buttocks.

Soon lips and tongue were working furiously against the swell of the plump, satin smooth cheeks, and Clare cried out with mounting pleasure as Miranda focused her entire energy and imagination onto the soft bottom she was mouthing wolfishly. With a velvety fold of flesh sucked deeply into her wet mouth, Miranda closed her teeth and took Clare up to – and then immediately over – the brink of self-possession. Still fixed between Miranda's firm, white teeth, she threshed in her hot, wet orgasm.

Susie whimpered as Jaya dealt her a tenth stinging swipe. She dropped the heavy medicine ball. Stooping to retrieve it, her little bottom received an extra taste of the length of waxed rope. She squealed in surprised pain and scampered down towards where she knew Miranda would be waiting with hands and lips to soothe and heal and proffer tender, loving care.

Miranda took the heavy medicine ball from Susie's exhausted arms and tossed it aside, taking the petite girl and encompassing her pale nakedness in a warm embrace. Miranda's glossy, thick tongue flickered across Susie's parched lips, them probed searchingly between them, taming and subduing Susie's own aroused tongue. As Miranda drank deeply from Susie's open-mouthed, sticky sweetness, the frantic greenband struggled to inch her fingers down between her loosening thighs. The dominant

175

blonde redband who held her so fiercely stayed the
gesture, quelling Susie's wandering fingers and re-
placing them in the wet shadows behind the pubic
fringe with her own. Soon Susie was mewing like a
seagull winging in a gale, her tone one of plaintive
surrender and sweet suffering, as waves of hot liquid
delight drenched her, breaking her small body under
their fierce force.

Miranda and Jaya sat in the cool darkness of Jaya's
dormitory. The honey of excitement oozed from
Miranda's clamped thighs, its sweet odour penetrating the oppressive darkness. They reviewed their
evening's training session clinically.

It had, they felt, been successful and so they resolved to repeat it, twice a day, until the cross-
country race at the end of the week. The psychology
of the plan Jaya had evolved was perfect. The three
girls were compelled between the extreme polarities
of the pleasure and the pain principles, veering wildly between the totem erected to Eros and the dark
altar of de Sade. It had already been firmly established in their muscles and in their minds that
Miranda proffered pleasure and Jaya promised them
pain. On the day of the actual race, both would be
waiting for them at the finishing line, to reward the
fleet of foot and chastise the sluggish and tardy.
Miranda kissed Jaya lingeringly and smoothed the
stubble of her closely cropped hair. She thanked her
for all her help and sound advice.

'As soon as you make blueband, you are within
reach of the door out of here. You will make it to
goldband, in time. Then comes your freedom,' Jaya
murmured softly, knowing how deeply the proud,
independent blonde had suffered.

Miranda silenced Jaya's soft lips with another tender kiss, burning to tell the dark beauty of her hastily scribbled SOS which would soon bring Aunt Emma to her rescue. But she thought it wiser not to do so. Let it be a complete surprise. Once free, she would return for Jaya. Be her saviour and secure her release. Miranda was determined.

'Where are you going now? To see Emily?' Jaya teased gently.

'No,' Miranda shook her head. 'I think I've left my armband down in the gym.'

She lied. She knew she had left her redband down in the gym. On purpose.

Miranda crouched down in the recess behind the pile of prickly matting. She had no idea of the time, having no watch or access to any clock, but she felt that the moment must come soon, was imminent when the gym door would swing open and both Miss Eaddes and the headmistress would enter in silence for their nightly ritual. The minutes ticked by. Silence.

In the solitude of the gym, Miranda conjured up the evening's events, summoning the images of Jaya playing the length of sinuous waxed rope across the bare bottoms as she encouraged the naked girls with successive strokes of increasing severity. How Zoe's breasts, so fulsome and gorgeous in their shiny splendour, had joggled and bounced as she had struggled to run under the weight of the heavy ball. How Clare's rounded bottom had swayed so sinuously along with her glistening hips and thighs as her long legs pattered across the polished wooden floor. Such a delicious bottom, so exactly perfect for the attentions of a caressing hand and searching teeth and tongue. Miranda shivered with pleasure as

177

she remembered how her cool saliva had silvered the rubicund buttocks.

And Susie. How Susie had willingly received Miranda's slim fingers in between, and then up inside, her opening thighs. Little Susie. Sticky little Susie. So pert. So docile, now she had been thoroughly tamed . . .

The door creaked. The neon light spluttered into a blaze of vibrant white life. Miranda ducked as Miss Eaddes entered the gym first, dressed in a tautly bound, black silk kimono. The thin, shining silk hugged every curve and swelling roundness of her svelte body as it clung like a second skin to her lithe form. A brilliant red sash drew it tightly to her slender waist.

Mrs Boydd-Black followed, attired in a loose, white towelling robe. Beltless, it gaped open, revealing her near nakedness within its soft embrace. To Miranda's voyeuristic delight, the two women clasped each other in a close, wordless clinch, Miss Eaddes bringing her small, foxlike face down onto the upturned lips of the headmistress. They kissed a long, unbroken, passionate kiss for several minutes.

Miranda's throat went dry. Her delta oozed wetly. She gazed hungrily as the maths tutor, under whose flickering strap Miranda herself had flinched and squirmed, rolled her head slightly from side to side as she ravished the supplicant mouth of Mrs Boydd-Black. In her darkened recess, Miranda held her breath as she thrilled to the dominant kiss, savouring the subtle drama as the fierce headmistress, held in awe by all around her, became almost abject in the fiercer embrace of Miss Eaddes.

Soon the maths tutor's hands found the edge of

the white towelling robe and slowly peeled it down to reveal sparkling shoulders, then down further to the honey-toned waist and slowly over the swelling hips of the trembling headmistress. The white robe now forgotten at her feet, Mrs Boydd-Black stood in splendour. Her brassière was snow white, the cups that clutched her full breasts deep and severely cut. The flesh within their quivering restraint bulged softly. Miranda wet her lips with the tip of her tongue as she noted how the thin strap stretched tightly around the back, cutting into the creamy flesh. Crisp white panties hugged the full buttocks, clinging to the swelling mound of the delta between the thighs. A snow white suspender belt clasped the swollen hips in its elastic embrace, and from the taut suspenders golden, bronzed stockings stretched down the full, shapely length of the lissome legs. The stockings were darkly seamed, the thin brown lines vividly tracing the feminine curves down from just beneath the bulge of the full, pantie-clad buttocks to the narrow heels of the arched feet.

Miranda had never fully realised just how beautiful, how breathtakingly and strikingly beautiful, how electrically erotic lingerie could be. Now she knew. And the image and its frissons of delicious responses pulverised her normally coolly controlled mind. The sculptured brassière, stiff and dazzlingly white, moulded each breast separately, cupping and bunching up the plump, firm flesh within its loving grasp. The cleavage, a sensuously deep valley, was steep and shadowed. The sense of weight and fulsomeness was heightened by the closely cut, figure forming brassière which held the firm flesh in its strict bondage.

Miranda's labia wept with joy as her eyes burned

with every detail, every nuance, every clear line and suggestive shadow. Around the sweep of the waist, the intriguing girdle dimpled the soft skin. Slightly below, the snow white panties clung to each separate rounded cheek of the full bottom, the tight fabric delineating the subtle swell of the proud curves. The second skin of sheer silk snuggled into the cleft between the buttocks, and from either hips embossed swallows delicately winged their way inwards, flying towards each other until their beaks collided on the soft pubic swelling between the clamped thighs.

The dry dust in the recess prickled Miranda's nose. She held back the sneeze, checking it just in time before it threatened to shatter the intense silence. In her high excitement, Miranda's nerves were as taut as the suspender belt's garters that kept the sheer bronze nylon stockings so disciplined and stretched tight. Miranda gazed longingly at the darker band of burnished bronze which denoted the stocking tops. The garter snaps bit into the darker shade of shimmering nylon, dragging little pyramids of the glistening material up the milky thighs.

With a gesture commanding silence, Miss Eaddes propelled the headmistress face forwards towards the wall bars. Using the red sash at her waist she blindfolded her submissive partner and then bound her spreadeagled body by the outstretched wrists and splayed ankles to the lengths of wood. From the left hand pocket of her luminous silk kimono the supple hand of the dominant Maths tutor took out a leather belt. Miranda, dry-mouthed and wet-thighed, judged it to be approximately four and a half feet long and an inch of soft, supple leather thick. The hand that gripped the leather belt paused, then doubled up the belt and allowed the teasing instrument of delicious punishment to tantalisingly dangle across Mrs Boydd-Black's right buttock and down the length of her stockinged leg.

As human skin recognised animal skin, and understood the sweet threat one posed to the other, the headmistress gasped softly and arched up on her feet, urgently offering her rounded buttocks up in a gesture of impatient submission. But Miss Eaddes was not to be hurried. She dictated the pace, the rhythm and the tempo of events, having established and sustained complete and absolute control.

The headmistress shivered with feverish anticipation in her taut bondage, but her indulgent tormentor merely brushed the wicked loop of leather against her bottom in delicious circular sweeps. Miranda saw her thigh muscles tighten and, behind their fragile shield of shimmering silk, the buttocks clench in expectation. Soon. Soon. Surely the choking tension would break with the first delicious stroke.

Her throat thickened as the excitement and impatience for the punishment to commence welled up inside Miranda's tense body. Soon. Soon. The arm would sweep back, be raised up and then *crack*, down the leather belt would whistle to scorch the patient peaches that awaited its savage kiss. But as Miranda stared, she saw the belt being trailed loosely up around the spreadeagled victim's shoulders, the blunt tip now skimming down the furrowed spine then out across the convex swell of the hip and thigh. Tantalisingly, teasingly, the tip of the leather belt was drawn in several circles around the outlines of the swollen rump. Miranda almost squealed with tension.

Then, in a single, fluid and graceful movement, like a ballerina dipping liquidly in her paces, the maths tutor stooped, shouldered her strap and eased down the crisp white panties as far as the bronzed stocking tops, the spread of the splayed legs forbidding further descent. The softly shuddering buttocks of the bound and blindfolded headmistress lay fully exposed in their total naked vulnerability.

Mrs Boydd-Black inched up slightly on arched feet, her nylon-encased toes grinding into the polished wood of the gym floor. Miranda noted that the left foot strained inwards, and her eye followed the dark seam of the stocking up to the left buttock, which now bulged like overripe fruit. The gesture caused a molten trickle to moisten her tiny white shorts. In her feverish mind, Miranda burned and yearned to wield the leather strap. Now. She wanted to whip that swollen left cheek, to please it, scald it, pleasure and torment it. A spasm of tormented frustration stabbed her belly. Miranda felt a physical pain grip her. If the punishment did not commence soon, she felt she would scream.

Crack.

The leather belt flickered and struck. The flexible strip of hide caressed the splendid bottom, hugging the curved contours and licking it with a tongue of raw fire. *Crack. Crack.* Again. And again. And yet again.

The cruel, withering strokes were measured, assured. Miss Eaddes was fully in control, reigning in her impulses and keeping in check her boiling desires. The strap spoke out against the scorched skin in modulated tones, neither stuttering or spluttering in anger or exhilaration. Each swipe controlled and delivered with deadly accuracy.

Miranda heard the passive flesh being lashed eight times and almost fainted with the rush of intoxicated joy that surged up and flooded her brain. The heady delights threatened to engulf and drown her. Mrs Boydd-Black was uttering sweet, delicious lust-thickened moans. The leather length flickered and struck, striping her swollen, punished buttocks again, again and yet again. Fifteen strokes left her searing buttocks criss-crossed with thin, pinkish blue, faint stripes. Miranda wanted that bottom. Now. She wanted it badly. Ached for it. Ached to hold it, kiss it, smother it with her tender after care of cool hands and wet lips, gentle lapping tongue and soft, oh so soft kisses.

Miss Eaddes rolled up the leather belt and placed it in the crotch of the stretched panties. Miranda watched, wide eyed, as the competent maths tutor's firm white hands dragged the panties back up over the buttocks, leaving the instrument of the recently administered sweet discipline coiled up tight between the punished woman's wet thighs. A wicked gesture, to leave the strap so close to the flesh it scalded, giving physical expression to the lingering memories. Such a sweet memento. A devilish touch.

The gesture caused a huge butterfly to unfold and spread its wings deep within Miranda's belly. She gazed, stunned and bedazzled, as Miss Eaddes lay down on the hard, polished wooden gym floor, wrenched open her silk kimono and greedily pleasured herself with both hands. There was no teasing with exploring, tentative fingertips here – she was hot and wet and hungry. The expert hands sought and found the spot in seconds, and the task was accomplished with clinical rather than sensuous perfection. Spine arched, breasts trembling loosely, mouth agape and slack with passion, the maths tutor climaxed long and loud, her soft bottom pounding its clenched cheeks against the hard, polished floor as the orgasm gripped her and wrung her out in its tight fist of fierce delight. Moments later, without speaking to the headmistress, Miss Eaddes turned off the light and strode out of the darkened gym.

Several minutes passed before Miranda felt it safe enough to emerge. She stole out of her hiding place on silent, stockinged feet and softly approached the headmistress. A loose board creaked.

'Who is that? Speak,' Mrs Boydd-Black commanded imperiously, her grim authority only slightly compromised by a flicker of anxiety in her voice.

Miranda positioned herself directly behind the recently whipped woman who still stood ensnared in the ruthless bondage. To allay all fears, she repeated the triple kiss signal, three on the white shoulder and three on the reddening left buttock. Mrs Boydd-Black sighed deeply, a sweet sigh of both relief and pleasurable anticipation.

'I wish I knew who you are . . .' she whispered pleadingly.

Miranda placed a warning finger against the parted lips of her happy victim and tapped them into silence with three curt taps. The headmistress shivered. Miranda stroked the spreadeagled woman along her outstretched arms, gliding her fingers from fleshy shoulders to sinuous forearm then on to where slim wrists writhed in the cords that gripped them. Invisible electric sparks flickered from flesh to flesh. The headmistress whimpered. By way of response, Miranda gently positioned her cool hands around Mrs Boydd-Black's waist and slowly, slowly peeled down the tight white panties.

The headmistress stiffened her arched body momentarily, then slumped into soft, passive acquiescence. The cleft between her recently scourged buttocks parted invitingly, the shadows yawning deep and wide. Miranda ran her fingers up between the punished buttocks, the tips skimming the hot, moist flesh within the glorious globes. The headmistress shuddered and emitted a thin scream which melted into a dying, curdling moan. Miranda's inquisitive thumb followed, probing and penetrating the warm dark secret place. The firm muscle of the hot sphincter trapped and engulfed the thumbtip, slowly accepting it into the warmth within. With a cruel twist, Miranda extracted her trapped thumb from the taut flesh, causing her victim to groan aloud.

The headmistress was beyond mere words now, and her feelings were expressed in primal sounds of raw pleasure, all rational thoughts banished from this realm of the senses. Miranda tapped the thick, sticky labial folds. They were already parted. Hot excitement dripped steadily down her fingertips. The headmistress was primed for pleasure, and accepted Miranda's three fingers willingly, hungrily, her rippling muscles devouring them with a savage appetite for more. The fingers worked with the spasms of the contracting muscles, seeking and finding the most sensitive reaches within, then pumping and plunging up and down with a controlled ruthlessness.

As she felt the belly tighten and the warm excitation drip, Miranda slowly inserted the index finger of her left hand in between the clenched buttocks, working it inexorably up against, and then into and beyond, the tightened whorl of the anus. The broad, soft buttocks bucked and bounced in a responsive spasm as the tightly bound body of the headmistress thrilled to the added delight.

Miranda smiled as her victim shuddered into a reverberating climax moments later, and as she stepped back slightly to peruse the writhing limbs tauten in sweet agony, a sudden surge of tenderness for this lonely, isolated woman crept into her young heart. Never really deeply touched by pity or compassion in her spoiled and privileged existence, Miranda suddenly reflected with tenderness upon the trials and tribulations Mrs Boydd-Black endured.

A widow, childless and burdened by the responsibilities of leadership and command. Wishing to make this brief session of undiluted pleasure an intensely memorable one, Miranda dipped her fingers into the panties and took out the coiled leather strap. Stepping back, she uncoiled it and cracked it down four times in rapid succession across the tremulous, domed buttocks that still shuddered under the force of the internal climax that had exploded within.

Fresh cries of pure joy were torn from the parted lips of the delirious headmistress. The cries were so deep and mellow, so liquidly passionate, Miranda could have been forgiven for thinking that the tongue that gave birth to them was rooted in the ravaged belly below.

Miranda stepped closer to the warm body that shivered in ecstatic surrender and unclasped the taut brassière. The wisp of airy nothingness fluttered down to the stockinged feet below, allowing the generous breasts, nipples peaked painfully in their alert erectness, to tumble and spill freely. Insinuating the

186

leather belt around the loose breasts, Miranda drew it tightly together across the soft flesh of Mrs Boydd-Black's back and bound it firmly into place. She examined the effect, nodding with satisfaction as she caught a glimpse of the bunched breasts bulging within the supple circle of hide.

Silvery hot droplets spangled the sheer bronze nylon stockings that graced the inner thighs of the shivering headmistress. Miranda traced her finger in the wetness, musing. As she dabbled her fingertips into the lava flow she struggled with an idea. Resolution flickered triumphantly in her eyes. Of course.

She dragged her sticky hands across the scalded bottom and smacked it playfully, resting her hand on the scorched skin for a moment before rubbing the hot flesh with the sticky wet warmth that dripped from her webbed fingers. As the headmistress screamed softly in response, Miranda skipped over to the recess and selected a thin Indian juggling club. She returned to where the near naked woman quivered in her taut bondage. Miranda placed the narrow shaft up against the parted lips. An inquisitive tongue peeped out and licked the smooth wood timorously, then rasped it with greedy, mounting confidence.

Miranda withdrew the tapered length of smooth wood. Mrs Boydd-Black whimpered for its return. Miranda spanked the exposed bottom sternly and then slowly sank down to her knees. Bending her face closely, she tongued the seam of the stockinged left leg up from the hollow behind the straightened knee to where it dissolved into the swell of the heavy buttock. Repeating and echoing the gesture, Miranda's little wet, pink tongue tip licked the seam the full length of the bronze-stockinged right leg, pausing to flutter and quiver at the cusp of the

187

curved bottom above. By now, the pupil was as wet and frenzied as the tightly bound and blindfolded headmistress.

'Who are you? I must know,' demanded the husky voice once more.

Miranda sharply spanked the naked bottom in a command for silence.

'Please ... please ...' sobbed the headmistress thickly, brokenly.

Miranda raised her strong leg up between the parted thighs before her and wedged it firmly into the shadowed, wet warmth. The splayed buttocks rested their heavy flesh on her flexed upper thigh. Miranda concentrated hard as she took a cheek in each hand and worked the pliant flesh, twisting and moulding it to her will, between the merciless talons that her fingers had become.

'Witch!' hissed the ravished victim, almost drunkenly. 'Bitch ... Devil ... Who are you? Tell me, tell me ... *please* ...'

Miranda squeezed the buttock flesh viciously, tenderly, lingeringly in several directions before dragging it wide apart, causing the deep cleft to yawn apart painfully. Miranda held it like that for a timeless moment, her own hot silver spilling freely down her legs.

'More ... please, I beg you. Do what you will with me. Please,' the lust-curdled voice begged her thickly.

Dragging the soaking panties down as far as the splayed legs would permit them to go, Miranda placed the blunt, thick end of the inverted Indian juggling club into the saturated gusset, carefully positioning the narrow, tapered shaft in between the glistening, parted labia above.

The headmistress responded with a shrill wail of

demonic joy, a scream that fragmented into sobbing joy and delight. As the panties slowly curled back up along the satin thighs, the nub of the tapered shaft was slowly forced up inside their owner. As the smooth wood disappeared, a quarter of an inch at a time, Miranda undid the leather belt. The bound breasts bounced free. Miranda steadied them, tweaking the stiff nipples painfully before applying the leather belt five times across the creamy orbs of Mrs Boydd-Black's naked buttocks.

Crack. Snap. Thwack. The crisp leather seared across the satin flesh. The buttocks bounced under the fierce lashes, causing the panties to unfurl more quickly, thus forcing the smooth shaft deeper upwards, inwards.

Crack. The headmistress screamed. The bottom bounced. The wood sank even deeper into the wet warmth. *Crack.* The fifth swipe seared the bunched buttocks savagely. The headmistress mouthed a torrent of endearments, obscenities and impassioned avowals of both eternal gratitude and revenge.

Smiling grimly, Miranda scooped up the discarded brassière from the floor and forced the soft material deep inside the parted lips. Checking to ensure that the Indian club was still penetrating the trussed, gagged, naked body of the delirious headmistress, Miranda kissed the punished bottom three times on each glistening cheek – and softly stole out of the gym.

Nine fifty-seven. A cold, dank winter night. The sort of night that kept taxis busy and London's pavements empty. Outside Liverpool Street station, a motorbike revved at the amber traffic light. The vast concourse shimmered in its swathe of golden light. Green. The engine snarled and roared. The bike flashed away, pulling up three minutes later outside a merchant bank that specialised in bullion and Far Eastern currencies.

The rider took the lift up to the eighth floor and handed over his small package. Six men immediately abandoned their flickering screens. Tokyo would not be up for an hour. The package was quickly unwrapped to reveal an unmarked cassette. The cassette was inserted into a video. Champagne and vodka cocktails flowed as the sweating men, all sporting the uniform of striped shirt and healthy tan, expensive haircuts and tired eyes, crowded around the large screen, their jaded faces alight with expectation.

On the screen, beautiful girls were being punished. A bottom, soft and creamy, was being hand spanked. Another, bronzed and proud, was being carefully swished with a supple bamboo cane. The men cheered lustily. Their ragged cries drew the eyes of a more senior colleague to the screen. A Bihar bullion expert, he had made his first million before they had learned to spell Porsche, let alone drive one. He frowned and shook his head sadly. These boys.

Then the Asian banker, who had merely popped in to confirm a meeting in Bonn the following day before going on to another tiresome Embassy supper, froze in his chair. His eyes narrowed to fierce slits. On the screen was the girl he loved. Jaya. Beautiful Jaya, whose family had whisked her off on some pretext or other instead of allowing the pair of them to sort things out. Yes. There she was, her luxurious hair cropped and cruelly shaven to the scalp, her large, sorrowful eyes brimming with tears as her buttocks flinched under a brutal, scalding strap.

'Where did you get that video?' he barked angrily. 'Where did it come from?'

Several pale, tired faces swung round. He was shushed impatiently. He repeated his questions, this time in a voice of icy calm.

'Little bloke I know. It'll cost you a ton,' an irritated voice snapped.

The Bihar banker opened his wallet, which contained a photo of Jaya smiling shyly up at him, and peeled off five twenties. An outstretched hand grabbed the notes and replaced them with a small business card. The Asian scanned it.

'And where can I get in touch with this Porteous fellow?'

'Fulham Road. The number's on the back. Now keep it quiet, Hazim. This bitch is getting it good and strong.'

Hazim tucked the solicitor's card carefully into his wallet and took a meditative sip of his iced lime juice. Tomorrow morning, the first plane to Bonn. He couldn't cancel. Back by nightfall. Sixish. His secretary would arrange a meeting. No. Better still, he'd phone from Heathrow first thing. Porteous would be told to wait. Where, he wondered, was Jaya now? And where, if they were needed, could a reputable international bullion expert get hold of a team of heavies if the need arose? He closed his eyes. The iced lime juice tasted sweet.

Miranda tapped gently on Emily Frobisher's green baize door. It opened, almost immediately. Miranda stepped quietly into the dimly lit, untidy room. As usual, paperbacks, tissues and a dozen other items – the flotsam and jetsam of a creative but disorderly temperament – littered the carpet. Miranda smiled as her toes crunched on a little pile of acorns and pine cones.

'Is it OK?' she whispered. 'Are you busy?'

The words sounded strange to her even as Miranda spoke them. In those almost forgotten times before the Academy, she would never ask anyone if her arrival was convenient. She simply arrived. Now, here, with Emily, she experienced a curious hesitancy within herself, a touch of humility tinged with both awe and expectancy.

Emily laughed warmly, delighted by Miranda's new-found, shy respectfulness.

'Of course it's OK. I'm never too busy to see you. We have all night together. I've swopped my rota. I'm off duty.'

Miranda grinned. Sometimes her nocturnal visits had to end abruptly if Emily was on night patrol duty. But tonight was theirs, entirely.

'Some wine, my dear,' Emily said, passing Miranda a large glass of chilled Chablis. Miranda's lips found it crisp, dry and delicious.

'There's some chicken salad for you over there,' Emily waved vaguely in the direction of her desk. She was delightfully undomesticated. Miranda found the white chicken breast, annointed with a light dressing which bore a trace of rosemary and garlic, and sank her teeth into the succulent flesh, tearing hungrily at her illicit supper with a keen, sharp appetite, all the keener and sharper after pleasuring the headmistress. Emily raised an arched eyebrow.

'My, we are lusty tonight, aren't we? I shall just slip into a bath I've been promising myself all evening. Relax, I won't be long.'

Miranda wolfed the chicken, and some bread and Stilton, as Emily bathed.

Emily Frobisher started to sing happily in her bubble bath. The silvery notes seduced Miranda's ears and drew her to the bathroom door. It was slightly ajar. Emily trilled an erotic coda from Mozart's Don Giovanni. Miranda recognised it as the passage which signalled the delicious moment when a strict and pious *duenna* surrenders to the promise of forbidden pleasure and wicked abandonment. It was the sound of a spirit struggling with the yearning flesh which imprisoned it, of cold chastity broken on the wheel of inexorable carnality. The triumph of the venal flesh.

The sensual music bubbled up from Emily's fluted throat and spilled out in a wanton cascade over her trembling, moistened lower lip. Miranda breathed sharply with acute pleasure as she watched Emily's tongue tip quiver in an effortlessly nightingaled arpeggio of liquid notes. The sweet ululation drew Miranda mesmerically to the side of the bath.

Down in the sweetly scented, shining bubbles, Emily lay pink and passive. Miranda knelt down and closed her mouth over the slightly parted lips beneath her. A slow, searching kiss. The hot steam made the bending girl perspire. Sharp beads of salt stung her eyes like tears of remorse. Emily reached up and licked them away, her breasts rising and glistening as she did so. Bubbles, large and small, spangling and shivering, nestled in her deep, shining cleavage. Miranda bent down and burst them, one by one, with the tip of her quivering tongue.

Emily had bunched her glorious hair into a disorderly top knot behind her, a large, black ebony clasp punishing it into place. Loosened by the steam, stray wisps dangled tantalising down over her left shoulder and along the snow-white, curved nape of her naked neck. Miranda's fingers found and fondled them, curling them around and around her lazy fingers. Emily's eyes sparkled invitingly. Miranda needed no further bidding. With trembling fingers, so certain yet so unsure, she loosened the ebony comb, allowing the glorious hair to tumble free. Fronds trailed in wet wisps as they spilled into the bath, or clung intently to the shining skin of Emily's bare, wet shoulders and upper arms.

Giggling naughtily, Emily rose from her screen of scanty bubbles to stand, proud and nakedly erect, in the bath. Her legs were splayed, her thighs open to Miranda's penetrating gaze or touch. Scented steam rose like an uplifted veil from her wet belly and glistening hips. Droplets gathered on the slender slopes of her fully rounded breasts, splashing down one by one onto her pubic delta, remaining there like sparkling spangles of a shattered diamond strewn on a cobweb of spun gold. Miranda closed her lips over the thrilling pubic fuzz and sucked the sweet, nectar-like moisture. She gazed up into Emily's eyes, her head swimming with giddy happiness.

'Dry me,' whispered the tutor, her brown eyes big and wide.

'Of course,' replied Miranda huskily, her blue eyes clouding to a pale grey.

Miranda gathered Emily up into a large, loose bath towel and hugged her warm, naked body closely, tenderly. She patted the soft towelling across the beautifully sculptured shoulders and then down the sweep of the splendid spine. Emily shuddered deliciously as the hands beneath the towelling sought and found her taut, dripping buttocks. Butterfly fingertips dappled the velvet-skinned orbs of joggling flesh as they gently patted the rounded bottom dry.

Slowly. Lingeringly. Often pausing to cup and weigh the breathtaking cheeks with infinite care and tenderness.

Emily closed her eyes and moaned sweetly like a sleepy dove as the patting became firmer, more assured. She felt the questing hands pause, then drag the swollen flesh of each buttock apart, outwards. She felt her cleft open and then gape, almost painfully. The torment was sweet. She shivered. The fluttering hands of her obedient tormentress swept up lightly over her swollen hips, skimmed across her tight belly and rose up to dry her breasts. Emily gasped, an audible bat squeak of raw sexuality as the hands closed over her exposed, defenceless breasts.

The attention was careful, lingering and extremely detailed. Palms swept up beneath the breasts to pat the skin dry with the ticklish towelling, then dabbed the ripe flesh at either side. Next, the upper slopes of sensitive skin were gently wiped, downwards, until the tiny beads of sparkling water disappeared. The hands toiled briskly then as their delicious labours continued. They kneaded, squeezed and shaped the soft, pendulous bosoms with increasing expertise, with mounting boldness. The power balance shifted subtly moment by moment as Emily first offered, then found herself surrendering herself to Miranda.

Miranda sensed the change. It occurred when she pressed her palms against the puckering, slightly swollen berry-like nipples. She was sure of it when she took each nipple between a fiercely tender finger and thumb, working the tiny erections assiduously, then between her lips. When her teeth closed over the nipples to bite and chew, and Emily screamed

195

like a wounded seagull, Miranda sensed that her dominance was completely assured.

She drew her head back and inspected Emily's face. It was pale, the features drained with exhausted lust, the tiny muscles slack with passion. Miranda returned her mouth to each nipple, bending to pleasure them one by one between her teeth. She nibbled with controlled precision, submitting each pink peak to extreme, maximum pleasure.

Extreme, maximum pleasure. The words, or at least the echoes of the blindly understood meaning, reverberated around her crimson mind. Pleasure, pure and perfect. Miranda, losing control, a spasm of urgent desire thrilling down along her taut thighs, buried her face deeply, totally into the creamy mounds of cushioning flesh. A trace of the scented foam pricked her lips. Her wetness streamed in spun sugar droplets from her tingling, opening labial folds of hot, tormented flesh. Her own breasts ached. Sweetly. Each erect nipple straining through the wet sheath of her soaking cotton vest. She squealed as they grazed against Emily's taut belly. Again. And again. Her hot joy splashed in a molten teardrop onto Emily's knee.

The tutor opened her eyes. Opened them slightly wider, then narrowed them with growing understanding. Emily slipped her cool hand to staunch the flow between Miranda's glistening thighs. They gazed, faces inches apart, intently. Who was to get the upper hand tonight? Who? Miranda's heart beat wildly. Eager to dominate, yet even more anxious to submit to Emily's fierce caresses, she was transfixed in the indecision of her own turmoil. Emily too was undecided. Her basic needs were to dominate, her deeper needs were to be dominated. Locked in their indecision, the two naked bodies closed together, after Miranda had cast aside her vest and shorts with an urgent abandon.

Urgent. At least they both instinctively knew that their wants and needs were urgent. They slipped to the floor, hips to hips, bare breasts pressed together, lips fused in a carnal weld. Forehead to perspiring forehead, like wild beasts locked in mortal combat, they drowned in one another's gaze. Slowly, with the wisdom of her age and experience, Emily dropped her hands down to Miranda's hips and turned the exquisite waist a quarter turn. She slowly sank her face down into the delicately blond-haired triangle of Venus, lips stretched apart, tongue glistening as it flickered.

As if echoing the balletic movement, Miranda grasped Emily's waist and brought her face down into its living honeycomb of oozing sweetness. With a sinuous glide, they each rolled, grasping the other's ankles. They lay, buried in each other's centre of delight, in absolute balance, in total equipoise. Miranda's body buckled as it wrapped itself into Emily's whiteness, Emily curled so that she was buried in to Miranda's clenched thighs. They licked, and lapped and they sucked and they bit and they mouthed and they tongued until, with a mutual scream of unbridled pleasure that threatened to waken the mournful owls in the bleak elms outside, they came.

Chapter Seven

The harsh, melancholy chorus of wheeling rooks woke Miranda. She emerged from her warm glow of restful sleep and delicious memories. Dawn. A quiet time, once the rooks had settled in their leafless treetops. Stillness. In the cool darkness of her spartan dormitory Miranda felt relaxed and contented. Soon she would rise, wash her face briskly and then go down to the bright, warm kitchen to prepare breakfast for the community.

Breakfast brought her mind to Sandstones, where she would have her mocha coffee served in the sunny drawing room and where her private telephone never stopped ringing. *Sandstones*. She wondered if Aunt Emma would sweep up the gravel drive today and take her away from the Academy. Why had she not already done so? Perhaps she was in Rome. It occurred to her that Aunt Emma's delay was not too great a disappointment. There had been, after all, Emily last night. The wine, the bathroom. And afterwards.

Jane and two of her sleepy-eyed greenbands were already at work down in the kitchen, busy at the vast Aga. The smell of toast and sizzling bacon greeted Miranda's nostrils. Her mouth watered. One of the stolen pleasures of early morning kitchen duties was to have a furtive rasher, crisply grilled, from the staff breakfast.

At Sandstones, Miranda could have wafer thin slices of Parma ham in a bed of diced, chilled honeydew melon. Or thick Braddenham gammons poached with peaches. But how much sweeter, she thought as she licked her fingers impishly, was a rasher of stolen streaky bacon! Forbidden fruit pricked the juices more keenly.

The large kettle had already boiled. She made a cup of instant coffee and sipped it. Jane was brisk with her greenbands. They seemed to be sulky and sluggish. It would not be long, Miranda reflected, before a cane would swish, or a strap would bark, across the pouting rumps of the resentful girls. Jane's tone became increasingly severe. The taller of the two greenbands turned and gave Jane a surly look. The scowl was intercepted. Miranda's pulse quickened, anticipating instant punishment, but a small saucepan of milk on the Aga suddenly seethed and threatened to spill its frothy contents. Eyes and hands were diverted to the rescue – and the moment of danger for the languid greenband's buttocks passed.

Miranda remembered her first ten days as a greenband. They had been fearful, terrible times. One's bottom was anybody's, it seemed. Merely the collective property of all who dwelt at the Academy, to be punished at will or whim. As a greenband, one walked on eggshells, never daring to transgress. Under the constant shadow of the hovering strap or flickering cane, punishment, and the very fear of punishment, dripped in the air like humidity in a torrid, tropical zone.

Crash. A sparkling white plate shattered on the

hard, flagstone floor. The taller of the two green-bands turned anxiously, guiltily, to where Jane was standing, trimming the rind from bacon rashers.

'Dustpan and brush. Get it cleared up,' Jane snapped waspishly.

The girl bent down on one knee and swept up the clinking debris. When she returned from the dust-bin, Jane was drying her hands slowly.

'Come here, girl,' she ordered.

With sorrowful eyes and hands clasped behind her back, the girl timorously approached the spot by the large wooden table where Jane stood impatiently.

'You've been asking for a sharp reminder ever since I got you out of your bed this morning. Bend over.' It was a curt command. Miranda noticed that Jane was tapping the wooden table top with one, outstretched finger. Such powerful control, she thought. How terrible to dominate with a fingertip.

Well trained and already highly disciplined in the ways of the Academy, the svelte girl instantly bent down over the table top. Breasts squashed, arms outstretched and face to one side, she parted her legs slightly, toes rising up from the cold flagstones. The punishment was briskly administered, but Miranda knew that it was as severe and undoubtedly painful as it was economical. Jane had snatched up a long-handled wooden spoon and had proceeded to spank the upturned, rounded buttocks eight times – four strokes to each cheek – in rapid succession. The curved wooden head of the spoon almost bounced off the taut white cotton shorts as it scalded the bottom within. Miranda flinched, knowing full well the measure of the accuracy and the blistering effect of the eight rapid swipes across the firm flesh.

Miranda caught sight of the second greenband. Frozen in the ambiguous grip of fear and curiosity, repulsion and attraction, the shivering girl peeped over her shoulder, wincing at the chastisement yet almost magnetically drawn to it. In her confusion, one of the eggs which she was cracking into a large china bowl missed the rim and slithered down onto the floor. Terrified, she wiped up the yellow mess with a nearby cloth and quickly nudged the tell-tale fractured shell under the Aga with her trembling toes. Miranda smiled to herself. How futile. All misdemeanours were eventually, inexorably, unearthed at the Academy. And punishment was as swift as it was certain.

'Now get back to your work and no more stupid nonsense out of you this morning. Understand?' Jane was tapping the wooden spoon against the palm of her outstretched hand, as if the spoon's work was incomplete.

'Settle down to your duties, or you'll regret it. Bitterly.'

Silence returned to the kitchen for a few moments, then the door creaked.

'Mrs Boydd-Black wants a cup of coffee in her office,' the third of Jane's greenbands announced.

Miranda had casually wondered where she was. She had wonderful cornflower blue, slightly frightened, eyes. She seemed to be terrified of Jane. Had Miranda pulled down the girl's white shorts and inspected her pale bottom, the faint pink stripes such an examination would have revealed could fully justify the fear brimming in the large blue eyes.

'I'll do that,' Jane said, taking down a tray.

Miranda nodded her agreement and started to cut up a fresh grapefruit for Miss Eaddes. As her hands dealt with the pliant flesh, opening up readily beneath her firm thumbs, Miranda suddenly thought of how the headmistress submitted and surrendered to the touch of Miss Eaddes. Those strong, capable fingers . . .

'Ugh,' gasped Jane. She had been wiping the tray with a cloth. The soiled cloth sticky with spilled egg. She held out her hands, glistening with yolk. 'Who did this?' she demanded crossly.

'Please, Jane. It was an accident,' whispered the guilty greenband.

Jane snorted and turned to Miranda.

'You'd better take her coffee, I've got my hands full here.'

She certainly had, Miranda reflected, as she assembled the cup and saucer, sugar, fresh cream and coffee pot on the tray. Jane dragged the whimpering, large-eyed girl over her knee and jerked down the taut shorts, her thumb under the elastic waistband. The large, bare bottom lay passive and vulnerable across her lap, patiently waiting for the punishment to rain down. The blows fell, a rapid staccato of spanks that stung the bunched buttocks harshly. The slaps and squeals echoed up the stairs behind Miranda as she bore early morning coffee towards Mrs Boydd-Black's study. The heavy walnut door was slightly ajar.

'But that is impossible, simply impossible, Mr Porteous,' the agitated headmistress was saying as Miranda approached.

Porteous. Miranda's hand froze inches away from the polished panel. Bending close to the narrow opening, she listened, her heart thumping wildly. From the silences between the concerned tones of the headmistress, Miranda realised that it was a telephone, and not a face to face, conversation.

'Sixty-five per cent? But you already get over fifty. There are the running costs, the overheads. The heating alone . . .'

Miranda suddenly understood. Porteous was more than merely the middle man, the family friend, the fixer. The quiet solicitor who referred errant girls to the Academy. He ran it. Owned it. Was in overall control, and profited hugely from the entire enterprise.

'But sixy-five per cent, Mr Porteous,' Mrs Boydd-Black protested.

Another pause.

'No, I cannot reduce the food bills. One cannot economise with the diet of growing girls. Protein is most important . . . No, I'm afraid those measures too are impossible. Quite impossible. Salary cuts? I will have to consider that, of course . . .'

Obviously, under considerable pressure, the headmistress was trying to reason and negotiate with the greedy solicitor. As he played his trump card her tone faded, tinged with resignation.

'The leasehold. Yes, I quite understand. Yes, your powers of administration are . . . I understand. You leave me with no option.'

Putting the squeeze on her for more. The Academy must draw in at least a quarter of a million every year. Half to run it, and the remainder went straight into his greasy little High Street suit pocket. And now he wanted more. Fifteen per cent more. Then a flash of anger sparkled in Miranda's greyblue eyes. Porteous had not merely suggested or recommended the possibility of the Academy to Aunt Emma. He had orchestrated the entire thing.

She suddenly realised the presence of his hidden, manipulating hand behind her downfall. Porteous raising the matter of the Brompton party with Aunt Emma. Porteous hinting at the scandal of those press snapshots hurting Uncle Peter's Cabinet post. Porteous. She was consigned to this place of privation, humiliation and severe discipline all because of him. And the weasel was getting handsomely paid for it. A crimson flush of rage stole into Miranda's pale cheeks. Then her face drained to a sallow, waxy white.

She suddenly remembered the letter. Her SOS to Aunt Emma. Porteous, greedily swallowing strawberry gateau and pocketing her letter. He would tell Mrs Boydd-Black – must have already told her – then her bottom would taste the full meaning of punishment. Probably a Chair and Half Exercise. A Chair. Oh God, thought Miranda, trembling slightly. The coffee pot and cup rattled dangerously on the shaking tray.

'Who is there?'

Miranda took a deep breath and tapped respectfully on the walnut door.

'Your coffee, ma'am,' she called.

'Enter,' the headmistress replied.

Miranda went into the study. The curtains remained closed, yellow lights burned softly. Paperwork told Miranda that the headmistress had been busy at her accounts since very early on, probably working on them since four that morning. Mrs Boydd-Black, her hand placed over the receiver, managed a weak smile as she nodded to her desk.

'Put it there. Thank you, Miranda.'

'Ma'am.'

Miranda closed the door firmly behind her, a surge of relief sweeping over her as she left the study. There had been no mention, by look or by word, of the letter after all. He had probably simply torn it up and thrown it away.

Back down in the busy, bustling kitchen, Miranda tried to put her troubled thoughts aside and concentrate on the tasks in hand. She began to prepare Emily's breakfast, taking an ovenproof dish, buttering it and placing a piece of white haddock in it lengthways. Emily enjoyed a breakfast of poached haddock and Miranda loved preparing it for her. It was a little act of love.

'Don't forget a bay leaf. Emily likes it that way,' Jane said as she passed by on the way to the fridge for another couple of pints of milk.

Miranda's eyes narrowed. She frowned, resenting the intimacy that lay buried within the remark. She hated Jane's intrusion.

'I'm cooking it. Leave me alone,' Miranda muttered.

'Touchy,' smirked Jane, closing the fridge door with her elbow. 'Didn't you know she liked a bay leaf? I knew that. But then I know all sweet Emily's little . . . likes and pleasures.'

'Shut up,' snapped Miranda, stung by a sudden flash of possessive, jealous anger.

It was not the first time that Jane had teased her about Emily. She waited until she thought she was not being observed, then slipped into the pantry and returned with a bay leaf. As she placed it on top of the fish, she turned instinctively. There, watching her with mocking eyes, was Jane. Grinning, catlike and triumphant.

The Lear screamed as it climbed steeply over Slough, the powerful thrust easing back slightly after the pilot banked the executive jet and pointed its silver nose through the crisp blue air towards Bonn. Hazim settled back comfortably in his luxurious seat. An attentive stewardess, sweetly perfumed and very generously bloused, placed her soft, scarlet-nailed fingers on his shoulder. He barely felt their light weight on his pure silk jacket.

'Breakfast, sir?' she whispered invitingly, the voice soothing but not entirely calming in its tone and effect.

'Juice and coffee,' he replied, his lips smiling automatically, his narrowed eyes hard.

'Of course, sir,' she cooed, as if promising prompt obedience and managing to suggest much, much more. Men with hard eyes paid well for whatever pleasure they took.

The Bihar bullion millionaire frowned. He had, unusually, been somewhat unsuccessful. He had been unable to make contact with that Porteous fellow, the one who might lead to knowledge of his beloved Jaya's whereabouts. The thought had crossed his mind to telephone Jaya's parents. He hadn't. It was a tricky business. Very delicate. Much discretion and tact would be required. He knew where he could buy a few hard men if the going got rough. Men he could rely on. Money spoke, and people listened.

That stewardess. Hazim's mind wandered. He pictured her kneeling for him in the gangway, in the airport toilet, in his hotel room. Kneeling, glossy lips open, cobra eyes shut tight. Kneeling, with the navy blue skirt riding high up over her splayed thighs. For a rustle of notes, in any denomination, he could have her. Any way he chose. In his brief fancy he chose the breasts. Blouse undone and swept open, he would take his full pleasure in the breasts.

Yes. The breasts. He swallowed hard as he imagined his hot erection, trapped under the lace strap of her wispy bra, nestling into the pillows of the cool, creamy cleavage, soon to spill the hotter seed over the deeply curved slopes held in brassièred bondage. Money. He licked his lips. His throat felt dry.

'Juice, sir,' the scented breath of the heavily breasted stewardess whispered. Her pale hand brushed the swelling in his trouser crotch as she adjusted his collapsible tray. The gesture was one of careful negligence, no more than a butterfly's wingbeat.

'Fresh?' he queried.

'Just squeezed sir. Are you stopping overnight in Bonn, sir?'

The engines roared lustily, drowning his reply.

Whatever her problems and pressures were, the headmistress showed no signs of them as she entered the refectory for breakfast. All the girls dutifully murmured good morning to her as she strode regally up to the top table. She sat down, undid her napkin and inspected it closely – causing the laundry girl's heart to skip several beats – and then surveyed the room. She nodded. The girls sat down to their breakfasts. Mrs Boydd-Black nodded again. At the lectern, Miss Eaddes began to read aloud from the life of Oliver Cromwell.

The maths tutor had a certain weakness for those who could shape events and control those around them. Heads bowed in silence, the girls, the greenbands shivering in fearful expectation and the red and bluebands living in constant hope, ate their breakfasts. Jaya, the only goldband, sat between Clarissa and Miranda. Since Matron's hurried departure it was now the custom for the headmistress to make all the announcements. She had only one to make that morning.

'The cross-country race will not take place as scheduled. I am reliably informed by my wireless that the weather will be quite wintry by the week-end. We shall, therefore, hold the race today. At two-thirty. That is all.'

Jaya's shoulder, soft and dusky, brushed Miranda's reassuringly. Under the table, Clarissa caught and squeezed Miranda's hand affectionately. Miranda was excited. She would have preferred to have had a little more time with Susie, Zoe and Clare. But they would, she knew, run well. Jaya's plans had seen to that. They would be spurred on by fear and drawn to the winning line by loyalty and devotion.

Miranda sipped her tea and gazed up at Mrs Boydd-Black. How cool and professional she seemed. How dedicated. It was intolerable that she should be in the clutches of a toad like the odious Porteous. How she would love to have him all to herself for just one hour. But even in her spurt of rage she softened slightly. Despite the Porteous connection, the Academy was different. Interesting. After years of bored privilege, aimless hedonism and wasteful, if conspicuous, consumption, the last few weeks at the Academy had been a sharp and not altogether displeasing contrast.

It had certainly been an adventure. An adventure into new physical and emotional territories hitherto unchartered and unexplored. How delicious a simple cup of tea or stolen biscuit had become. How thrilling to share a piece of stolen cake in the dormitory of a friend after lights out. How beautiful were the bodies of the girls around her, displayed not in sultry bikinis but in the strictly severe white uniforms.

208

And Miranda's sharpened senses now knew that no liquefied golden droplets of the most exquisite perfume could excite as much as a freshly soaped girl being towelled dry. Carbolic won hands down over Diorissimo. Miranda had never realised just how delicious a freshly washed girl could smell at close, very close quarters.

Other senses and sensibilities had been honed to a razor-like acuity. There was Jaya, beside her. Trusting, gentle and wise. Still innocent in her realm of richly dark experience. Then there was dear Clarissa. Fun loving, reasonably virtuous and frequently delightfully naughty. Emily, the art tutor, who had taken Miranda tenderly by the hand and led her through the gates of paradise, there to eat plentifully of forbidden, golden fruits. The darker pleasures, of chastising and, yes, of being chastised. Of punishing and being punished. To whip a naked bottom, or to have one's own bare buttocks spanked. The darker pleasures, of punishment and dominance, of submission and surrender. Of these and other forbidden fruits Miranda had eaten full and plentiful measure. And the fruit was exceedingly sweet and luscious.

Discipline. The hot, wet thrill of discipline. Of reigning supremely for the absolute moment over a bewitchingly thrashed bottom. There was also a new sense of inner strength, purpose and resolve. A gritty determination had blossomed and flowered within her even over the short space of time she had spent at the Academy. Miranda suddenly felt herself – for many, many reasons – interested in those around her. Where once contemptuous neglect or bored indifference had held sway, now she truly cared for the fate and future of many of the wayward girls incarcerated

at the Academy. For the most part strays and un-
ruly misfits, they too would, once firmly disciplined,
be released to live rewarding and fulfilling lives.

And it was all due, acknowledged Miranda, to the
dedication and the care, the firm supervision and the
strict control of one person – Mrs Boydd-Black.
That lonely figure who loomed large in Miranda's
concern. An isolated, burdened woman, whose secret Miranda had discovered. Yes. The Academy
had such memories for her. The headmistress was
doing sterling work. It was, thought Miranda, a
pleasure to serve her. Especially down in the
darkened gym at night . . .

After lunch, the two teams of girls lined up at the
start. The girls bounced up and down to keep warm.
Zoe, being so generously endowed, bounced slightly
more than her fellow competitors. The route of the
course was pointed out to the six runners, three rep-
resenting Jane's hopes for the blueband and Zoe,
Clare and Susie running for Miranda. The entire
estate being completely encompassed by a high,
crumbling red brick wall, there was no hope of making an escape bid.

'And I'll skin the backside off anyone who even
thinks of trying to look over it,' Mrs Boydd-Black
warned them grimly.

Susie, the least capable of scaling the wall,
blushed transparently.

'I wasn't going to, honestly,' she lied prettily.

Within the extensive park land that surrounded
the Academy there was ample scope for the two and
a half mile run. The runners were instructed to make
their way down the gravel drive towards the gate
lodge, then bear right and run clockwise within the
perimeter wall.

'Run through, not around, the spinney. Take your marks,' the headmistress ordered.

The six girls bowed their heads and flexed their thighs.

'Ready . . . wait for it Susie . . . steady . . . go.'

They scampered off, their pumps, especially provided for the event, crunching the gravel underfoot. Miranda noticed that Jane trotted off around the back of the imposing Queen Anne house as soon as Mrs Boydd-Black had withdrawn to make some phone calls.

'There's not much we can do but hope,' she said, turning to Jaya.

'Don't worry, Miranda. They will run well for you. You inspire them.'

The minutes ticked by. It was dank and chilly in the raw November air. From time to time, Miranda stood up on her toes, hoping to catch a glimpse of the returning runners.

'Relax,' Jaya comforted her. 'Two and a half miles. That will take twenty minutes at least.'

A little later, the headmistress rejoined them.

'Eighteen minutes gone. They should show up soon. Jolly good.'

Jane returned to their group, red-faced and sly-eyed. Miranda caught the ugly, cat-like grin of mocking triumph in her rival's expression. She shivered. She knew, intuitively yet decisively, that there had been mischief afoot.

The small figures emerged out of the distant mist, disappeared behind the line of thick holly bushes and then reappeared. Jane's three runners took the first three places, winning the contest unopposed. Clare limped home, followed by an equally lame Zoe. Of Susie there was no sign whatsoever until, almost half an hour after the start, she trailed in, dripping from head to toe in stinking black slime. Tear tracks washed single clear lines through the sticky mire.

'A decisive victory. Most decisive. Well done Jane's team. Now off into hot baths, all of you.'

Clare's white rump wobbled slightly as she stepped over and into her bath. She looked up in alarm when Jaya entered the steam-filled cubicle.

'I'm sorry,' she shuddered. 'I couldn't help it. My feet . . .' she explained.

Jaya frowned, bent over the side of the bath and picked up Clare's pink feet, examining them carefully one by one. The toes were red raw. Calming the frightened girl, and reassuring her that no punishment would be administered just yet, she stooped and picked up the mud-spattered, soaking black pumps. Her fingers felt their way blindly down into the toe section. She smiled grimly as she extracted a thin ribbon of wire wool, torn from a scouring pad, from each pump.

'You said you could not run properly?'

'No,' said Clare, 'my feet hurt. It was very painful.'

Jaya entered the next cubicle where Zoe was running cold water over her reddened toes.

'Jaya. They put something in my pumps . . .'

Jaya grimaced and picked up the left pump. A ribbon of wire wool fell to the bathroom floor.

Susie was sitting on the edge of her bath. Jaya approached her and placed a consoling arm around her shoulders. Susie sniffled and buried her tear-stained face in Jaya's gently heaving bosom.

'She jumped me from behind that big juniper and I went straight into a quagmire and the mud went

212

in my eyes and I swallowed at least a ton of it and
I bet I die and then she'll go to prison or at least
be –'
    'Who?' Jaya asked, stemming the outburst at last.
    'Jane, of course,' Susie sobbed.

After the clinical, clockwork precision of Bonn,
London felt scruffy, infuriating and was totally irre-
pressible. Hazim paid the taxi then paused, gave the
cabbie an extra fiver and asked him to wait. The
cabbie spread out his hands in a gesture of disbelief.
Already the air was bruised by impatient horns.
Six-fifteen, he implied in mime because of the din,
was no time to sit down in the Fulham Road. Hazim
shrugged and nodded. The cabbie smiled sympathetically and offered to return the fiver.
    'Double or quits?' Hazim grinned.
    'Quits,' the cabbie grinned ruefully, handing back
the note. Hazim pocketed it alongside the double-
headed dollar with which he quietly amassed a tiny
fortune and stepped across to the glass door. Behind
the frosted glass, he discovered Mr Porteous at his
desk.
    'My name is Dhingra,' Hazim lied, giving one of
many aliases. 'I telephoned from Bonn at lunchtime.
Thank you for waiting to see me, Mr Porteous.'
    The fat solicitor fussed with some papers on his
desk with self-important vigour.
    'It is a little strange, perhaps, the request I am
about to make. I will of course respect your decision
if you do not wish to divulge the information I seek.'
    In his early days of bullion dealing, Hazim had
paid the price for appearing too eager.
    'Quite so, quite so,' said the solicitor, nodding, his
busy little brain immediately detecting the possibi-

lity of money behind all this careful preamble. Already, it was not a question of whether or not it was to be a lucrative inducement, but how much it might be.

'I do not deal in cash. I thought these might interest you, if you find them acceptable.'

Hazim placed two gold bricks on the desk top. The yellow metal winked under the light above. The solicitor's eyes grew momentarily wide with wonder. The foxy little brain whirred into life. At so much an ounce, and if one sold when the market was high, why, one could gross . . .

'Sixteen thousand pounds,' supplied Hazim, accurately timing the answer to complete the equation the greedy solicitor was struggling to calculate and solve.

Porteous frowned. He did not like being so transparent to another in business matters. He preferred to be in control. The chess master, not a pawn on the board.

'Quite so, quite so,' he purred softly.

He suddenly speculated if he could sell this gold in a way that avoided tax and bypassed his books.

'Tax free if you go to the right quarters,' anticipated Hazim. 'No VAT and no one need know a thing about it.' He was matching the solicitor thought for thought.

'What is it that you are seeking, my good fellow?'

Hazim winced. The expression jarred on both his pride and on his nerves. 'My good fellow' indeed! He wouldn't even employ this rat as a latrine cleaner.

'An address. An address that I will not contact or approach. I just need to satisfy my curiosity.'

'Well, I am sure that we can come to some satisfactory arrangement. In relation to what, exactly, do you require this information?'

Hazim gathered up the two gold bricks and gently clicked them together. The dull yellow metal made a haunting sound. Porteous licked his lips.

'This girl. My cousin. I do not speak with her parents, there has been a family quarrel.' Hazim spoke in as casual a voice as his boiling rage within would allow.

Porteous picked up the photograph and recognised Jaya, looked up at Hazim and then back down at Jaya.

'A cousin?' he countered.

'Sixteen thousand pounds,' replied Hazim.

Supper was over and Mrs Boydd-Black rose. She had several things to say. She commenced by commenting that Miss Eaddes had expressed her grave concern over the results of the latest maths tests. Certain girls would be wishing that they had worked harder during the tutorial tomorrow morning. Clarissa, whose algebra was weak, shuddered. Miss Eaddes caned one so slowly, so searchingly and so mercilessly.

The next item was a note of personal concern. Mrs Boydd-Black deprecated the cleaning team who seemed to have neglected the dust on the furniture in the hall. There would be an inquiry. They had made such a very poor job of it. And after the inquiry, conclusions would be reached. There was, she hinted darkly, the distinct possibility of punishments.

'But now, girls, a success story. Jane's team raced well today, no doubt due to her creative and imaginative efforts. I am happy to announce that she is to be made a blueband forthwith.'

215

The news was greeted with a subdued murmur. Jane was widely feared, and now, as a blueband, her lash was licensed to reach farther, cut deeper.

'I have another change to announce. As you know, Miranda is at present a redband.'

Jaya looked at Miranda in delight. She had not seen her since the race – Miranda had sought a little consolation with Emily – and had much to tell her. But all that could wait. It didn't really matter now about Jane's cheating. Miranda, too, was going to be promoted.

'Miranda will no longer wear a redband.'

The tone of the headmistress's voice was neutral and cool. Miranda looked up, smiling expectantly.

'Miranda will revert to green and attend in my room for a Chair and Half Exercise after supper.'

Gasps of fearful dismay greeted this announcement. Miranda turned pale and clutched the wooden table for support.

'This belongs to you, I believe?' the headmistress held up the letter Miranda had scribbled to Aunt Emma and entrusted to Porteous. 'It was returned to me in this afternoon's post.'

The room started to spin around Miranda. She felt Jaya's steadying hand and heard the reassuring voices of Clarissa and little Susie. But Miranda's mind reverberated with one word only. The Chair. *The Chair*. Her dry lips opened and closed soundlessly. *Porteous*. The swine had betrayed her. Delivered her up to the Chair.

An hour later found Miss Eaddes humming pleasantly. It was her favourite song from *Pirates of Penzance*. She was not only a light operetta buff but a G & S (as she coyly referred to them) fanatic. Up in the gallery that ran three-quarters of the way

216

around the large study, she busied herself with the video camera. She intended to try something a little different tonight. Yes. The flick of the hair as the head jerked. A poignant detail. Punished girls had a habit of tossing their hair as the cane sliced or the strap snapped across the bare bottoms. She would try to capture the delicious moment with her lens, catch the flounce as it spread into a wild fringe over Miranda's eyes. Her golden mane would toss proudly as each stroke kissed her exposed buttocks.

Such a wonderful subject to work on, a punished blonde. Yes, she giggled. Miranda was in the Chair tonight. Blonde. Most impressive. A fine, shapely, athletic girl. Nice thighs, splendid hips. And a most attractively shaped bottom.

Whistling a snatch from *The Mikado*, she checked the cassette. The little green light blinked. All set. Splendid. Miranda should come out well in colour. Red stripes are so becoming on a golden tan. For a maths tutor, Miss Eaddes showed a surprising awareness of the possibilities of colour.

Head down, arms painfully stretched out and bare bottom raised up for the impending punishment, Miranda closed her large eyes as the first rapid double explosion of pain seared across her taut rump, bathing the satin skin stretched so tightly across her firm flesh in fierce fire. Ten hands had been nominated to ply the springy table tennis bat for the painful, humiliating Half Exercise.

The first, Clare, wielded the bat competently, striking the upturned cheeks smartly and severely, the bat cracking down swiftly and firmly on the exposed buttocks. Other feet shuffled up to the Chair, other hands picked up the table tennis bat and other eyes gazed down on Miranda's suffering. After each

217

double swipe of scorching pain, Miranda stretched and strained to press her trembling lips against the warm surface of the dimpled rubber. Obedience to the bat and submission to it was a strict stipulation and all who suffered a Chair had to kiss the instrument that caused their pain.

The humiliating First Position, the jackknife posture that rendered the bare bottom totally exposed, came to its painful conclusion with Mrs Boydd-Black herself. She strode purposefully up to the Chair and stood, legs astride, her feet planted firmly apart. Weighing the table tennis bat momentarily, she judged the distance and then raised it up. Miranda felt a tingle of fearful anticipation thrill down the arched curve of her naked spine.

Crack. Crack. The broad bat swept down and splatted into the juddering cheeks, swooped back to shoulder height and cracked down again in a savage twinkling. The rubicund buttocks jerked as they were kissed with scorching pain. The headmistress paused a fraction to inspect the glowing bottom and then thrust the bat up against Miranda's lips. The punished girl kissed it obediently, penitently.

'Second Position,' came the curt command.

Slowly, awkwardly, Miranda clambered across the broad seat of the polished Chair and lay there, belly down. Her head and shoulders were framed and trapped by the left arm rest, her thighs and legs lay stretched out behind her under the right arm rest. Trapped and imprisoned, her naked body lay supine, waiting anxiously for the chastisement to recommence.

Her bottom, less taut because of her horizontal position, wobbled slightly as she adjusted herself. Her tummy stuck to the clammy wooden seat. Her full, rounded cheeks lay closely pressed together, the cleft hardly discernable. Unlike the First Position, which spread the taut cheeks apart to reveal the valley of the shadowed cleft, in the Second Position her bottom was rendered pliant and passive for the imminent pain.

Clare, followed by two redbands, then Zoe and then Clarissa came and went, approaching the Chair and kneeling down before it to administer the searing double swipe across the defenceless, jerking buttocks. In turn, they rose, presented the hot rubber surface of the bat to Miranda's parted lips and returned silently to their place amid the silent ranks of punishers.

Then Jane stepped up and approached the Chair. Taking the bat in her hand, she knelt down. Miranda glanced up sideways at her tormentress. Jane's eyes flickered like a cobra stirring in a troubled dream. Reaching out languorously, she rested the surface of the bat down acrosss Miranda's passive cheeks. The skin crawled and flinched beneath the warm, dimpled rubber, the muscles twitched under the potent weight. Looking down in absolute triumph, Jane ostentatiously adjusted the blueband that encircled the bronzed, sinewy muscles of her upper right arm. Miranda shuddered softly and groaned inwardly as Jane slowly reached out and grasped the handle of the bat, dragging its dimpled rubber face even more slowly across the double domes of hot, tormented flesh. The bat rose and fell.

Crack. A blinding flash of golden light exploded in Miranda's brain. Jane swiped down the bat with all her venomous strength. Maximum effort was invested for a return of maximum pleasure. The scalded buttocks juddered and bucked as the bat rose up once more. Miranda clenched her taut cheeks. A feint. Too soon. The bat remained poised aloft. Miranda relaxed slightly, the flesh softening a little.

Crack. The cruel bat sliced the air and exploded once again four square across her creamy, red streaked cheeks. Miranda's hiss dissolved into a protracted groan. Jane grimaced and stood up, steadying herself as she rose by placing her outstretched, taloned fingers onto the simmering bottom. She squeezed it viciously in fond, fierce farewell. As she winced, Miranda knew that it was *au revoir*, not *adieu*.

Miranda suffered the final strokes of the Second Position as the headmistress stepped up briskly to deliver two deliberate swipes down across her naked bottom. *Crack. Crack*. Memorable blows.

'Third Position, girl. Snap to it.'

Miranda's tummy peeled away from the flat wooden seat of the Chair. She glanced down and was relieved to see that no tell-tale splashes of excitation remained where her pubic mound had pressed down into the polished wood. This was punishment, pure and simple. If Emily or Jaya had been wielding the bat, in a more intimate setting, then Miranda knew that the Chair would have been left slippery with her sticky juices. But here, before the assembled community of the Academy all she felt was the searing pain and burning shame.

There was no violent tenderness, no fierce joy or rush of delight as she happily surrendered her spirit and flesh to the domination of a loving partner. There were no emotional peaks and depths, no breathless expectations. Nor was there the whimpering, the pleading, the husky beseeching for the sweet

220

punishment to scald and blister until orgasm, raw and violent, clenching its velvet fist within her molten depths. It could be like that. It had been like that. But the Chair was barren of bliss, denuded of joy, stripped bare of such precious consolations. Its purpose was dedicated to pain, humiliation and suffering. Miranda rose and sullenly assumed the Third Position, these thoughts and reflections burning darkly in her tormented mind.

Or so she thought. How frail such certainties can prove to be. Self-deception is such a curious thing. It shimmers on the mirage of false horizons, changing like a chameleon crossing the emotional colourings of the ravished mind and turbulent spirit. As Miranda bent down over the high back of the Chair and reached out to clasp the arm rests beneath, toes just inches above the floor, she felt the swollen fig between her white thighs part, blister and open imperceptibly.

Confused and ashamed, she struggled to choke down the darkly delicious ideas that danced in her crimson brain. An image of the moist fig, oozing its ripeness, flashed across her mind. Of Clare, then Zoe, then Clarissa, stepping up to punish her exposed, pert bottom, each gasping as they paused, bat in mid-swipe, transfixed by the beauty of her juicing Venus which they held in frank admiration. Clare, accidently brushing it with the hot rubber surface of the bat, leaving the dimples gleaming and glistening with her inner wetness.

Zoe, succumbing to the implacable temptation to insert her thumb top in an effort to examine the forbidden inner pinkness. Clarissa, bending, breasts bulging, to place a wet kiss on the even wetter lips now parted like a velvet curtain. Dizzy with delight at these, and other, phantasms of exhibitionism, Miranda lay across the harsh wood as if impaled upon the sweet and deeply wounding thorns of masochistic narcissism.

Let them come and punish me, she triumphed. Let them do their worst. But let them linger, let them gaze, let them look ... and wonder. And in their wonder let there be want, and may yearning fan the flames of their cruel, consuming want. Let them want me. Want and desire me. Let them tremble in their liquid chains of desire as they gaze upon what they may just touch but not taste. And punish what they cannot have but most desire.

Yes. *Yes*. That too. Lash at what would be licked, blister what should be blessed with the benison of a kiss. Swept along on this surge of violent emotions, devastating insights and fresh awakenings, Miranda parted her thighs slightly and dared the potent bat to do its worst. Her pain might be much, but the pleasure, the dark, delicious, disturbing pleasure of teasing and taunting, displaying and provocatively exciting her tormentors, was deep.

Crack. Crack. The bat barked twice. Clare brought it across the full moons. Darkening scarlet clouded their creamy shine. *Crack. Crack.* The bat had found the gift of tongues. It spoke in words of anguish. The second girl blazed her double imprint of controlled fury across the supine rump.

Crack. Crack. The buttocks bounced and bucked, writhing in exquisite agony. Miranda's heart sang, certain that her punishers now yearned for that which was punished. *Crack. Crack.* Silvery droplets oozed like honey, spilled in haste from the sweet, sweet comb between her glistening thighs. *Crack. Crack.* Her bottom jerked and screamed in mute protest at the withering strokes and their fiery onslaught.

Then Jane approached the Chair. As she assumed her dominant stance, planting her feet firmly apart, Miranda willed her thighs to open even wider. A long spindling dribble of nectar sparkled as it splashed down like quicksilver against her inner thigh. Jane gasped audibly. Miranda flexed and unflexed her thigh muscles, rippling her buttocks invitingly, enticingly. Jane barely managed to suppress the carnal moan of desire. Her very soul seemed to be in pain, torn by the sight that welcomed and greeted her, offered yet denied such a glimpse of paradise.

Slowly, wantonly, wickedly, totally controlled yet on the brink of abandonment, Miranda stretched her cheeks apart, allowing her punisher a lingering glimpse of the pink sphincter's tight rosebud whorl buried in the warm depths of the mouthwatering cleft. Jane mewed like a stray kitten and held out her hand to steady herself, almost tipsy with desire.

'Do your worst, bitch,' hissed Miranda, who, despite her abject position, felt strong enough to dictate terms.

Jane's eyes flashed dangerously then narrowed into fierce slits. She swiped the bat down. *Crack*. Again. *Crack*. Again. *Crack*. Miranda grinned through the red mist of pain.

'Stop,' cried the headmistress. 'Two strokes only. Those are the rules.'

Crack. *Crack*. In a frenzy of frustrated lust Jane brought the bat down repeatedly across Miranda's bare bottom.

'Stop it this instant,' shrieked Mrs Boydd-Black. You're spoiling everything. Stop. Two strokes.

Those are the rules. You must do the Exercise properly.'

Miranda laughed softly as she heard the headmistress, helped by two members of staff, drag Jane away.

'Back to your rooms, everyone. Back to your rooms this instant. Jane. Get that blueband off your arm at once. You have completely ruined my Chair and Half Exercise. Ruined it. I will see you and thoroughly punish you personally tomorrow morning. And you'll be wearing a greenband, my girl, for a very, very long time . . .'

Chapter Eight

'Roll over onto your tummy. I have something for your poor bottom.'

Jaya's soothing words were soon augmented by her cooling hands. She peeled back the single sheet to reveal Miranda's nakedness. She had sought sanctuary in Jaya's bed after the recent turbulent hours. The chill air of the darkened dormitory kissed her hot buttocks. Miranda shuddered and sighed. Then Jaya's trembling fingertips, dipped deeply into a pot of Pond's cold cream donated by a sympathetic Emily, dappled lightly across the scalded domes of punished flesh. Gently at first, then more firmly and assuredly, they wove around in expanding circles, spreading the soothing balm into the ravished skin.

Skin as soft as that of a silken peach, Jaya marvelled. A bruised peach. Cheek by cheek the dusky hands, slender fingers anointed with the gelatinous cold cream, the hands themselves rendered invisible in the darkness, worked by sense of touch on the equally invisible rounded buttocks. Following the swelling contours, the blind fingers sought and found the firm, pliant flesh. Jaya paused, lingeringly, then slid a slippery finger along the deep furrow of the cleft in between the blazing buttocks.

Miranda sighed deeply and let slip a shallow moan. Emboldened, Jaya slipped her cream dripping fingertip between the firm cheeks once more, tracing the depths of the cleft that nestled between the heavy domes on either side. Domes of quivering flesh. Hot, punished flesh. Her fingertips paused and stopped their gliding motion, hovering tremulously over the tight anus, hesitated audaciously and then, gently, almost shyly, probed the warm flesh. Miranda gasped into her hard pillow.

Withdrawing the finger with infinite slowness, Jaya bent down low over the glistening bottom spread softly before her and, pursing her wet lips, blew a gently healing zephyr of sweet breath over every tiny pore of the scorched flesh which was already healing under her tender ministrations.

Miranda murmured her pleasure and relief. Easing herself up alongside Miranda's prone, naked body, Jaya lay her own soft nude body face down on the narrow bed. They snuggled closely, shoulder to shoulder, hip to swelling hip, thigh to trembling thigh.

'Sleep, now. Sleep,' whispered Jaya with quiet authority as she stroked Miranda's soft, blonde hair. Miranda strained to kiss Jaya's sweet, wet lips and curled up into the warmth of the limbs beside her. On the very brink of drowsy sleep, she felt Jaya's hand alight gently on the swelling curve of her bottom. The fingertips dappled on the dimpling flesh as though the cheeks were some musical instrument upon which Jaya played a silent tune. The fingertips ceased their butterfly dance, tensed imperceptibly then closed over the supple flesh, dragging the cheeks slightly apart.

As Miranda tumbled in slow motion down into

the eddying vortex of sleep, she sensed rather than felt the comforting warmth kindle within her as a questing finger probed, slipping up and remaining in the softness between her quivering buttocks.

Immediately after breakfast, Jane was summoned to appear before the headmistress in the large study. Reduced to the rank of a mere greenband, Jane trod warily past those she had chastised and tormented with her leather strap during her brief spell of redband tyranny.

Miranda had learned of Jane's treachery during the cross-country race, of how the running shoes of Zoe and Clare had been spiked and how Susie had been so ruthlessly ambushed, but what particularly rankled was Jane's jealous sniping and bitter resentfulness. Miranda had given Jane no cause for such emnity. Other than her close friendship with the art tutor, Emily.

Mrs Boydd-Black contemplated the situation and then decided to postpone Jane's punishment. It needed, she opined, more fulsome consideration. A certain special something to match the wickedness of her actions. The ritual spell of the Chair had been broken. Utterly spoiled. Now, the headmistress knew, something else would have to be devised.

Jane was assured in no uncertain terms that something would indeed be devised, and that Jane would be the very first to learn of it. To Mrs Boydd-Black's credit, a fitting punishment was designed and delivered just before lunch. Each girl and every member of staff were marshalled in two lines leading up to the entrance into the refectory. The aroma of oxtail soup haunted the air, only lightly masking the sweeter smell of treacle pudding. Jane was instructed to slip out of her cotton vest and take down her shorts. She did as she was told, a sullen scowl of resentment twisting her usually pretty features.

'Hands on head,' came the crisp command.

Jane obeyed, her breasts rising up and thrusting out as she performed the action. Proud, swollen, splendid breasts. It was not only the treacle pudding that made so many mouths water.

'Take up your canes, everyone,' the headmistress ordered in a tone of barely controlled excitement.

Innocent greenbands and seasoned staff, the tentative and curious along with the expert and capable, all hands present picked up the short whippy canes provided for the formal chastisement.

'Jane will, when commanded to do so, sprint through our ranks at a brisk pace. Each of you will deliver one, and only one, stroke across her bottom.'

The irony in the emphasis on the words one, and only one, was not lost on Jane. She gulped and cast her sorrowful eyes down at her white socks.

'Canes at the ready, everyone,' ordered Mrs Boydd-Black, slicing the air with her own length of supple bamboo. The canes rose and quivered in an instant salute to Pain, the goddess of discipline. The headmistress, High Priestess, nodded. The unholy ceremony commenced.

Hands on head, eyes flashing resentfully, the votive offering scampered down between the lines of twitching whippy canes. Her thighs flashed white and her breasts bounced in their freedom.

Swish. Swish. Swish. Whack. Swipe, Crack. Jane squealed as, one by one, unerringly and inexorably, the short, supple canes cut through the air and swept down at an angle of 45 degrees to slice her rounded buttocks. The air throbbed with the whistle and slice of cruel wood across bunched cheeks. The rounded flesh, swollen and shaped by her long strides, was striped accurately, painfully and intimately.

Swish. Swish. Swish. Like tyres in a rain storm, the sound of the strokes hissed as the wicked bamboo was brought down across the stinging, reddening flesh.

Jane's white-stockinged feet fluttered along the crimson and blue carpet as she dashed headlong between the ranks of her assembled punishers. Head down, her face scalded by tears of shame and pain, the punished girl ran headlong towards the sanctuary of the refectory door which gaped wide open at the end of the bamboo forest. Every pace meant a withering, slicing stroke across her hot buttocks.

Halfway down the line of shame, Jane's bottom was ablaze. Already her beautifully rounded buttocks, which symmetrically echoed her beautifully rounded breasts, were glowing, each cheek showing several pinkish stripes. Jane sobbed, lost her concentration and stumbled. Stooping, she proferred her gorgeous bottom upwards, perfectly formed for punishment.

It was perfectly punished. A slicing stroke whipped the swollen rump. Jane squealed and staggered up onto her legs, pounding down between her tormentors towards the open door.

She approached, and then came level with, Miranda. Yellow cane poised, Miranda judged it exactly. *Swish. Slash.* The lash kissed the convex curves of Jane's bottom viciously. A scorching swipe. Jane flashed a look of pure, undiluted hatred t Miranda. Nearer and nearer the open door loomed. The quivering thicket of upraised canes thinned in density. Seven remained.

Swish. Swish. She yelped, twice, the strokes now landing across the stripes of previous lashes, darkening the pink to burning red. Nearer. Five canes left. *Swish. Swish. Swish.* Her buttocks blistered, the invisible flames licking the glistening cheeks. *Swish.* A cruel cut that swiped the rump four square. A searing taste of agony. Only one trembling cane remained. It quivered in the raised hand of the headmistress. Instead of swooping down to savagely caress the ravished flesh it checked the scampering girl in the middle of her anxious stride, the tip firmly tilting back her chin. Jane stopped dead in her tracks.

'On your knees, you wicked girl,' seethed the headmistress.

Slowly, disbelievingly, Jane sank to her trembling knees. The tip of the cane rested against the white nape of her neck. Passive yet potent. Under the gradually increasing dominance of the cane tip, Jane's head bowed.

'Down. Forehead on the carpet. Give me your bottom.'

Shivering, Jane obeyed. Her breasts bulged as they swung, the nipples just grazing the carpet. Raised up behind her, her bottom presented its delicious rounded globes, the cleft widening noticeably. The cane hovered over the whipped bottom, then alighted on its crimson cheeks, tapping them three times. Jane shuddered. Anguish twisted her frightened mouth.

'Kneel, head up, arms outstretched,' the headmistress thundered.

Jane obeyed with alacrity, the tremulous cane

only inches from her buttocks. Kneeling upright, she held out her arms as instructed. Mrs Boydd-Black addressed the assembled community.

'We shall go in for lunch. Each of you will give Jane's bottom one more stroke as you enter the refectory. Jane will collect the canes from you for your convenience. She will carry them around with her for the rest of the day as a sign of her transgression and atonement. Proceed.'

The file of uniformed girls and the staff walked towards the open refectory door. As each one approached the kneeling, penitent girl, they paused, raised their canes and delivered a single stroke across the clenched, suffering buttocks. As they stepped past Jane, having swished at her rump, they deposited the yellow whippy canes into her outstretched arms.

The collection of canes grew heavy. Jane's bottom grew redder and redder as the file dwindled down to the last five punishers. Miranda approached and cracked her length of wood down across the rounded cheeks, casually tossed the cane into Jane's arms, and went in to take her place at the polished wooden dining table. As she sat down, she heard the concluding strokes.

Swish. Swish. Swish. A rose of pleasurable satisfaction opened its dewy petals in her fluttering belly. She found the punishment deeply satisfying, appropriate and fitting. It was theatrical, ritualistic, humiliating, controlling and very, very severe. Miranda licked her lips at the prospect of the hot oxtail soup.

Crack. The punishment concluded as the headmistress delivered the final, withering swipe. The bamboo sang and sliced Jane's perfectly rounded cheeks. Miranda thrilled to the sound of the cane kissing the scalded bottom, that delightful note of the liquid slicing ending abruptly in the lash of supple wood on taut, blazing flesh.

'Gather up the canes, Jane,' Miranda heard Mrs Boydd-Black instruct the kneeling girl. 'You will carry them with you wherever you go for the rest of the day. Should you give displeasure or even the slightest offence, they will be redistributed and all will be invited to chastise you once again, singly and severally. Now go on in and sit down. Luncheon is served.'

It was shortly after tea, when the late November afternoon had crept up and surrounded the mellow Queen Anne manor house in gathering darkness, that the inevitable confrontation between Miranda and Jane spluttered, ignited and flared up into a fierce conflagration.

Miranda had been gathering fir cones and acorns, delicate fronds of fern and interesting samples of dried bark. She had carefully arranged them into a delightful still life which she hoped would excite Emily's pencil and inspire her artistic mind. Holding the delicate still life in both hands, she was making her way along a narrow corridor towards Emily's green baize door. Halfway along the confined passageway, she encountered Jane.

'A little love token for her?' snarled the sullen girl, still burdened by the twenty or so yellow whippy canes, her visible mark of public shame.

Miranda ignored the taunt, electing to pass by in dignified silence.

'Silly old tart,' mocked Jane. 'Apple for teacher?' she smirked.

Miranda paused, her loyalty to Emily pricked.

232

Her eyes narrowed dangerously. She placed the delicate burden carefully down at her feet.

'I'm getting pretty sick of you, Jane. Sick of your spiteful, cheating tricks and petty jealousy. Just keep clear of me from now on. Keep out of my way, understand?' Jane scowled and took a threatening step closer. The canes rattled in her arms.

'You think you're so damn clever, don't you?' she hissed. 'I'll get you back for this,' she growled, thrusting her newly awarded greenband into Miranda's face.

'That?' Miranda replied, shrugging impatiently. 'You've only yourself to blame.'

'Get lost, stupid bitch,' Jane hissed, lashing out with her foot petulantly at the still life. Miranda's painstakingly assembled little offering shattered into forty pieces.

Like feral cats they sprang, grappling, clawing and scratching wildly. The canes clattered to the floor. Miranda held Jane firmly in a tight headlock; Jane replied by pulling at her opponent's fine golden blonde hair. Panting, they sank down onto the cold lino, rolling over in a short burst of fury. Jane's teeth bit into Miranda's shoulder; Miranda threshed in surprised pain and snatched at Jane's vest. It ripped from belly to throat, spilling out the proud, firm breasts. Miranda pushed her hand up under Jane's chin, forcing the frenzied face back, and almost had the advantage when Jane's knee jerked into her belly and winded her. Miranda lay gasping on the cold, hard lino. Jane straddled her, pinning her arms down between her knees, pinioning her body down beneath the weight of her soft buttocks and spreading, straddling thighs.

'Now, bitch,' Jane leered, bending down to gloat into Miranda's anxious face. 'Suffer.'

Her rounded breasts, shiny and bouncy ripe, spilling out in their freedom from the split in the tight cotton bondage, almost brushed Miranda's lips as Jane struggled to yank up the vest she straddled. Dragging up the soft cotton, she exposed the heaving bosom beneath. Miranda tried to struggle, causing her naked breasts to wobble and shudder fleshily, but she was firmly pinned down beneath Jane's expertly placed knees. Resistance was futile. She sank back beneath the dominating victor. She was at Jane's mercy – a quality she knew to be in distinctly short supply.

Jane took Miranda's exposed left nipple in between her finger and thumb and squeezed it, twisted it savagely and then tugged at it, pulling the pale pink flesh at least an inch from the creamy breast. Miranda choked on her scream of pain. Jane slapped the face beneath her. Miranda blinked with surprise.

'Shut up, you bitch. Take your medicine,' Jane hissed.

Jane clamped her vicious fingers over the right breast, pinching and clawing the soft, tender flesh. Once more the cruel pincer closed over the vulnerable, quivering nipple. Once more, the elastic skin was painfully tweaked, pinched and stretched. Miranda cried out. Jane slapped her face, twice.

'You've been begging for this, your ladyship, and now you're going to get it.'

Both nipples were ravished with searing pain. Miranda writhed, thrusting her bottocks up off the hard lino in a desperate effort to dislodge her abuser. Jane teetered but remained intact, her squatting buttocks spread firmly over Miranda's belly. Jane bent down and clutched the fine blonde hair in a fierce grasp. Now she controlled the head of her victim, and could savour her cruel domination. She bent closer, gripping the hair more firmly.

Miranda's head was jerked back. She stared up into the hate that brimmed in Jane's spiteful eyes. Suddenly, lunging forward, ignoring the searing pain caused by her trapped blonde hair, Miranda nipped her teeth at Jane's left nipple. Jane squealed and relaxed her clutch. Miranda seized her moment and bucked her hips upwards. Jane, nursing her savaged breast, toppled over. Miranda was astride her in a flash.

The positions were now reversed. Jane now lay panting between Miranda's firm white thighs. Miranda slipped her hand down over Jane's belly and reached down into her tight shorts. She wove a strand of her victim's pubic hair around her finger and pulled. Jane gritted her teeth but her scream was still shrill. Miranda pulled again.

'You have given me no alternative. I am going to teach you a lesson your jealous little heart will never forget. Never,' Miranda whispered, inches from Jane's contorted face. Miranda's tone was cold and even, free from rancour and revenge. It was the firm voice of controlling discipline. Strong, steady and cold. The sober tone of stern retribution, not the hysterical, cruel excitement that had sullied Jane's spitting lips.

'Bitch,' hissed Jane, squirming like a cornered cobra.

Miranda rolled her helpless victim over onto her belly, squashing the ripe breasts down into the cold lino. Gathering up a yellow bamboo cane, Miranda pressed it firmly against Jane's face, as if in an attempt to quell and tame the demon of rage that twisted her beauty. The cane was applied firmly across Jane's full, wet lips.

'This,' Miranda warned, tapping the cane, 'is for your own good. Believe me, Jane, you will thank me for what I am about to do to you. Not now, perhaps. But one day.'

Miranda jerked down the tight shorts and fondled Jane's creamy buttocks. Jane bucked and threshed, stung into fresh paroxysms of fury by Miranda's words. Miranda tapped the writhing rump.

'Keep still and quiet while I beat you, Jane,' she said, and raised the cane.

'Stop. Stop it at once. What do you think you are doing? Get up at once, Miranda. How dare you bully that poor girl.'

It was the shrill, sharp voice of Miss Eaddes.

'But she –' blurted Miranda, anxious to explain.

'Silence, girl. I will not tolerate bullying. Jane. Get up. What has been happening here? Come along, speak up.'

Jane detected the note of concern and craftily seized her chance.

'She attacked me,' Jane sniffled, wiping her eyes with the back of her hand, determined to milk the situation. As she rose, her foot trod on an acorn. She winced painfully and was suddenly inspired. Not encumbered by Lady Miranda Gordon-George's sense of fair play, she honed her cunning.

'I was bringing you a little gift. Just a little thank you for teaching me geometry so well. You make things so clear and easy,' Jane lied artfully. 'Miranda smashed it.'

Stooping, Jane gathered up the pathetic fragments.

'I made this for you, Miss Eaddes. I called it 'Autumn Rumours'. It was just a little present . . .'

'She's lying!' Miranda shouted hotly.

'Silence, Miranda. Silence. I will not tell you again,' Miss Eaddes thundered. 'Carry on, Jane,' she murmured encouragingly.

Jane managed a passable sob of sorrow as she told the vain maths tutor how Miranda had supposedly smashed her token of esteem out of jealousy. Miss Eaddes swallowed the lie completely, vanity clouding her better judgement. She refused to countenance the possibility that Jane could be saying anything other than the simple truth. Besides, she reasoned to herself, what could be more perfectly natural than for this pretty, charming girl to express her affection in the form of a little love token. And, she considered sententiously, her ego now quite bloated, it was equally natural for another pretty, charming girl like Miranda to flare up with jealousy. Miss Eaddes felt momentarily dizzy with delight. To have two such beauties wrestling and fighting for her favours was heady stuff indeed.

Jane's primitive cunning was alerted to the maths tutor's train of thought.

'Miranda said that you were an ugly old bitch,' Jane blurted out, as if reluctant to say the words. 'Then she smashed your present.'

The effect was calculated, the result devastating. A careful deceit. Miss Eaddes flushed crimson and dragged Miranda down onto her knees.

'Jane,' she gasped, barely in control of herself. 'I want you to take one of those canes and punish Miranda severely. She must be taught, as swiftly and as painfully as possible, that bullying is not tolerated here at the Academy. Her days of gilded privilege are over.'

Miss Eaddes, like Jane, resented Miranda's cachet

of aristocratic elegance and well-bred poise and self-assurance. The charge, verdict and sentence, however, remained totally transparent to both Miranda and Jane. Mere wounded vanity lay behind Miss Eaddes's judicial measures.

'Shorts down, girl. At once,' rasped the furious maths tutor.

Miranda knew that Jane had won. Had outwitted and outmanoeuvred her. To protest would only enrage and inflame the maths tutor all the more. She knelt down on all fours, then pressed her forehead into the cold lino, her naked bottom shivering in fearful anticipation as her shorts hugged her knees tightly, binding them together and making all movement impossible.

Jane, breasts still spilling freely from the rent in her vest, took up a supple cane and fingered the yellow length of bamboo with malice in her dark heart and triumph in her sparkling eyes. Miranda's stomach muscles contracted with fear as she heard Jane thrum the air with the cane.

'I want this to be a very special punishment, Jane. Do not stripe her bottom too quickly. Pace yourself. Allow for a deliberate pause between each stroke. You young things do not seem to know how to deliver an effective thrashing. It is an acquired skill. I will supervise you carefully. Grip the cane more firmly girl. That's better. No, leave your thumb where it was. Good. Step back a little. Right. Commence.'

The final command was delivered in a squeak of sexual arousal, the tone a thin falsetto of anger and excitement.

Swish. The bottom, bare and offered up to the cane, shuddered as the bamboo whipped across its double domes of creamy flesh.

'Stripe her well,' urged the maths tutor. 'Do your duty.'

Miranda dipped her belly and arched her taut spine, catlike, as the surge of scarlet pain swept along her punished body. *Swish. Swish.* The strokes swiped at her bare bottom relentlessly, remorselessly. For a brief moment of misery, Miranda glimpsed the awful truth of eternity. *Swish. Swish.* Hypnotically, inexorably, the chastisement continued. Pain, pain, pain without end. Little tongues of flame errupted across her creamy cheeks, scorching the taut sheen of smooth skin.

'Firmer,' commanded Miss Eaddes, now down on all fours herself, her face only inches away from Miranda's jerking bottom. 'Harder.' The maths tutor's eyes burned like coals. Her words of command were harsher and more brutal than any obscenity Miranda had ever heard.

Down in the cool, dark womb of the gym, Miranda crouched painfully in the recess. Jane's cane had been brutal.

Mrs Boydd-Black would be in dire need of some comfort tonight. She had passed through turbulent, difficult times, Miranda reflected. The pressure from Porteous. Then there was the disappointment of discovering Miranda's letter. The breach of trust, the disloyalty of it all. And Jane, ruining the tradition of the Chair and Exercise, breaking the ritual and utterly destroying the ceremonious spell cast by the formal punishment held so dear by the headmistress.

Yes. Difficult days, Miranda concluded. Days of distress for her headmistress who deserved delightful nights. The door to the gym swung open. Miss Eaddes, as usual, led the way. They kissed and clasped each other straight away, melting in an embrace of fierce tenderness.

Miranda noticed immediately that tonight Mrs Boydd-Black was completely nude beneath her white towelling robe. The robe was removed by the brisk, efficient maths tutor and the utterly naked headmistress submitted herself to be arraigned and arranged at the wall bars. Miranda's eyes sparkled as she gazed at the splendid figure of the shapely woman stretched out and spreadeagled before her against the wall of the gym. The lightly muscled arms, milky and sinewy, slender and strong. The hint of power in the gleaming shoulders. The narrow waist, the slender yet full hips, the rounded thighs, svelte and tapering, supple and smooth. And the bottom. The large, full and softly fleshed buttocks. The cheeks heavy and swollen with potent promise. Tantalising. Adorable. Kissable, biteable, spankable. Yet a somewhat regal bottom. Serene, splendid and superb. Not a minx's rump or a Rubensesque glory. A bottom to be appreciated, savoured and, yes, honoured. Knelt before, even. Certainly embraced and revered. A round, white bottom of perfect proportions. A bottom to constrict the throat and thicken the tongue with admiration and desire. A bottom before which the quickening heart must bow and worship – prior to the rendering and receiving of exquisite pleasures.

Miss Eaddes left the gym, leaving the light on as she departed. Moments later, satisfied that it was safe to do so, Miranda cautiously made her soft, stealthy approach. Reaching her quarry, pantherlike, she stretched out her arm and gently trailed her fingertips down the captive white spine before her, sweeping them out over the swelling cusp of the curved rump.

'Do not be gentle with me tonight,' the husky voice of Mrs Boydd-Black whispered.

Miranda's heart hammered as she grazed her belly against the broad buttocks. So be it. Bending down closely against the warm, naked flesh of her captive prey, the huntress gave the hunted the customary signal. Three lingering kisses on each buttock. She both sensed and actually felt the taut body in her thrall slacken in a swoon of recognition and delight. Easing down her shorts, and then stepping slowly out of them, Miranda clasped her arms around the warm, white waist of the spreadeagled, naked woman and thrust her pubic delta against the soft cheeks of the joggling bottom. The headmistress gasped as the pubic fuzz rasped against her sheen of silky flesh.

The satin buttocks buckled and collapsed slightly under the pressure of Miranda's pelvic bone as they yielded their warmth up to her insistent, primal force. The sapling ensnaring the seasoned beech, the slender shoot of mistletoe clinging to the fruit-laden bough.

Up on her white, flexed toes, Miranda slowly, slowly sank back down onto her heels, dragging her pubic fringe down, down, down across the silken, shivering moons. Mrs Boydd-Black moaned as Miranda's soft white belly eclipsed the buttocks beneath. Up on her toes once more, Miranda again sank slowly, slowly down, down, down, dragging her labial flesh folds against the rippling buttocks. And again. And again. Clasping the soft waist tightly with one encircling arm, and the softer bosom with an even tighter embracing arm, Miranda repeated the intimacy eight, ten, fifteen times, her own breasts squashed into the warmth of the broad back, her lips, parted and wet, dragging down across the shoulders and spine.

Then, with increasing tempo and intensely concentrated fervour, the hips that covered the passive rump beneath them gyrated slightly, then with a more pronounced sweep. Miranda's labia silvered a tell-tale trail of weeping joy to mark their circular presence and passing. Suddenly, as if gripped by a higher force, as if obeying an unquestionable command, the blonde pupil increased the pressure and tempo of her thrusts with which she sweetly tormented her headmistress.

Both wept openly from their throbbing orifices, the sticky silver dripping like raindrops from a spider's web. Mrs Boydd-Black shivered and shuddered and groaned with delight. Faster and faster, faster and faster, until her oozing, parted labial lips were skimming up and down the pillows of taut flesh beneath them, Miranda straddled, pleasured and dominated the buttocks with complete sovereign mastery. As her own quicksilver spilled down the slopes of the dominated buttocks, and was smeared into the pliant cheeks, Mrs Boydd-Black seemed to collapse into a sweet swoon of utter surrender. A loose-limbed, soft-spined total submission to the fierce joy. Miranda's fingers sought and found the yearning breasts and pinched the erect, straining nipples.

'Yes,' the pleasurably punished headmistress screamed aloud. 'Yes. Harder. Harder. Hold me. Hurt me. Hurt me . . . please,' she moaned.

Miranda grasped both swollen breasts and squeezed, ravishing their pulpy firmness, jerking her hips savagely from side to side as she climaxed herself against the soft, sticky buttocks. The body beneath her buckled and spasmed as it too was first

242

paralysed, then galvanised in its own shattering orgasm. Welded together, skin kissing skin, bonded tightly by their freely flowing lust juices, the younger girl collapsed into the firmer flesh of the older woman. Spring melting into summer. The nascent bud suffused into the open rose.

Suddenly the headmistress turned, her hands and feet completely free from their supposed bondage. They had never been tied. It was a honey trap, in which the curious headmistress was determined to ensnare the bee that browsed on her nectar and stung so sweetly.

'Miranda. It is you. I hoped . . . I wanted . . . I am so glad . . .' she crooned, clasping her nocturnal visitor to her warm bosom. Miranda gasped in alarm. She was stunned, completely shaken. The firm arms swept around her and crushed her closely, possessively, triumphantly. Miranda gazed up out from her dizzy confusion. Mrs Boydd-Black gazed down with tenderness.

'Oh my dear, dear Miranda. What on earth am I to do with you?'

Bolting out of the gym, ignoring the imploring cries from her headmistress to return, Miranda ran down the silent passageways and along the deserted corridors. But where to go? She instinctively knew that Jaya would comfort her. Miranda ran to her friend's dormitory.

It was empty. Miranda slumped down onto the empty bed in the still, dark room. Long, lonely minutes ticked by. Where was she?

Soft sounds approached. Rustling and stifled, giggling whispers. Jaya shushed somebody sternly. She in turn was shushed. By a man. Miranda's heart thumped. It was a man's voice.

The fact registered like a flash of lightning in Miranda's brain. A man. And they were about to enter the dormitory. She dropped to the floor and rolled under the bed, shivering as her limbs kissed the cold lino. Just in time. The door opened softly and she saw four feet enter. Two were Jaya's dainty white-stockinged feet, two were clad in soft, supple pigskin. Italian cut. Very, very expensive. Miranda's eyes grew wide with wonder.

'Close the door. Quietly,' whispered Jaya. 'Oh, Hazim. It is wonderful to see you.'

'I have come for you. I love you. Marry me if you will. Either way, I am taking you away from this place tonight.'

'You gave me such a fright. I nearly screamed.'

Hazim sealed Jaya's babbling lips with a slow, lingering kiss.

'How did you find me?'

'Later. I will explain everything to you later. But I must know. Tell me. This marriage arranged between us. Our parents are old-fashioned, and they mean well. But come to me only if you wish it. I love you, but your father never let me tell you. Then you disappeared. I have not slept. I have been like a madman.'

'You . . . you love me?'

'Did you not know?'

Silence ruled supreme. Miranda knew that kisses had replaced the fervent words.

'Hazim' Jaya squealed, thrilled.

'Forget those parents of ours. Marry me, have many sons for me, go to your university and read law . . .' Hazim murmured against her soft throat.

Jaya nestled happily into his strong, broad chest.

'I knew nothing of this hell they put you in, I swear.'

244

'Hazim, Hazim,' she wept happily.

They sat down together on the edge of the bed. Miranda ducked instinctively.

'I am frightened,' Jaya announced suddenly.

'Do not be afraid. I came undetected. We will leave just the same. I have a car waiting . . .'

'No. Not that. I am safe with you. It is . . . it is that I may not . . . please you.' Her voice was barely audible.

'Please me?' he repeated, genuinely baffled.

'I want to. Very much. To please you. But I have not known a man, in that way . . .'

'I hoped it would be so,' Hazim replied huskily.

Bet you did, Miranda thought to herself as she shivered beneath them.

'But I have . . . I have known the pleasures of . . . there are no men here at all, only . . .' Her voice died away.

'You have found pleasure with the girls here?' he asked swiftly, his voice charged with excited curiosity.

'Yes,' she whispered, her tone frank and honest.

'Do not worry. Our marriage will be fine. Trust me. Promise me that you will trust me?' he implored.

'Yes, I promise,' she murmured silkily.

Furtive rustlings and soft silence ensued. Miranda heard flesh rasp against flesh. The bed sagged beneath their combined weight. Oh God, Miranda thought. He's going to have her here and now. Jaya moaned as feverish hands fumbled over her swelling curves.

'Er, excuse me,' Miranda said sheepishly.

'What the . . . ?' snarled Hazim, leaping up from the bed, tucking in his shirt tails and smoothing back his glossy hair.

'Come out, Miranda,' Jaya giggled.

'Sorry, I didn't mean to.' Miranda shrugged as she emerged from beneath the bed.

'Just in time, perhaps,' Jaya smiled, pulling down her tight vest over her bare bosoms. Her shorts – Miranda smiled secretively as she noticed them – had been dragged back on in haste. Back to front.

'Just in time,' Jaya echoed, wistfully. 'Hazim,' she spoke softly.

'Yes?' he replied in a voice thickened with frustrated lust.

'Our marriage will be fine. Of that I am quite certain.'

'Darling,' he replied, huskily.

'We must take Miranda with us. She is a true friend,' Jaya urged.

Hazim drew back the curtain and turned to peruse the sight of the young blonde's splendid curves in the moonlight.

'Yes,' he said, approvingly.

Twelve minutes later, the shivering girls clambered into the soft, warm leather seats of Hazim's Mercedes. His hands drummed the stitched yellow leather of the steering wheel. He looked over his shoulder.

'If I had known about that uniform I would have brought something warm for you to wear, Jaya. Here, drink this.' He passed back a thermos of hot coffee.

Liar, Miranda grinned to herself. Hazim was a sensualist. Jaya would be seeing more of her thin vest and tight shorts. Theirs was destined to be a climactic relationship, the endless hours crowded with frank pleasures and the celebration of honest lust.

'Did all the girls wear uniforms?' he asked curiously.

Miranda groaned. Jaya giggled.

'Just drive,' they chorused, snuggling into each other for warmth.

'London?' queried Hazim, looking up into his mirror.

'Yes, please,' Miranda nodded. 'I have an appointment with a solicitor.'

Hazim looked at her directly. Their eyes met.

'So have I,' he smiled, mirthlessly.

Miranda stirred, opened her eyes and looked around her at the unfamiliar luxury of Hazim's Holland Park flat. The rich Regency furnishings puzzled her sleepy brain. Then she suddenly remembered, and the puzzle was solved.

The long drive in the warm Mercedes. Jaya's soft limbs and body heat. The dirty orange glow as London had loomed up through the tinted windscreen. The busy inner city streets still shining with traffic at the dead of night.

Christmas was coming. The shops were garish in silver and golden displays. Police vans had tinsel wrapped around their stubby aerials.

She remembered the scratch supper of caviar and champagne. Hazim wandering into her shower in case she needed some shower gel. How solicitous. His eyes had widened like a child's as he caught a glimpse of her sparkling limbs. How they had narrowed with vexation as Jaya had called him away. Miranda giggled.

Bed. On a sofa for her. Long hours of sleeplessness, the lonely hours between midnight and dawn. Pensive hours. Far from savouring her sudden liberation she felt a pang of loss. She nourished the pang with sweet memories. Four times during her lonely wakefulness she had caught the cries of carnal joy from Hazim's master bedroom.

The first two had been the deeper grunts and groans of male satisfaction. Jaya was getting it hot and strong, she reflected. Good and hard. Then, after a long silence, Jaya's thin wail of wanton delight had ripped the air as though it were taut silk. Miranda had risen up on one elbow, thrilling to the sounds of her friend's ecstasy. She stroked her left nipple, dragging it up to a fierce peak of pleasure. She tried to picture Jaya. Was she face down, hugging her pillow, or were the lovers pressed belly to belly, the dusky legs of the beautiful young Asian wrapped around her saviour's thighs, her heels drumming his firm buttocks? Or had Jaya found the courage to go on top, sinking down slowly to be speared exquisitely while the raw male between her glistening thighs snapped and sucked at her loosely swinging breasts?

Miranda curled up under the heavy duvet. The cool silk caressed her lovingly. Fired by images of the lovers next door, she fingered her hot wetness with relentless fervour. Joy flickered into the flames of delight, and her delight melted into molten pleasure.

The fourth scream from the master bedroom was more a series of cries of enmeshed joy. Intertwined, the low carnal grunts of satisfaction and the high squeals of ecstasy, like the male and female bodies from which they were torn. Even by the time the dying cries faded away, Miranda's back was arched as, belly thrust up, her inner thighs flooded with her own spillage of excitation. After her orgasm, she slept like a puppy.

Breakfast, which Miranda prepared and brought in on a tray, was a silent though not a solemn affair. Hazim and Jaya sat up, naked and unselfconscious, in their rumpled bed of pleasure. Hazim munched toast hungrily, Jaya nibbled an apple, a secretive smile playing on her warm, generous lips. As Miranda sat and watched them she felt assured that the marriage would be a good one. Placing her coffee cup down on the bedside table, she reached over and kissed Jaya gently.

'I am so happy for you,' she murmured.

Jaya smiled, delight dancing in her large, liquid eyes.

'Hazim told me that he found me, us, through a video. Show Miranda, Hazim, while I shower.'

Miranda frowned, not understanding. Hazim nodded and sprang out from the bed. Miranda gazed up appreciatively at his lithe, lightly muscled body. He stooped, rustled about in a cabinet and then strode over to a video at the foot of the king-size bed.

Click. Whirr. The machine hummed, the large silvery grey screen flickered. Instantly, Miranda was transported back to the Academy. There, on the screen, Clarissa was sobbing silently as her beautiful bottom jerked responsively to the repeated strokes of a cane. Miranda swore softly. Hazim picked up the remote control. Fast forward. Hold. Play.

Jaya appeared on the screen. The scene must have been videoed some time before Miranda's detention at the Academy. Jaya's hair was thick and luxuriant and she wore a blueband. On screen she appeared before Hazim and Miranda in a giant close-up of her pain and shame. An unseen hand was lashing a broad strap against her buttocks. Silently, she

249

gasped her cries of distress. *Click*. The screen darkened to a silver dot.

'See? I had been trying to trace her for over three months. Her parents told me nothing, other than some damn lies about her choosing to go to Geneva. Then I came across this, through which I tracked down a very sinister little chap called Porteous . . .'

'Porteous?' cried Miranda. 'You mean . . . ?'

Hazim told Miranda all he knew. She completed the picture. Between them, they had the solicitor framed.

'Are you going to Sandstones? They might be worried. Miranda lives in Wiltshire,' Jaya explained to Hazim, after her shower.

'Perhaps,' Miranda replied. 'I'll ring soon. But first, I think Hazim should show you the video. Then I am sure that you will wish to come with me to the Fulham Road.'

'I'm coming too. I've one or two things to discuss with that bastard,' Hazim remarked, yawning deeply after his night's exertions.

'No, Hazim. Thanks, we may need your help but Jaya and I have to do this ourselves. We will need a few things.'

'Things? What sort of things?' Jaya asked, puzzled.

'A dozen cream cakes and a couple of stout leather belts,' Miranda replied, her eyes narrowing. 'Hazim, play the tape for Jaya.'

Jaya watched as, on the screen, Clarissa was being whipped. Hazim watched Jaya's face intently as she focused on the punishment.

Chapter Nine

The dialling tone sang in Miranda's ears. She kicked off her shoes and unzipped her tight skirt.

'Sandstones,' the impeccable voice said.

'Hello, Brompton. May I speak with Aunt Emma?'

Miranda inserted her thumb into the tight elastic of her white lace panties. She eased them down over the fulsome bulge of her heavy buttocks.

'Certainly, Lady Miranda.'

Silence followed. Miranda shivered as her hips and thighs goose-pimpled in the chill morning air.

'Are you there, is that you?' Aunt Emma boomed. 'Little minx, what the devil is going on?'

'And a very good morning to you, Auntie,' Miranda replied, grinning broadly. 'I'm calling from the London flat.'

Miranda grunted down into the phone which was now tucked under her chin. Unclasping her brassière with difficulty, she sighed as it fluttered down to join the panties on the floor. Her breasts swung loose and lovely in their freedom.

'Have you got a man there?'

'No, Auntie.'

'Then why are you groaning like a tart?'

'Undressing for a shower.'

'If that's what you tell me I'm bound to believe you. I don't, by the way. You have behaved incorrigibly in all other matters. The Academy phoned first thing this morning. Mrs Boydd-thingummy –'

'Black,' supplied Miranda.

'Don't quibble. They were very upset. What the hell is going on?'

'I'm coming down to see you at teatime.'

'Better had, my girl.'

Miranda stepped into her shower and luxuriated in the sparkling stream of hot water. She soaped her neck and outstretched arms, then her shining, plump breasts, massaging their pliant flesh with the tablet of soap. The creamy curds of lather gathered and amassed down in her glistening pubic triangle. She rinsed them down her inner thighs and watched them spin away beneath her small white toes. Towelling herself dry, she paused to admit Jaya. Hazim remained at the door.

'Girl's work, Hazim. But be at the Fulham Road office for one-thirty sharp.'

'Very well,' he shrugged, and went.

Miranda strode back into her bedroom. Jaya was sitting on the bed.

'War paint and feathers,' Miranda said, casting aside her long towel. Standing nude before a full-length mirror, she admired herself briefly. Turning, she glimpsed the faint red stripes, the legacy from Jane's merciless caning. Her eyes clouded momentarily with anger.

'Strip off,' she ordered.

Jaya peeled off her sinuous silk sari, every gesture more revealing and erotic than the one before. In moments, she too stood in proud, splendid nakedness. She joined Miranda before the mirror.

Miranda's creamy skin contrasted deliciously with the warm amber, glistening honied tones of Jaya's flesh. Miranda's breasts were fuller, riper, heavier. Jaya's belly rounder, her hips slightly broader. Both had superb legs.

Turning, they gazed over their shoulders at each other's pertly rounded bottoms. Imperceptibly, they jostled closer, squeezing their cheeks together. Skin kissed soft skin. Miranda dropped her arm down and allowed her hand to smooth Jaya's rounded buttocks gently, fondling and squeezing the tight, supple flesh. Jaya sighed deeply and stroked the cleft between Miranda's joggling cheeks.

'I will miss you so much,' she whispered huskily.

In the long looking-glass, their eyes met. Miranda squeezed Jaya's bottom with a fierce tenderness.

'Our loving friendship will continue, don't worry. We will meet from time to time. Feed the flames of our precious fire.'

'But Hazim . . .'

'You will be very happy with him. But that which he cannot give you as a man, I will give you as a woman. Do not be afraid.'

Jaya turned to embrace Miranda, her soft, dusky bosoms nestling into the creamy breasts of her beloved, her lover and sweet disciplinarian. Slowly, she kissed and tongued Miranda's throat, then the valley between the rounded breasts below. Finally, and firmly, she attended to the swelling bosom.

Taking each cherry red nipple in between her lips, she sucked hard, then slipped her tiny white teeth over the stiffening peak and tongued it fiercely until Miranda rose up on her toes in sheer ecstasy. The warm, wet mouth worked down across the smooth, milky skin, the hot, thick lips dragging against the silky sheen of tight skin beneath them. At the hip, the lips worked sideways towards the outer curve.

Jaya turned Miranda's naked body within her firm, slim dusky hands. Miranda responded, presenting her soft bottom to the worshipping mouth. Jaya eased back and sank on her heels, gazing steadily and longingly at the quivering cheeks. So soft, so round, so heavy. Inching her face closer, closer still, she licked the sweeping curve of the left buttock. First with a tentative, tremulous tongue tip then more boldly, using the full length of her strong, pink tongue.

The freshly washed skin of the buttocks tasted faintly of luxurious soap. It filled her mouth. It filled her mind. Down, down, down into the white hillock of soft flesh she pressed her face, squashing it in her attempt to lose herself and drown in the warm, satin smooth glory.

Miranda swayed slightly as she felt first the hot breath, then the wet lips, then Jaya's full face caress and adore her bottom. For five long, silent minutes Jaya enjoyed the buttock, before turning tongue and lips to the other. Five long, languid minutes later, her hot tongue was probing and flickering along the length of the shadowed cleft between the creamy mounds. Into the warm, dark, steeply sloping valley of flesh, her long tongue flicked. Soon her frenzied mouth was sucking and kissing, biting and gorging on the soft, quivering flesh. Spreading the tight cheeks apart between her firm thumbs, Jaya opened up the cleft to expose the single pink rosebud of the anal whorl. Her tongue tip flickered across it. Again. Miranda shrieked and dragged Jaya back up to her bosom in a close embrace.

'Spank me,' pleaded Jaya, drowning in her liquid

longings, having paid fulsome homage to the one she adored. 'Spank me, please.'

Miranda took Jaya's nipples between her pincered fingers and thumbs and forced her backwards down onto the bed, belly down. Still imprisoning the tightening nipples, the blonde positioned the dusky Asian girl beneath her against the mattress, straddling the wide, warm hips with her own, dominating the soft bottom beneath her with her firm pelvic girdle. Jaya squealed as she felt the shock of the pubic coils rasp against her velvet buttocks.

'You are beautiful,' Miranda spoke softly, quietly. 'Your bottom is superb. Such beauty is painful. It hurts the eye of the beholder, wounds the heart of the admirer. For this reason, such beauty must be punished.'

Jaya thrilled to the words, thrilled to the threat of pain and promise of dark pleasure they carried with them. She thrust her bottom up eagerly for the delicious punishment to come. Miranda merely drew her outstretched finger down the dusky spine of the bending girl and, turning her outstretched hand into a claw of sharp fingernails, dragged them down across each plump buttock. Jaya shivered and moaned, wriggling her bottom in eager, openly unashamed impatience. Miranda steadied the quivering buttocks with a firm hand.

'You will be punished when, and only when, I deem it fitting. When you surrender to me, your surrender and submission must be complete, utter and absolute.'

'Yes,' whispered Jaya hoarsely. 'Yes.'

'Your bottom is mine,' Miranda hissed, stroking t tenderly.

'I give it to you, completely,' Jaya whimpered.

'I take it, absolutely, to pleasure and enjoy,' Miranda replied.

'Do it, please, do it now, I beg you. Spank me, spank me hard. Please, do with me what you will.'

Smack. The sepia-hued cheeks wobbled provocatively under the first of six firm spanks. *Smack. Smack. Smack.* Jaya hissed with pain and delight. *Smack. Smack.* Miranda's slightly curved hand rose and fell rapidly, cracking down with fierce tenderness across the exposed, upturned buttocks. Already both hands and cheeks were warm.

'Beat me harder, harder,' implored Jaya, her voice thickening with frenzied lust, sweet anguish and the desire to be dominated.

The cruel spanking continued, the crack of firm hand across soft buttocks echoing around Miranda's luxurious bedroom like pistol shots.

'Beautiful, beautiful, beautiful Jaya. Beautiful, beautiful, beautiful bottom,' whispered Miranda severely between the sharp slaps.

Jaya squeezed her thighs together and thrust her hot bottom up for more.

'Spank me, oh my love, spank me. Hurt me, love me, own me,' she cried.

Miranda gripped Jaya's breasts and squeezed them tightly. Bending down she whispered into the small, perfectly formed ear that met her hot dry lips with its cool silky skin.

'In my arms you are safe. Safe and loved. Remember that. Always and forever there will be a place in my arms, in my heart and in my bed for you. I will tame you, spank you and give you the love no man ever dreamed of giving or receiving. I burn with fierce joy to possess you. Like a jewel, I treasure you. Your bottom is soft. So soft. Your

256

bottom is round. So round. Your bottom is mine, all mine.' *Spank. Spank. Spank.*

Tears of joy spilled freely down Jaya's face. To be so desired, possessed, owned and lovingly dominated was pure heaven. She felt her body melting into liquid surrender. Swollen breasts and taut belly, moistening thighs and burning buttocks – all became one molten offering dedicated to her love in whose arms she was rocked, soothed, savaged and enjoyed. Her mind trembled on the very brink of delirium as she fluttered on the edge of a swoon.

This firm blonde, so strong, so beautiful, so proud. This blonde wanted her. Loved her. Pleasured her. Owned and controlled her jerking nakedness. The experience was both shattering and uniquely, deeply fulfilling.

Jaya screamed as she sensed Miranda's mouth hovering above her hot bottom. A trickle of warm saliva dribbled down into the shadow of her cleft. The kiss of warm, perfumed breath drew closer. Closer still. The wet, fleshy lips brushed her punished rump fleetingly. Again, the kiss was a slow, lingering caress. Then the tongue. Now the teeth. They sank into Jaya's generous bottom softly, silently and slowly. The mouth opened and then, tantalisingly, closed. The teeth tortured the scalding flesh for several minutes. Golden waves of crimson delight. Jaya threshed, hot silver sluicing from beneath her tingling pubic curtain. Miranda sprang back, spun Jaya over and knelt down over her upturned face. Jaya's mouth lay exactly four inches beneath the sweet, soft centre of Miranda's splayed thighs. Jaya gazed up in total adoration.

'You will kiss the sweet honey that flows from

257

within me. Taste me. Drink from our love cup that will never run dry.'

The golden pubic hairs grazed Jaya's nose as Miranda lowered herself, inch by inch, down onto Jaya's mouth. The soft, wet flesh enfolded itself, the labial tissue opening to greet the lips and quivering tongue. Jaya sucked and mouthed the open sex. Miranda bucked and shuddered as her very soul trembled. The juices poured out from one mouth into the other.

Firmly pinioned beneath the hot, white thighs of her mistress and tormentor, the dusky girl squirmed and wriggled, her domination complete. Miranda's orgasm broke suddenly and savagely. She arched her spine then rode Jaya's face with her scalding, open wetness, grinding down into the upturned face between her powerful thighs. With a mutual, echoing scream, they collapsed into a sweaty heap of drained passion. Spent and exhausted, they curled up into a close embrace.

Later, after soothing cups of Gunpowder tea served with slices of lemon, Miranda became business-like and practical.

'Perfume. Opium, I think. The Jicky by Guerlain is too subtle for our purpose.'

She dabbed the heavy, sweetly toxic scent between her breasts, at the base of her neck and onto her wrists. She was both liberal and slightly reckless as she splashed the perfume all over Jaya's naked, softly glowing body.

'Good. Now for some panties. Gold for you, black for me.' She tossed Jaya a flimsy wisp of gold lace. Jaya held them up in amazement on the tip of one finger. Miranda looked over her shoulder in the mirror as she pulled her scantily cut panties up, deep into her parted cleft. They felt good. Nice and tight, snuggling closely against her pubic mound. Jaya followed, dipping her lissome legs one by one into the fragile golden lace.

'We'll go bra-less. Suspenders – these for you,' Miranda said, tossing Jaya a crimson suspender belt. 'I'll stick with black.'

They both adorned themselves with the belts, thrilling – as many women do – to the close, sensuous embrace that kissed and clung to their skin so tightly.

'Stockings. White for you, with a nice, thick seam. I've got a pair of really vampy fishnets somewhere here . . . got them,' said Miranda triumphantly.

Jaya flexed, then straightened, her left leg as she rolled the sheer stocking up along the full length of it. At the fullest part of her rounded thigh, she snapped the suspenders down into the stocking top. Arching her foot, she examined the effect critically, seemed satisfied, then sinuously and sensuously stepped into the other.

'Seams straight?' she asked, standing with her back to Miranda, peering down over her shoulder at her pert, freshly spanked bottom. The cheeks wobbled slightly so she clenched them. Miranda, adjusting her glossy fishnets, looked up. She squinted, head inclined, then grinned.

'Perfect,' she purred, appraising the effect of the sheer stockings on Jaya's sweeping, curved long legs.

'Now for our battledress. Something loud, sexy and brash. Now what have we got in here?'

She thumbed through her capacious wardrobe, selecting and rejecting several items.

'Here we are,' she smiled wickedly, pulling out two tight bolero jackets, severely cropped and open

259

down the front with no fastenings. They were both cut from a seamless roll of electric blue velvet. Two jet black micro skirts enhanced the lascivious, leggy look.

'Shoes,' Miranda speculated pensively. She passed Jaya a pair of red, strappy ultra-high heels. The effect was stunning. Jaya's tight rump was thrust upwards and outwards immediately. Miranda selected a pair of high-heeled leopard skin sandals. Fully dressed, or at least partially covered by the clothes Miranda had chosen so deliberately, they looked like a couple of call girls in the car park of the Dorchester.

'We'll take a cab.'

They took one. The cabbie refused any fare. He had driven them to Knightsbridge with his tongue hanging out like a labrador slobbering over liver sausage.

First stop was at an exclusive patisserie, from which they emerged with a large silver carton topped off with an outrageous crimson ribbon. In the vast Knightsbidge emporium, they made several rather more bizarre purchases, raising eyebrows among the female assistants – and much more among the men who served them so promptly and attentively. A brief stop in a magic and novelty joke shop in the Brompton Road was all that lay between them and their visit to the solicitor's Fulham Road lair.

'In we go,' Miranda said, grimacing.

They dismissed the startled receptionist and locked the outer door behind her. Miranda strode towards the inner sanctum. Jaya, unaccustomed to the height of her heels, teetered tipsily in her wake.

Porteous gasped as they burst into his office.

'Good gracious,' he exclaimed, his eyes bulging.

'Oh, dear Mr Porteous,' Miranda gushed in tones of simpering treacle, 'I simply had to come and thank you for all you have done for me.'

'Me too,' chimed in Jaya, musically. 'I owe you so much and must repay you somehow.' She let her cropped bolero swing open. Her breasts bounced and wobbled deliciously with a rubbery naughtiness.

'What is the meaning of –' spluttered the solicitor.

'We owe so much to you we simply had to pop in and thank you, properly,' Miranda cooed. 'You must let us reward you. Name it and it is yours . . .' She waggled her hips and unzipped her black micro skirt. It dropped down the length of her glossy fishnets revealing the black suspender belt and silk panties beneath. 'Name it,' she said, pouting through her heavily glossed, Max Factor High Definition cherry red lips. The solicitor's hands gripped the desk. His eyes stared hungrily. Jaya kicked off her skirt and shed her jacket completely.

'But you must punish us for leaving the Academy without permission. We need disciplining,' Miranda whispered excitedly.

Porteous mopped his perspiring brow. He spluttered in an attempt to speak but was too flabbergasted to do so. Jaya approached him, turned her bottom into his face and wiggled it. The suspendered thighs sparkled inches from his eyes.

'Spank me, Mr Porteous. Be firm with me, ooh please spank me, spank me,' she squealed. She skipped around to the back of his chair in which he sat transfixed. She cradled his head in her Opium clouded bosom, crushing him in between their fleshy softness.

'Spank my bottom very, very hard,' she hissed, tonguing his left ear.

261

'Really, I must protest,' Porteous exploded. 'I really must . . .' he choked, confused and delighted, amazed and astounded by the events unfolding around him like a dream.

'Before you punish our naughty bottoms, have some cake,' purred Miranda, who, smoothing her fishnets along her shimmering thighs with the palms of her scarlet-nailed hands, teasingly unpicked the ribbon and opened the silver carton. Jaya stretched over, her breasts smothering the upturned face of the spellbound solicitor. She picked out a *frais du bois Pompadour*, swollen with fruit and fresh cream and a *chocolat de Veronique*, oozing with sinfulness.

Holding the two delicious cakes between erotically prinked fingers, Jaya stood behind the solicitor and bent down over him. Her breasts brushed his slobbering lips, then the cakes were tantalisingly drawn before his piggy eyes. Frozen between greed and lust, he mouthed silent obscenities. Miranda stood before him, bunching up and squeezing her breasts between her slim, sensual fingers. Porteous attempted to scramble up to his feet, but Jaya held him down, gently but firmly, with her elbows on his shoulders.

'Enjoy,' she whispered, dragging the two cakes alternately across his wet, trembling lips.

Porteous lunged at the *frais du bois Pompadour*, his sharklike teeth snapping greedily. Jaya whisked it just out of reach. Porteous strained after it, whimpering tormentedly.

'Now,' commanded Miranda harshly.

The solicitor blinked, startled. For a fraction of a second, he stared up, frightened and afraid. Jaya slammed the two cakes down into his eyes. Blinded and panicking, the solicitor threshed in his chair.

Jaya rammed two more thick, oozing cakes into his eyes, blinding him completely, then squashed more cakes up his nose and into his gasping mouth. Struggling frantically for breath, the solicitor flapped his arms above his head. Miranda and Jaya, working to their pre-arranged plan, took an arm each and brought them savagely down behind his back, handcuffing them crisply into passive helplessness. Porteous was a strong man. A bull. In his rage, he spilled over the chair and crashed into a filing cabinet.

'Get his balls,' Miranda cried.

Jaya obeyed immediately. She reached down and caught the solicitor fiercely by the crotch. The effect was electric. He stood stock still, trembling and quivering with rage and fear.

'OK, you bastard,' Miranda hissed. 'I've waited for this moment and I'm not going to hurry it. This is where you get yours.'

Jaya forced a huge wedge of coffee and almond Beaumarchais into the solicitor's mouth, effectively gagging him and rendering him helpless, before ripping his trousers down. With Miranda's assistance, she forced him face down over his desk and cut away all his clothing with a Stanley knife bought especially for the purpose. A second pair of the handcuffs secured his ankles tightly together before they felt it safe enough to stagger back and catch their breath.

'Gag and blindfold,' Miranda instructed. Jaya obeyed in a trice.

Miranda uncurled the two leather belts purchased in the menswear boutique and handed one of the cruel lengths of supple leather to her partner. They took up their positions on either side of the larger,

263

flabby buttocks spread out across the desk before them.

Crack. Miranda struck first. Porteous screamed through the tight gag. *Crack.* Jaya's vicious cut seared the pale flesh, striping it red immediately. *Crack. Crack.* With relentless, unerring fury the two girls rained the lashes down. Porteous squirmed and threshed but his bondage was firm and his escape impossible. A dozen swipes later, Miranda tossed her belt to the floor.

'Carry on, as hard as you like,' she commanded. 'I've got other fish to fry.'

Jaya, who had never whipped a man before, warmed and then thrilled to her task. She raised her leather belt up, snapped it twice in the air and applied it ruthlessly to the solicitor's buttocks. Again. Again. And again. He screamed through his gag. She lashed him yet again. Administering corporal punishment felt strange. It felt good.

Crack. Crack. Jaya's belt whipped the angry red buttocks. The victim squealed and groaned.

'Got it,' Miranda exclaimed in triumph. She had been rifling through the open safe and had discovered the lease to the Academy. She had already thrust Hazim's two gold bricks and a half dozen videos marked *The Academy: Disciplining and Punishments*, into a black plastic bag. The lease joined her earlier finds.

Anything else? she wondered. Of course. The accounts. Remembering the computer in Mrs Boydd-Black's office, she searched for discs. And found them. Six of them. Scanning their contents briefly, she realised that she had tumbled across the complete financial and administrative operations of the Academy. She threw them into the bag along with her other booty. One-fifteen. On the desk, Porteous was still being soundly whipped.

Miranda rootled around in the bowels of the wall safe and unearthed a stout iron box. It was locked. Intuitively, she pounced on Porteous, turned him over and spotted the small key on a chain around his neck. Wrenching the key away, she returned to the box, leaving Jaya to ponder the possibilities of a naked, manacled full-frontal victim at her complete mercy. And mercy was a quality in extremely short supply with the angry girl. Memories of her humiliations, pain and suffering at the Academy flooded into her crimson mind. Memories. She leaned forward. Three seconds later, Porteous screamed. And screamed again.

Miranda scattered the contents of the secretive cache on the carpet. Inspecting them briefly, she knew she had come across a blackmailing sideline. The slim dossiers, printed on the solicitor's own headed paper, contained detailed records of the financial and sexual peccadilloes of several important Establishment figures. A plan evolved in her mind quickly.

She faxed the documents to sources she knew would be able to deal with Porteous effectively. Not TN, or New Scotland Yard. Too obvious, too easy. No. She faxed them to the five most exclusive and prestigious of the City's Masonic lodges. When the Establishment closed ranks, it crushed anyone caught up in its outrage. Her actions, she knew, would not only destroy the bastard, but tuck him away for a six year stretch.

'We've got six minutes left. Give me a belt,' Miranda hissed.

Porteous was stretched across the desk, writhing

in agony. Jaya had devilishly attached bulldog clips to both of his pale nipples and to the fold of yellowish foreskin at the tip of his flaccid penis. Miranda nodded with grim approval, then turned him over onto his belly. *Crack. Crack.* Each girl lashed the already punished rump with their lengths of quivering leather, their faces glowing with excitement as they drew closer together.

Crack. Crack. Their eyes met and locked in a tender gaze of mutual delight. *Crack. Crack.* Their lips brushed, and then they kissed, the limp belts dangling down over the twitching buttocks.

One twenty-seven. Miranda phoned Reuters, giving a restricted password she had overheard from her Special Branch protection squad to the duty officer.

'Be outside the entrance to the Law Society at 13.50. Two photographers, you won't be wasting your time,' she snapped briskly.

One twenty-nine. Miranda and Jaya donned Donald Duck masks, scooped up the naked solicitor and bundled him out to where Hazim sat behind the wheel of his Mercedes. Fulham Road stopped and stared as the two scantily, raunchily clad girls bundled the naked, manacled solicitor into the Mercedes.

'Christmas has come early for that lucky bastard,' remarked a greengrocer, absently bursting a greengage between his excited fingers.

'What the hell . . .?' marvelled Hazim. 'Hey, mind the seats. That bastard is covered in cream!' he protested, laughing.

'And he's got a strawberry arse to match,' snarled Miranda, her voice muffled beneath the outrageous Donald Duck mask.

Hazim eyed the flimsy lingerie of the two shivering girls appreciatively. The two sets of bosoms bounced delightfully as they clambered into the car.

'Where to?' Hazim grinned.

'Law Society. Quick.'

The Mercedes roared off. They made it to the august portals with 45 seconds to spare. Three photographers lounged idly on the steps, the two from Reuters trying to ignore the freelancer who had followed them in the hope of a coup. The grapevine was humming. Even as the thick wheel kissed the curb, three more photographers arrived for the scoop. Jaya and Miranda worked rapidly. They dragged Porteous out and draped his hand-cuffed hands over the black iron railings, whipped off his blindfold and draped a crudely printed sign around his neck. The lettering on the sign pro-claimed that a senior member of the Royal Family was romantically linked to a notorious serial killer, recently in the headlines.

'Cold, isn't it boys?' Miranda said to the gaping pressmen. 'This should warm things up a bit.'

Flashbulbs exploded in an orgy of blinding light. Bare-bosomed, the two girls posed provocatively, applying their belts to the solicitor's naked buttocks. Exactly six minutes later, the Mercedes roared off once more, just as the approaching police sirens split the cold air of the London afternoon.

Witherspoon, footman to the butler Brompton, brought a tray of tea, golden buttered toast, an-chovy spread, cucumber sandwiches, a raspberry sponge cake, some chocolate-covered shortbread, brandy snaps, a plum cake, a rich walnut and date cake, potted shrimps and some tiny egg and cress sandwiches the size of postage stamps. Witherspoon was renowned throughout the shires for his teatime trays. He, and those taking tea at Sandstones, frequently staggered under them. Miranda wolfed the golden buttered toast spread thickly with anchovy paste. Sir Peter nibbled a slice of the heavy, moist plum cake.

'So you intend to return to the Academy?' Aunt Emma said after demolishing the egg and cress in a way that brought a gleam of pride to Witherspoon's rheumy eye.

'If they'll have me, of course,' Miranda replied demurely. 'I'd like to. They do very useful work with the girls. Very useful.'

Miranda's tone was simple and sincere. Aunt Emma gazed at her shrewdly, secretly delighted with the new sense of purpose the girl displayed.

'You never cease to amaze me, minx,' she commented. She had been listening attentively to Miranda for the preceding 40 minutes, and certainly was amazed.

Witherspoon cleared away the remains of the sumptuous tea and withdrew. Aunt Emma turned to business matters. A settlement on Miranda, some ten thousand a year, was quickly achieved. A cheque was written to redeem the lease.

'I will turn the financial side of things around in eighteen months, Auntie. You will get this money back. Every penny. The Academy, now free of Porteous, will thrive.'

'Rum business, that,' Sir Peter remarked to nobody in particular. Miranda and Aunt Emma smiled and exchanged knowing glances.

'Had a very peculiar phone call. Seems the fellow went native in the middle of London earlier on. Facing some very odd charges in Bow Street tomorrow morning. And there's more to follow. Most distressing.'

Later, before her departure, Miranda made a present of the six videos to her Aunt.

'They show some of the methods the Academy uses to get the desired results,' Miranda grinned. 'For your winter evenings. Should keep you warm.'

Later still, Aunt Emma played the first of the six videos. Witherspoon was just entering the library with a nightcap of sherry when Clarissa's striped bottom loomed large on the screen. Aunt Emma's hand paused over the box of orange creams she was guzzling. Behind, Witherspoon's tray crashed to the floor.

Freddie the chauffeur nosed the Audi carefully through the narrow country lanes. There was little traffic. The countryside in wintry Wiltshire was a pretty tame affair. The car phone warbled. Freddie picked it up and passed it straight back to Miranda.

'Hazim, how lovely,' she cooed.

They chatted happily for half a mile. There was a pause.

'What did you do with all those videos?' he asked, hesitantly.

'Don't worry. They are out of circulation. Jaya's reputation is safe.'

'I am glad. It infuriates me to think that anyone dared lay a hand on her gentle body . . .'

Miranda grinned and remained silent.

'Of course, I could never spank Jaya . . . I couldn't possibly . . .' He left the sentence hanging, like his hopes, in the air.

Miranda came to his rescue.

'The disciplines of love, Hazim, the disciplines of

love. You will soon learn their dark secrets, Jaya will make a perfect teacher, and,' she added enigmatically, 'a willing pupil. Good luck.'

The Audi pulled up outside the gate lodge. Miranda said goodbye to Freddie.

'How long you reckon on staying this time, m'lady?' he grinned.

'Five minutes, perhaps. Five years, I hope.'

Mrs Boydd-Black welcomed Miranda with a warm embrace at the front door. The reunion was poignant and intense.

'I knew you would come back,' she beamed. 'Jolly good.'

In the hallway, a little redband was being soundly spanked over the knees of a blueband. The small, white bottom squirmed under the fluttering hand and stinging slaps that rained down upon it. *Smack. Smack. Smack.* The thin wail of miserable protest. The stern voice warning the punished girl not to wriggle and squirm. *Smack. Smack. Smack.* The stifled sobs of the chastised. It was good to be home.

Up in her study, the headmistress poured Miranda a gin and tonic.

'You have no idea how relieved I am to be rid of that swine, Miranda. He was ruinous.'

'The lease is perfectly safe now. And you have the discs. The Academy is absolutely in your hands now, under your control.'

'With you as my assistant, I trust,' the headmistress smiled. Miranda raised her glass as a sign of her willing acceptance.

'Headmistress,' she said, tentatively.

'Yes, my dear?'

'About the girls' uniforms. Instead of shorts, I

wondered, perhaps, and of course only if you approve . . . opaque tights. They fit so superbly, and we could insist on . . .'

Deep into the night, and for many long winter nights later, the two sat almost head to head, drowning in the delicious proposals for new rules and regulations, new penalties and punishments . . .

The following morning, Mr Porteous was denied bail and, because of the distinct possibilities of more serious charges, he was remanded into the custody of Pentonville to appear before the Crown Court in the New Year. From the dock, Porteous saw the legal men gather around like crows as they huddled together. He also saw his defence exchange a Masonic handshake with the prosecuting barrister. His heart sank. Porteous sensed the shadowy hands of the Establishment pulling invisible strings. Terror dried his throat and choked down any protests.

Back in Pentonville, he was whisked away to a remote landing reserved for difficult cases. Here, men were fed and watered twice a day – and left locked up to their own wretched devices. The door creaked and slammed shut with an echoing thud. Porteous sat down on his bed in the rank urine-scented gloom. Moments elapsed before the slurred vowels of Bethnal Green broke the terrible silence. Porteous froze, his pulse quickening.

'Wotcha, sweetie. I'm big Cecil. Sweet-tooth Cecil. Got any choclit? I likes choclit. You gonna be my best mate for the next few months, eh? 'Ere, get em orf. Let's have a butchers at yer lily white arse . . I likes a nice soft arse, I does . . .'

* * *

Breakfast was in progress when Miranda, dressed in a soft yellow polo neck jumper and stretchyblack ski pants, arrived down in the refectory. She carried Aunt Emma's riding crop nonchalantly under her left arm. Susie squealed with delight and, breaking all the rules, waved excitedly. Miranda grinned, then frowned and raised the tip of the whip to her lips in a sober gesture for silence. Susie cast her eyes down sorrowfully, but on looking up was thrilled to see Miranda gazing at her fondly.

'See me in my study immediately after breakfast, Susie,' Miranda said gently.

Susie's face looked anxious for a few seconds.

'We must think about the Christmas festivities, and I'd value your advice.'

Susie preened, basking in the jealous stares of the girls at her table.

'Jaya phoned earlier this morning. From St Moritz,' Mrs Boydd-Black remarked as Miranda sat down to her plate of bacon and kidneys.

'She's going to marry him, you know,' Miranda grinned.

'Already done so. Special licence. The gal has spirit.'

'Thanks to you, and the Academy.'

'You really think so?' the headmistress queried.

'Absolutely,' Miranda replied.

'Jolly good.' The headmistress nodded and tackled her kippers.

The life of Cromwell drew to a desultory close as Miss Eaddes read out the concluding sentences from the final paragraph. The girls, in neat rows with their heads bowed and their breasts bulging through their tight, white vests, ate their breakfasts in dutiful silence.

NEXUS BACKLIST

Where a month is marked on the right, this book will not be published until that month in 1994. All books are priced £4.99 unless another price is given.

CONTEMPORARY EROTICA

CONTOURS OF DARKNESS	Marco Vassi		
THE DEVIL'S ADVOCATE	Anonymous		
THE DOMINO TATTOO	Cyrian Amberlake	£4.50	
THE DOMINO ENIGMA	Cyrian Amberlake		
THE DOMINO QUEEN	Cyrian Amberlake		
ELAINE	Stephen Ferris		
EMMA'S SECRET WORLD	Hilary James		
EMMA ENSLAVED	Hilary James		
FALLEN ANGELS	Kendal Grahame		
THE FANTASIES OF JOSEPHINE SCOTT	Josephine Scott		
THE GENTLE DEGENERATES	Marco Vassi		
HEART OF DESIRE	Maria del Rey		
HELEN – A MODERN ODALISQUE	Larry Stern		
HIS MISTRESS'S VOICE	G. C. Scott		Nov
THE HOUSE OF MALDONA	Yolanda Celbridge		Dec
THE INSTITUTE	Maria del Rey		
SISTERHOOD OF THE INSTITUTE	Maria del Rey		Sep
JENNIFER'S INSTRUCTION	Cyrian Amberlake		
MELINDA AND THE MASTER	Susanna Hughes		
MELINDA AND ESMERALDA	Susanna Hughes		
MELINDA AND THE COUNTESS	Susanna Hughes		Dec
MIND BLOWER	Marco Vassi		

MS DEEDES AT HOME	Carole Andrews	£4.50	
MS DEEDES ON PARADISE ISLAND	Carole Andrews		
THE NEW STORY OF O	Anonymous		
OBSESSION	Maria del Rey		
ONE WEEK IN THE PRIVATE HOUSE	Esme Ombreux		
THE PALACE OF FANTASIES	Delver Maddingley		
THE PALACE OF HONEYMOONS	Delver Maddingley		
THE PALACE OF EROS	Delver Maddingley		
PARADISE BAY	Maria del Rey		
THE PASSIVE VOICE	G. C. Scott		
THE SALINE SOLUTION	Marco Vassi		
STEPHANIE	Susanna Hughes		
STEPHANIE'S CASTLE	Susanna Hughes		
STEPHANIE'S REVENGE	Susanna Hughes		
STEPHANIE'S DOMAIN	Susanna Hughes		
STEPHANIE'S TRIAL	Susanna Hughes		
STEPHANIE'S PLEASURE	Susanna Hughes		Sep
THE TEACHING OF FAITH	Elizabeth Bruce		
THE TRAINING GROUNDS	Sarah Veitch		

EROTIC SCIENCE FICTION

ADVENTURES IN THE PLEASUREZONE	Delaney Silver	
RETURN TO THE PLEASUREZONE	Delaney Silver	
FANTASYWORLD	Larry Stern	Oct
WANTON	Andrea Arven	

ANCIENT & FANTASY SETTINGS

CHAMPIONS OF LOVE	Anonymous		
CHAMPIONS OF PLEASURE	Anonymous		
CHAMPIONS OF DESIRE	Anonymous		
THE CLOAK OF APHRODITE	Kendal Grahame		Nov
SLAVE OF LIDIR	Aran Ashe	£4.50	
DUNGEONS OF LIDIR	Aran Ashe		
THE FOREST OF BONDAGE	Aran Ashe	£4.50	
PLEASURE ISLAND	Aran Ashe		
WITCH QUEEN OF VIXANIA	Morgana Baron		

EDWARDIAN, VICTORIAN & OLDER EROTICA

ANNIE	Evelyn Culber	
ANNIE AND THE SOCIETY	Evelyn Culber	Oct
BEATRICE	Anonymous	
CHOOSING LOVERS FOR JUSTINE	Aran Ashe	
GARDENS OF DESIRE	Roger Rougiere	
THE LASCIVIOUS MONK	Anonymous	
LURE OF THE MANOR	Barbra Baron	
MAN WITH A MAID 1	Anonymous	
MAN WITH A MAID 2	Anonymous	
MAN WITH A MAID 3	Anonymous	
MEMOIRS OF A CORNISH GOVERNESS	Yolanda Celbridge	
TIME OF HER LIFE	Josephine Scott	
VIOLETTE	Anonymous	

THE JAZZ AGE

BLUE ANGEL DAYS	Margarete von Falkensee	
BLUE ANGEL NIGHTS	Margarete von Falkensee	
BLUE ANGEL SECRETS	Margarete von Falkensee	
CONFESSIONS OF AN ENGLISH MAID	Anonymous	
PLAISIR D'AMOUR	Anne-Marie Villefranche	
FOLIES D'AMOUR	Anne-Marie Villefranche	
JOIE D'AMOUR	Anne-Marie Villefranche	
MYSTERE D'AMOUR	Anne-Marie Villefranche	
SECRETS D'AMOUR	Anne-Marie Villefranche	
SOUVENIR D'AMOUR	Anne-Marie Villefranche	
WAR IN HIGH HEELS	Piers Falconer	

SAMPLERS & COLLECTIONS

EROTICON 1	ed. J-P Spencer	
EROTICON 2	ed. J-P Spencer	
EROTICON 3	ed. J-P Spencer	
EROTICON 4	ed. J-P Spencer	
NEW EROTICA 1	ed. Esme Ombreux	
NEW EROTICA 2	ed. Esme Ombreux	
THE FIESTA LETTERS	ed. Chris Lloyd	£4.50

NON-FICTION

FEMALE SEXUAL AWARENESS	B & E McCarthy	£5.99	
HOW TO DRIVE YOUR MAN WILD IN BED	Graham Masterton		
HOW TO DRIVE YOUR WOMAN WILD IN BED	Graham Masterton		
LETTERS TO LINZI	Linzi Drew		
LINZI DREW'S PLEASURE GUIDE	Linzi Drew		

Please send me the books I have ticked above.

Name   . . . .
Address   . . . .
           . . . .
           . . . . Post code   . . . .

Send to: **Cash Sales, Nexus Books, 332 Ladbroke Grove, London W10 5AH**

Please enclose a cheque or postal order, made payable to **Nexus Books**, to the value of the books you have ordered plus postage and packing costs as follows:

   UK and BFPO – £1.00 for the first book, 50p for the second book, and 30p for each subsequent book to a maximum of £3.00;

   Overseas (including Republic of Ireland) – £2.00 for the first book, £1.00 for the second book, and 50p for each subsequent book.

If you would prefer to pay by VISA or ACCESS/MASTERCARD, please write your card number here:

Please allow up to 28 days for delivery

— — — —   — — — —   — — — —   — — — —

Signature: _____